SKIN

Insatiable Series

Book 1

Patrick Logan

Books by Patrick Logan

Insatiable Series

Book 1: Skin

Book 2: Crackers

Book 3: Flesh

Book 4: Parasite

Book 5: Stitches (Summer 2016)

Family Values Trilogy

Mother

Father (Summer 2016)

Daughter (Fall 2016)

Short Stories

System Update

Prologue
Burnt Grass

COME.

The word was not spoken, but it was heard nonetheless. One lonely syllable, so benign on its own, yet laden with unprecedented authority.

Come.

Simple. Straightforward. Candid.

Lacking context, it was like any other word, just a directionless command that, if heeded, would send one wandering aimlessly.

Come.

Come where? Come to whom?

These logical questions should have arisen, *would* have arisen, but this was different. This word, this *command*, reverberating inside the Leader's head somehow offered a course, a *purpose*.

It was not of his mind — even his limited intelligence grasped this realization. Like the sun, like the air, like the ground beneath his feet, it was exogenous. Yet it was also *inside*, which in and of itself should have been troubling. But these facts, like everything else now that he had heard the *word*, seemed to lack significance.

What mattered was that *it* was calling to him — like a celestial beacon, *it* summoned him, and this took precedence over all else.

The seven Askergan tribesmen had been following the fire in the sky for more than six hours. Over hills, creeks, and through the heavily wooded terrain they ran, their wide feet grasping the varied landscape as effectively as the feet of their ancestors. They did not speak during their trek, but this was not a consequence of fatigue; the trained long-distance hunters that they were, running for six hours or more was not challenging, particularly given the slow trajectory of the flaming object that traced a line through dawn. No, there was another reason for their lack of exchange: there was something disturbing about the way it slid through the atmosphere, not like a wayward, tumbling asteroid, but determined, as if the object had a purpose. It was this *directness* that put all seven tribesmen in a state of unease and stiffened their tongues.

Although the Askergan didn't see the object touch down, they heard it. There was a slight fizzle, and then a crack like dry lightning boiling the warm air only moments after the flaming ball dipped below the tree line.

The Leader pulled into the clearing first, and as soon as he broke through the wooded area, he stopped fast, a clear indication for the others to stay. The man's eyes, usually even and emotionless, scanned the field like a starving animal seeking prey. Then, like his forward advance, his saccadic eye movements suddenly stopped as they focused on something in the middle of the clearing: a radius of burnt grass—blackened in some places, more charcoal grey in others—surrounding a large hole that was roughly six feet in diameter.

The Leader calmly bent and grasped a branch that lay beside his fan-like feet. Then he took two aggressive steps toward the hole, the deliberate act a signal to the other Askergan members to spread out.

With several deliberate steps, he closed in on the burnt radius. It was only when he reached the charcoal-colored grass that his advance slowed and began prodding the scorched earth with an inquisitive foot. To his surprise, the burnt undergrowth seemed cool to the touch. Curious, and not completely trusting the soles of his calloused feet, he bent and cautiously reached for the darkened lawn.

Rubbing the ashy remains between thumb and forefinger, the Leader confirmed that it was indeed cool—maybe even cold—to the touch. The air was also thicker down near the hole where he crouched, and it forced him to breathe more deeply, his diaphragm fully contracting in order to pull in the requisite oxygen. There was something in that strange air; something that evoked a desire, a *need*, to look into the hole.

Something deep inside whispered to him, told him to stand, to collect his tribesmen and flee this space. To head back to the village, to migrate as far west or east or anyway, so long as it was far from this place.

But then there was the voice. The one that was not his own, the one that had become more excited over the past few minutes, the one that had taken on a strange begging quality. *Come come come come.*

As before, the Leader was helpless to resist.

The hole was roughly four feet deep, a perfect cylinder in the earth, and nestled at the bottom, as if carefully placed instead of having just fallen from the sky, was a translucent oval roughly the size of a human skull. When the Askergan tribe leader tentatively tapped the egg-shaped orb with a branch, the jelly-like exterior appeared to harden and a pink substance swirled beneath the transparent membrane. The object also seemed to thrum upon impact, releasing a bizarre electrical energy that vibrated the man's crooked brown teeth and made the hair on the back of his shoulders and arms stand at attention. But instead of being frightened, the man with the calm blue eyes grew curious.

Come.

The Leader withdrew the branch from the hole, and the cloudy substance within the object rapidly dissipated until it regained its liquid-like state.

Intrigued, he brought the branch back above the opening in the earth, but instead of tapping the object as before, he flipped the branch with a sharp twist of his wiry wrist and forearm so that the jagged, broken end hung over the opening like a spear. Then he thrust the sharp end of the stick into the opening, the branch sliding effortlessly through his open palm.

Unlike when he had struck the object, this time it didn't harden and go dark. Instead, the sharp end pierced the rubbery skin and the liquid inside instantly churned, tiny pink beads moving about each other faster and faster, increasing not only in speed but also in number.

The Leader dropped to his knees and leaned closer to the hole in the earth, watching in awe as the gelatinous skin reformed around the wound that the makeshift spear had made. But before the lesion could close completely, the pink fluid began to accumulate around the edges of the branch, rapidly building into a froth. As he watched, a few ounces of the foamy pink fluid began creeping up the shaft like tendrils — no, more like *fingers* — twisting and curling around the knots in the wood like new, malignant vessels.

The Leader leaned closer, and although his eyes remained calm, he became acutely aware that the thick air down by the hole in the earth was again making it difficult for him to draw a full breath. When the creeping pink liquid reached halfway up the branch, the Leader shifted his body to one knee with the intention of standing.

In that instant — in that fraction of a second before he pushed his palms flat against the burnt grey grass and stood — it happened.

A massive cloud of pink dust shot from the earth and engulfed the Leader's head. After hovering in the air for a moment, the pink mist coalesced into seven individual strands, twisting in the air like ethereal cotton threads, before each one was individually *inhaled* by every orifice on the Leader's face: one for each tear duct, ear, and nostril, and a large, tumbling rope that didn't enter his gaping mouth so much as it *burrowed* down his throat. The Leader's head suddenly snapped back, and the cloud was gone, sucked into his face with alarming speed. This—the puff of pink air, the condensation, and the inhalation of the odd pink cloud—happened so fast that it would have been easy for the tribesmen to chalk it up to their imagination, fueled by the unrelenting sun beating down on them.

Nevertheless, when the Askergan tribe leader's head whipped forward violently and he crouched on his knees, fists embedded in the burnt grass, none of them stepped forward to lend a hand. It could be that they were just obeying his last order—*stay*—or, more likely, it was the strange smell that suddenly wafted toward them, a stench that reeked like wind through the ribs of a decaying deer. Or maybe it was their memory of the fiery object that had streaked across the sky for the better part of a day. Whatever held them rooted in place kept them there for a good minute until their Leader slowly raised his head.

Even at a distance, they could see that his eyes were closed and that his cheeks were slightly puffed, as if he were holding his breath. A moment later, the Leader's back hitched and he expelled a surprisingly tight cloud of pink air that, unlike the previous ball that had engulfed and then entered his head, quickly dissipated into the atmosphere. Then he said a word in a voice that was not quite his.

"Oot'-keban."

The tribesmen's eyes went wide when the word reached them—it was a word they hadn't heard in a very long time. It was a word that went unspoken, one that brought about visions of an evil that had nearly destroyed the tribe many decades prior, an ancient Askergan lore that transcended generations. It was a term that meant, quite simply, *evil skin.*

The Leader opened his eyes, and when the tribesmen saw the dark pools that were hidden behind those thin brown lids, they turned and ran.

*   *   *

The Leader knew he had made a mistake even before he had caught and killed the last three tribe members. The first two had been easy, almost too easy, and, in the end, this was his downfall.

Within minutes, he had caught the two nearest tribesmen, and moments after stripping them of their skin, he had consumed their entire bodies whole—their blood, their guts, their bones—leaving nothing but their skin to dry in the hot sun like thick, moist sausage casings. The next took a little more time—not much, but more than the first two—as his already bloated and stretched body was becoming difficult to propel across the uneven terrain. After consuming this tribe member his sides tore slightly, the skin around his ribs splitting in ribbons. Even the corners of his mouth were torn, necessarily so to permit the consumption of some of the larger bones—the femurs, the hips, the skull—and inside these tears, a milky green pigment peeked through.

Despite his massively distended body, the Leader managed to catch the last three Askergan tribesmen. Although the men shouted and screamed, *"Keban! Keban! Keban!"* — *Evil! Evil! Evil!* — they did not fight, the fear induced by his appearance doing nearly as much damage as his calloused hands and long, pointed fingers. But now, as his tan-and-green-striped flesh soaked in their blood, he realized that he had eaten too much, too soon: his ribs had broken, the front halves flipped outward to contain the meat within his torso, and his neck had been stretched nearly as wide as his shoulders.

A pain shot through his body; despite what he had already consumed, he needed to eat, and he needed to eat *now* — he needed to feed his children, his *palil,* and he needed the tribe members' skins to incubate them.

Squatting amidst the wasted skins of what had once been his loyal followers, he closed his eyes and drew foul, thick air from somewhere deep within his core into his mouth, filling his flaccid cheeks. Then he let the vulgar gas out in a pink puff and opened his eyes.

"Come," he uttered in a baritone whisper that seemed to skip across the terrain like a flat stone over water.

Even though the sound came from the Leader's mouth, it wasn't his word. There was something else inside his head now, something ancient, something sent from the heavens with but one goal: to consume — to consume and then to *breed.*

It was no use. They had traveled so far that even if the other members of the tribe heard his call, they would never reach him in time.

The beast tilted its head and listened; nothing — the forest was silent, all of the inhabitants having fled beyond the reaches of his summons.

But *Oot'-keban* needed to eat now.

The beast shifted its weight and stood, feeling the skin that once belonged to the Leader tear completely off its left side and fall away like a hunk of ice off a warming glacier.

A noise partway between a belch and a moan—a bastardized expression of pain—exited the thing's ragged mouth. The membrane peeking through tears in the Askergan leader's skin was immature; a milky white green that had not yet fully developed.

Too fast, I ate too fast.

Changing focus, the thing pivoted and lumbered back in the direction it had come, its body tumbling ungainly with every step.

The shambling green mass, trailing tendrils of what once had been the Askergan tribe leader's skin, eventually made it back to the gelatinous pink orb, but by then it was too late.

I should have been more careful, I should have taken the time... my palil *need time to grow.*

It was a fruitless hubris, but with this realization came expectation.

Expectation of returning, expectation of future success.

The beast collapsed on the cool circumference of burnt grass that surrounded the hole in the earth, taking minor comfort in the sensation.

Come   Come

Come

Come   Come

Come

With a final effort, the beast rolled its massive body into the hole, and what was left of the Leader's shoulder struck the gelatin orb within with a dull thud. As before, the object hardened, the pink liquid swirled, and the thrum that ensued brought with it a final moment of clarity.

Oot'-Keban will return—and when it does, it will not make this mistake again.

Earth spilled into the hole, choking out the hot sun, burying the strange, celestial object and its lone inhabitant beneath several feet of charred grey soot.

Come.

Chapter One
The Storm is Not Coming

1.

"LEAP PAD, DADDY."

Cody Lawrence flicked on the wipers, clearing the thick snowflakes that had settled on the windshield.

"Sure, Henrietta," he answered, briefly glancing in the rearview mirror. His three-year-old daughter was wrapped so tightly in her jacket and snow pants, and wedged so firmly in her car seat, that her head and face barely peeked out from beneath the folds of fabric and faux fur. She looked like a submarine sandwich that had been squeezed too tightly at one end.

"Marley, couldn't you have at least taken off her boots?"

His wife turned to him from the passenger seat, and although he had meant the comment to be more humorous than malicious, her stern look made it clear that she was not amused. Cody quickly turned his attention back to the road.

"Leap Pad, Daddy," Henrietta repeated.

"Yes, sweetheart," Cody answered, but despite his affirmation, he doubted that wrapped up the way she was, the girl would be able to lift her sausage-like arms to hold the thing, let alone use the pen. He turned back to Marley.

"Maybe you can reach back and pull down the zipper of her—"

"I had to do everything to get the girls ready," Marley interrupted.

Cody recoiled. He opened his mouth to say something, but

his wife quickly continued before he could speak.

"*And* I had to pack all of our bags, including yours. So before you go on saying that Henri looks uncomfortable, maybe you could have helped out *just* a little."

Cody cringed.

Henri.

He hated when she called their youngest daughter that.

It wasn't like I was doing nothing, Cody thought, and then, as if Marley had read his mind, she added, "Your writing could have waited, you know."

Yet despite her harsh words, Marley's tone had softened somewhat.

Well, if it were up to you, my writing could always *wait.*

Cody closed his eyes for a brief moment, trying to clear the negative thoughts.

Keep it together, Cody. This is supposed to be a fun trip, despite the circumstances. A time to relax, recollect, maybe even — dare I say — rekindle?

"Leap Pad, Daddy."

Marley twisted suddenly in her seat and spoke in a tone that was probably — hopefully — more aggressive than she had intended.

"For Christ's sake, Corina, get your sister's Leap Pad out of the bag and give it to her!"

Marley's frustration went unnoticed.

"Corina!"

Cody glanced in the rearview mirror at their eldest daughter who, although not yet thirteen, already appeared to be adopting an attitude typically reserved for the dreaded mid- to late-teenage years. She sat with her head pressed against the car window, the breath that puffed out from between her full red lips leaving rhythmic condensation on the cold glass. It wasn't that she was ignoring her mother—at least not intentionally. Rather, the white headphones from which even Cody could hear the Top 40 beats emanating were the underlying cause of her disobedience.

"Corina!" Marley shouted again, this time grabbing her daughter's leg.

Corina removed one of the earbuds and finally turned to face her mother.

"What do you want, Mom?"

Cody turned his eyes back to the road and instinctively increased the windshield wiper speed. The snow was coming down heavier now, blanketing the already white road and trees with thick, fresh flakes.

"It's too loud, Corina! And pass your sister her Leap Pad!"

As if suddenly reminded of her request, Henrietta raised her round face.

"Leap Pad, Daddy."

Cody sighed and wondered, not for the first time, if making the long drive north in the snow had been a mistake.

Rekindle? Yeah, right. Survive is more like it.

2.

OXFORD LAWRENCE AWOKE WITH a start, a scream caught in his throat. The veins in his neck flexed and jutted and his eyelids pulled back so far that he felt his eyes bulge from their sockets, precipitously close to falling out of their orbits. A few painful, diaphragm-paralyzing moments later, he finally managed to gulp air like a guppy struggling for oxygen on land.

What the fuck—?

But when he looked down, Oxford immediately knew '*What the fuck*'.

A hypodermic needle lay embedded in the crook of his left elbow, a belt—his belt—loosely wrapped around his biceps. A sigh bubbled in his throat then, but he caught it before it could escape his lips.

No— I will not feel sorry for myself. I did this. Not Mom, not Da—

Ironically, it was another sigh that broke his self-deprecation; although, this time, it wasn't *his* sigh.

Startled, Oxford turned to his left and for the first time since waking, realized that he was not alone: a woman lay beside him on what he now recognized as a bare mattress. She was lying on her stomach, her acne-riddled back bare, her buttocks covered only by a worn pair of greasy—*good God*—white boxers. His wide eyes slowly traveled upward from the small of her back all the way to her matted black hair, which was splayed almost artfully around her head; the woman was face down on the filthy mattress. Another thought crossed his mind then, and it too was accompanied by a barely stifled sigh.

Did I...?

He looked at the red spots on the woman's back again and realized that what he had first passed off as acne wasn't quite accurate; the bumps were swollen and red. Fucking *sores*. And her skin...the entire surface of her mottled skin looked dry, chapped, *textured*.

Oxford shuddered and after pausing only to pluck the needle from the crook of his elbow, he glanced down at his body. Although relieved that he was still wearing his purple boxers, this offered him little solace. He glanced quickly at the woman with the sores, then cautiously pulled the waistband of his underwear away from his scrawny body and gave himself a rudimentary once over. Everything *looked* normal, although he wasn't sure what—*chlamydia, AIDS, herpes, hepatitis, crabs, gonorrhea*—he had expected to find. Either way, normal couldn't be bad, could it?

Oxford took another quick look at the woman beside him and, confident that there was no chance she was going to wake, he kept the waistband of his underwear pulled back and bent his neck downward, drawing in deeply through his nostrils.

And everything smells normal too, Oxford thought, but he wasn't really sure what that meant either.

He unhooked his thumbs from his waistband, and the *snap* as it slapped against his pale, thin stomach made him cringe. Thankfully, the woman beside him continued to sleep. In fact, Oxford thought that he could hear her snoring softly, but straining to listen made his head hurt. And hurt did it ever.

After another deep breath, Oxford looked around, trying to catch his bearings. He remembered the peeling beige paint of the small apartment as much as he remembered the unconscious woman who lay less than a foot away. Equally as foreign to him was the black leather couch and the small tube TV—*who still has a tube TV?*—that was currently showing a portly man with a dark, manicured beard hawking the newest oxygen-powered cleaning agent. Oxford didn't remember any of this. He remembered going to the Western Widget for a drink, he remembered... well, that was it, really; that was all he remembered. There were flashes of things—an alley, a green hat with a shamrock, a leather carrying case—but nothing even remotely coherent.

Oxford turned his eyes to the syringe that he had pulled from his arm and tossed on the floor beside the mattress.

Fuck. This has to end. Too many nights not remembering, too many mornings wondering how I didn't wake up dead.

After one more deep breath—*in through your nose, out through your mouth*—he gathered enough courage to stand, careful not to disturb the woman beside him.

White flecks flashed brightly behind his tightly closed lids and his world spun. For a moment, he thought he might come crashing down. Standing as still as possible, holding his breath, Oxford fought the sensations and they eventually passed. The relief was short-lived, however, as the void they left was quickly filled with the pounding of his headache.

Tiptoeing like a toddler sneaking downstairs on Christmas morning, Oxford made his way to the couch where he spotted his jeans and sweatshirt. He dressed quickly, only now noticing a funk in the apartment that all of his previous deep breaths had failed to unearth. Oxford also noticed six or seven used syringes on the coffee table along with the usual accoutrement: a spoon, a lighter, and some aluminum foil.

As predicted, these items brought with them the mental lip service that seemed to have become so common as to verge on verbatim.

This has to stop—how many chances are you going to get, Oxford? How many times are you going to fuck up and let everyone—Mom, for Christ's sake, and Dad, wherever he was now—down? When are you going to grow up and stop being so selfish?

Oxford did his best to drown out his meddling conscience as he dressed, his eyes trained on the sleeping woman, ready to bolt the second she woke, dressed or not. But her only response was a snort, a horrible, thick sound, and her head remained buried in the mattress. On the counter by the front door he found his coat and hat, and he put those on, too.

As Oxford reached for the doorknob—*almost home free*—his eyes fell on a black leather cosmetic case on a section of counter between the stove and the door, and he hesitated. It was the same black case that had pinwheeled through his memory like a loosed hubcap, and although he could not recall its contents, he had been in the game long enough to know what was inside.

Hand still on the doorknob, the cheap, brass sphere half turned, he paused and licked his dry lips, his tacky tongue skipping unevenly across the chapped surface.

How many chances, Oxford?

His mother's voice, her kind face.

Oxford turned the knob and threw the door wide, but instead of leaving, he offered one more furtive glance toward the junkie with the black hair and sores on her pale back. Then he darted back inside the dilapidated apartment, grabbed the case, and fled, all before the door slammed closed behind him.

3.

SHERIFF DANA DREW PULLED into the Askergan police station parking lot just before nine. He walked briskly across the parking lot, the cold air stinging his nostrils with every breath. He was about to pull the door open, but a gust of wind hit him in the side of his face, and he turned away from it. When it died down, he opened his door again and he found himself staring at the illuminated sign on the lawn, the one that read 'Askergan County Police Department'.

Beautiful Askergan County, approximately one thousand residents spread out over roughly sixty square miles. Askergan County, where the Sheriff's Department and the Police Department were one and the same, where crime was nearly non-existent, where the residents and the authorities did things their own way. Askergan County, where being rebellious meant skinny dipping before the sun had completely dunked below the skyline.

Dana shivered and made his way inside, a wry smile on his face.

Askergan County, boring as hell.

It would make for shitty marketing material, and an even worse slogan, but that was just the way he liked it.

Inside the small, three-room police station, Sheriff Drew was greeted by the smell of fresh coffee and the static crackle from the CB radio that sat on the unmanned front desk.

The sheriff's smile fell off his face.

It was the third time this week that Alice was late. And when she was late, he couldn't help but think that maybe—

Stop it, he scolded himself. *Just stop it.*

"Last day," he murmured to himself. "Christmas Eve—the

last day before ice fishing and drinking beer and... and..."

...and the last day to stop worrying about Alice. After today, she will be with Mrs. Drew. Safe.

As he made his way across the room, voices from the back — the unmistakable voices of his two deputies arguing — grew louder.

"...and dealing with those two."

Rather than going directly into the back room and being undoubtedly dragged into whatever inane sports-related "debate" that they started every morning with, Sheriff Drew went to the sink and emptied his thermos instead. He stood there for a brief moment, watching the cold black liquid swirl in the aluminum basin before being swallowed by the drain.

He offered a quick glance at the dispatcher's desk. He hadn't meant to, but he couldn't help it. Just like he couldn't help the next thought that entered his head.

Where are you, Alice?

Sheriff Drew ran the faucet to wash away the coffee before refilling his thermos with coffee from the pot — it tasted like shit, of course, as Alice was the only one who could make a decent cup, let alone pot — before making his way to the back room.

Seated at a round table across from each other were his two deputies — the only other two officers of the law serving all of *(empty, boring, safe)* Askergan County — a pile of playing cards tossed haphazardly in the middle. His most senior deputy, a large black man named Paul White, clutched a fistful of cards between his meaty fingers. Even from ten feet away, Dana could see that some of them were folded and bent, and as he watched, the deputy twisted and warped them even further in frustration. Sheriff Dana Drew grimaced.

Another deck? I'm going to have to get another *deck?*

"That is such bullshit, and you know it," Deputy Paul White said, his tone, like his expression, taut. It was not yet nine, but the vein on the deputy's heavy brow was already pulsating, and his gaze was so intent on the man seated across from him that he failed to notice that Dana had entered the room.

Deputy Bradley Coggins, a pale, thin man with hawkish features and the beginnings of a red beard, was leaning back in his chair, the cards in his hand held so loosely that from where Dana was standing he could see that he had a stacked house: jacks full of threes.

"Ha, c'mon now, Whitey—there is no way those old-timers would even be able to hold a candle to new stars like Ovechkin, Karlsson, or Crosby."

The much smaller deputy paused and leaned forward slightly, his tiny dark eyes glinting. He was liking this—really liking it.

"Not. A. Chance," he said, laying his full house down on the table for full effect.

Sheriff Drew, moderately amused now, could literally see beads of sweat form on Deputy White's forehead. It was only when the much larger deputy slammed his cards down—two pairs, Dana noted—that the Sheriff decided to announce his presence and alleviate some of the tension.

"Morning, boys," he said calmly, making his way to his desk at the back of the room.

Both men turned simultaneously, one face grinning, revealing teeth so small that they were almost sinister, while the other attempted, and failed, at a neutral expression.

"Morning, Sheriff," they replied in unison. For some reason this collective act seemed to further anger Deputy White, and he shot a scowl at the other deputy. Dana couldn't help but smile.

"One day, Brad, Paul is going to come across the table—"

The much smaller deputy didn't let the sheriff finish, interrupting him with a loud laugh.

"Can't do it, Sheriff, 'cause I'm too fast."

The man bobbed his head from side to side as he spoke, imitating evasive maneuvers, and even Paul's tight expression relaxed somewhat. Coggins noticed this too and he laughed again—a short, and rather obnoxious *bleet*.

The niceties didn't last, though, as the two Askergan County deputies resumed their argument—hockey, always about hockey—even before the sheriff had removed his hat and coat.

"Hold a candle?" Deputy White said, any humor that had crept into his face following Deputy Coggins' comical head-bobbing having long since vanished. "What does that even mean, hold a candle?"

Dana decided then to end the argument before it degenerated any further. Although his deputies' morning tiffs never developed into anything more than verbal affronts—for all his size and intimidating facial expressions, Paul White was as gentle as they came—he had no desire to see this one get any more heated. With the blizzard touching down any time now, they needed to keep their heads screwed on straight. Although Askergan was no stranger to the odd winter storm, this one was chalking up to be one of the worst in recent history.

"Easy, guys," he said softly, just loud enough for them to take notice. He waited a moment for them to turn, especially Deputy White, who was now sitting with his back to him, before continuing. "Have either of you heard from Alice?" he asked, trying to keep his own frustration from creeping into his voice.

The deputies exchanged looks, and he knew in an instant that he had done a poor job of masking his emotions. Sheriff

Drew brought a hand to his face and absently rubbed at the deep grooves that lined the corners of his mouth; clearly, there was no hiding things with this face. Nearly two decades being Sheriff, even in as uneventful a place as Askergan County, had weathered him—would tax anyone.

"Nuh-uh," Deputy Coggins answered. "Only person who has called this morning is Mrs. Wharfburn."

Again, the two deputies exchanged looks.

Dana took a swig of the bitter coffee, grimaced, and then ran a hand through his short grey hair.

"What is it this time?" he asked, holding back a sigh.

An image of Mrs. Wharfburn, her rust-colored hair frizzled and unkempt, with an absolutely revolting cat—more like a damn overgrown sewer rat—clutched in her arms passed through his mind and he shuddered.

Mrs. Wharfburn. One of the few residents that had contributed to his lined face.

It was Deputy White who answered.

"She called six times already."

"What did she want?"

Deputy White opened his mouth to answer, but Coggins piped in before he had a chance to speak.

"A new husband?" he offered, raising his thick black eyebrows.

"Unkind," Dana said with a tight frown before turning his attention back to Deputy White.

"She called six times, and each time it was about the trees out by the road; says that with the storm coming, they were gonna fall and she would be left without power and—her words—'freeze her purple nipples off'."

When Dana's frown deepened, Deputy White raised his palms defensively.

"Her words, not mine."

Deputy Coggins, who had since turned his attention to picking up his full house and shuffling them into the rest of the warped playing cards, added, "She said she is going to call back; wanted to speak to you directly."

Of course she did, Sheriff Dana Drew thought. *Of course she did.*

The sheriff turned his gaze to the window and admired the thick snowflakes while his mind wandered.

Mrs. Wharfburn may have contributed to the deep lines on my face, he thought, *but Alice was probably the one that caused them. Safe, boring, completely ordinary Askergan County... and yet she still finds ways to get into trouble.*

As the window continued to be accosted by more blowing snow, Sheriff Dana Drew couldn't help but think that Askergan County was in for one hell of a ride.

4.

AN HOUR INTO THE drive, Cody found the car unnervingly quiet. His youngest daughter, Henrietta—her Leap Pad obsession satiated for the time being—had since fallen asleep, her chin resting lightly on her chest. In the end, his wife had managed to undo her jacket and had pulled off the girl's boots. His eldest, Corina, was still listening to her music, forehead pressed against the cool glass, but either her music had mellowed or she had turned it down because the tinny reproduction from her earphones could no longer be heard throughout the car. Marley was staring ahead blankly, apparently lost in thought.

Probably thinking about the snow, Cody thought.

The flakes were coming down even thicker now, and despite what he had heard that morning, it didn't look like it was going to let up anytime soon.

To break the silence, he switched on the radio, making sure to keep the volume low to avoid waking Henrietta. A quick glance at his wife suggested that either she hadn't noticed or didn't care. He couldn't help thinking about that word again—*rekindle*—and wondered if perhaps he should say something to her. He felt inclined to say something, *anything*, that might push her out of this funk of indifference she had been wallowing in for the past week or so.

What happened to us, Marley? We used to be so happy.

But, as with most relationships, financial struggles and raising two children so far away from family had strained their relationship.

Still... he couldn't help but think that perhaps there was

someone else.

"Mar—" he started, if for no other reason but to cease his careening thoughts, when the local weatherman interrupted him.

"This winter storm system is here to stay, it appears. So all of you wishing for a white Christmas, well, you are in luck!"

Cody grimaced and quickly went to change the station, but Marley caught his hand before it reached the knob. Evidently, she *had* noticed that the radio was on. He slowly put his hand back on the wheel, knowing that she was glaring at him, but unwilling to give her the satisfaction of acknowledging it

"Bitterly cold temperatures and massive precipitation are expected..."

Cody cringed.

Yeah, we get it. Shut up already.

He didn't need to look or speak to Marley to know what was she was going to say.

Cody! You said the storm would blow by us—that we wouldn't be getting more than an inch or two at most!

He would shrug—his go-to move.

That's what they said this morning.

Who's they?

The weatherman.

Well, how many different weather channels did you look at?

One.

"...rural Askergan will be hit especially hard over the next few days..."

He could literally feel his wife's eyes on the side of his head like lasers—tiny red spots that burned his skin.

Marley had made her disapproval of heading north for the holidays well known, and it had taken all of his effort to convince her to come along with the girls. Truth be told, if it hadn't been for the recent death of his father, he wouldn't have hesitated to forgo the trip altogether.

A quiet place to reminisce, to mourn, he had said. That wasn't selfish of him, was it?

To relax to rekindle… ah, fuck it—not happening.

Cody lasted another ten seconds before cracking.

"Damn," he whispered, trying to sound distressed, "they said it would blow over, pass us by."

He kept his eyes straight ahead and swallowed hard.

"They? Who's they?" Marley asked, venom on her tongue.

Cody was about to answer—to offer his pathetic defense—when someone in the car screamed.

5.

IT WAS NEARLY NOON by the time Oxford got back to his small apartment, and it was two hours after that before he had cleaned himself up and packed his overnight bag. His head still hurt, but the pain had regressed to a dull throb after chasing his fourth Tylenol with about a gallon of warm water. If he could draw solace from anything in his decrepit state, it was that the hole the needle had made in his arm after having been left there dangling all night, however unsettling, had stopped bleeding.

What if I had rolled over in my sleep? I could have torn a vein and bled out.

His mind returned to the pale woman with the pustules on her back lying face down on the mattress and thought it unlikely that he would have rolled too far *that* way. But if he rolled away from her—if he had rolled in the other direction? He would have fallen off the mattress, which surely would have woken him up—maybe.

Or maybe not.

Oxford left his apartment and headed for the train station on foot. He had had a car once—a blue Chevy that was more than ten years old—but he had sold it when he'd needed to pay some bills. Of course, once that few hundred—*four-hundred and ninety-five dollars*—was in his pocket, well, it had made a quick exit. And at the end of the week, he had had a massive headache—not all that much different from the one he suffered from today—and his bills had remained unpaid.

The thick woman at the ticket booth gave Oxford a warm smile when he handed her a crumpled twenty from his pocket.

"Goin' to Askegan to see your family for the holidays?"

The question made him uncomfortable—guilty—and he found himself nervously adjusting the collar that peeked out from his crew neck sweater.

Family.

He wondered what his mother might say if she found out he had relapsed again—worse, he imagined what she might *do* to him.

There will be no second chances, she had said.

Second chances.

It broke his heart to think about how many *second* chances he had actually had. And if that broke his heart, thinking about how many times he had lied to her made him feel like less than nothing.

If I could take it all back, 'Ma, I would. If I could take it all back and never put you or anyone else through this, believe me I would.

The woman in the ticket booth spoke again, and he snapped out of it.

"Yeah," he croaked, "visiting the family."

The woman was nodding, the thick fat wobbling beneath her chin like rooster wattles, and Oxford felt himself nodding back. Anything to get this woman to shut up and let him get on that train.

"My Mama is from Askergan—born and raised. Moved here just after I was born. Beautiful place, she says, though I ain't never been."

Oxford offered a slow blink as a response.

The lady missed the hint and glanced at the overnight bag Oxford clutched in one sweaty palm before continuing.

"Well, I hope you packed some warm clothes in there."

She sat back in her chair and turned her gaze to the train station entrance. It was clear that she wanted to turn her whole body to face the doors, but her girth made swiveling in her chair a significant task.

"*I'nt* gonna stop," she informed him, referring to the thick snowflakes

The woman was holding the ticket just out of his reach, and all he wanted to do was snatch it from between her chubby, manicured fingers and get the hell on the train. And sleep. Oh God, sleep would be great. He brought two fingers to his temple and rubbed. The Tylenol were wearing off.

"And it's gonna get cold, too. Colder than it's been in some twenty years. Hey, you know what else my Mama say?"

Oxford shook his head.

No, I don't know what your diabetic, wheelchair-bound mother says. The better question is, why the fuck would I care?

"Mama says that there is something buried there, that there is something bad in Askergan—something *wrong*." She lowered her voice to a mere whisper. "She says every time the snow comes, she hears it."

The woman's face suddenly went dark and she aimed a chubby finger at her temple.

"She says she hears it *inside*."

Oxford just stared, dumbfounded, wondering what the fuck this obese woman was prattling on about. Their eyes remained locked for a few moments, neither sure of what to say next.

The lady broke first.

"Anyways, that's why I ain't never been. They say it's beautiful 'n' all, but I don't want to be messing with no—"

When the ticket lady leaned forward, Oxford seized the opportunity; he reached under the plastic partition with surprising dexterity and snatched the ticket from her hand.

"Thank you," he said under his breath, ignoring the way her smile—obnoxiously white teeth peeking out from red lipstick that was two shades too cheery—faded.

"Hey!" she shouted, but Oxford just kept moving.

It wasn't until much later that he realized he had forgotten to ask for his change.

Merry Christmas, he thought glumly, his sweaty palm massaging the last ten dollars he had to his name.

Merry fucking Christmas.

*   *   *

Oxford awoke to an announcement over the train's intercom.

"Final stop: North Askergan County."

His headache was gone, and after a few deep breaths and a long stretch, Oxford realized that he actually—surprisingly—felt pretty good. So good, in fact, that his mind was free to think of other things. It wasn't his brothers, or his recently widowed mother that he thought about, however, but something else—something inert, but oddly more powerful: the black cosmetic case he had stolen from the pasty, sleeping woman.

It was powerful, that case, and like a magnet it pulled at him.

No, Oxford scolded himself, squinting his eyes so tightly that he saw bright flashes. *No fucking way.*

Another deep breath and the *tug* subsided to a level that left him feeling comfortable enough to open his eyes. Still, he was helpless to prevent his gaze from flicking to the bathroom door—a door that he knew could be locked from the inside, a place where he could be alone.

The train slowed and then stopped, and less than a minute later he found himself standing, grabbing his overnight bag, and disembarking before he succumbed to any of his urges.

Inside the station, Oxford made a brief stop in a small, brightly lit souvenir store. He bought a cream soda, a stuffed owl, and a QueenPop magazine, reluctantly handing over his last ten dollars. This time, he made sure to take his change.

As annoying as the woman at the ticket desk had been, at least she hadn't lied to him; the snow was coming down so heavily that it was difficult to see more than a few feet across the train station parking lot. A brief glance back at the tracks the train had made in the heavy snow and he was grateful that he had taken the early train; if the snow kept up at this rate — and if the completely impenetrable grey sky was any indication, it most definitely would — he doubted any other trains would be making the trek north tonight.

Oxford had only been waiting outside for a few minutes before he realized that the ticket woman's other prediction also held some truth to it. Despite the falling snow, it was damn cold — a dry, brittle chill that pricked at his exposed flesh. He tossed his bag down on the snow and, unzipping it just enough for his hand to fit in, but not wide enough that it would fill with snow, he reached inside. Unfortunately, nothing he touched felt anything like his hat. With a frustrated grunt, he unzipped the bag all the way and peered inside. Of course, his hat was *right there*, near the top, right beside the —

Oxford's hand hung in midair.

His black-and-white-striped cap was *right there* beside the inconspicuous black faux-leather cosmetic case.

You could go inside, a voice in his head implored. *You could go inside and keep warm. Head to the bathroom, wash your face, maybe go into a stall and —*

A vision of his mother's eyes, sadness and disappointment clinging from her green irises, flashed in his mind.

Oxford closed the bag forcefully and zipped it with such vehemence that the zipper overextended and pinched the fabric like tiny teeth biting down on canvas.

Again his mind returned to the woman in the train station, her hand pointing at her temple.

What did she say her mother told her?

Oxford thought about it for a moment before it came to him.

She hears it inside.

"Yeah, well," he said to the snow, "your mother *ain't* so special. Other people hear voices *inside*, too."

6.

ALTHOUGH IT WASN'T THE world's loudest scream, the noise was so unexpected that Cody instinctively yanked his head around to look at his girls. This simple and arguably dangerous act likely saved their lives. When Cody turned his head, his arms, which had been firmly and obstinately locked at ten and two to avoid the impulse to look at and thus fuel his wife's anger, turned slightly in the same direction and their car avoided the skidding silver sedan by mere inches. The fishtail drew Cody's attention back to the road, and after a brief lateral slide, he managed to right their SUV.

Holy shit.

He realized then that he had been holding his breath, and he quickly released the stale air and sucked in a fresh lungful.

"Everyone all right?" he gasped, still unsure of who had spotted the swerving car in front of them and screamed.

When no one answered, he offered a quick glance at Marley and was surprised that she was still staring at him. Her eyes, wide and bright, expressed not so much fear or relief as something else—anger, maybe, or disgust.

What the hell is going on with you?

"I'm fine, Daddy," Corina finally replied from the backseat.

He glanced back at her and noticed that her white headphones lay in her lap. Unlike Marley, she looked frightened.

"The storm's not coming my ass," Marley grumbled angrily, and Cody turned his attention back to the snow-covered road in front of them.

In the backseat, Henrietta started to cry.

*   *   *

It was almost an hour after their near collision before tensions eased enough to allow conversation to return to the vehicle.

Tentatively, Cody posed what he knew was a clichéd question, but his words held no other purpose but to break the unease.

"Are you guys excited?"

He ignored Marley's sour expression and turned his attention to his girls. To his dismay, Marley's look was mirrored on Corina's young face. Even without the matching expressions, they were near replicas of each other: small, almost upturned noses, full lips, roundish faces. Only their eyes differed significantly, Corina's being a bright green, while his wife's were a deep hazel.

"Who's going to be there?" Corina asked, not bothering to look up from her cell phone.

Definitely not whoever you have been texting for the last half hour.

"Well, Mama, of course, and your two uncles."

"Uncle Jared?"

"Yes," Cody replied hesitantly, "he is one of your two uncles."

"Is he coming alone?"

Cody shook his head slowly.

"I think he's bringing Seth."

Corina finally stopped texting and looked up. When their eyes met briefly in the rearview mirror, she quickly turned back to her phone, but not before muttering, "Gaylords."

Cody was so taken aback by the comment that it took a moment before he came to terms with what she had said.

"Corina!"

"Gaylords!" Henrietta repeated with a giggle.

"Corina!" Cody scolded again, turning to Marley for support. Either she hadn't heard, or worse, she had chosen to ignore the comment.

"That's terrible! Why would you say that?"

When his eldest daughter failed to respond and instead continued to click away on her phone, he once again turned to Marley.

"Are you just going to sit there?"

Marley flicked her long, dark hair over her shoulder and finally faced the backseat.

"Give me the phone," she demanded sternly.

When Corina ignored her, she repeated herself.

"Give. Me. The. Phone."

This time, she didn't wait for a response, and instead reached back and snatched the phone from her daughter's hand before she had a chance to react.

"Hey!" Corina cried.

Marley switched off the phone and put it in the cup holder between the front seats.

"You are not to use those words," she said with a sigh.

Finally you back me up, Cody thought. *Maybe your icy demeanor is cracking. Selfish or not, the idea of a peaceful holiday with my family to mourn Dad's passing maybe, just maybe, won't be a complete debacle after all.*

Corina crossed her arms and sulked.

"Gaylords," Henrietta chanted in a sing-song voice, and Cody scowled.

Or maybe not.

7.

THE TWO ASKERGAN COUNTY deputies had stopped bickering, and a calm had settled over the station, broken only by the incessant telephone ringing. Sheriff Dana Drew glanced at the phone on his desk for a moment before deciding to just let it ring. They would call back, he knew; or, more specifically, *she* would call back. For some reason, on this final day before his holidays, he was feeling somewhat nostalgic, and the last thing he wanted to do right now was talk to Mrs. Wharfburn. His gaze drifted from the black telephone to his two deputies—Deputy White, head firmly entrenched in paperwork, and Deputy Coggins, staring blankly into space—and he counted his blessings. These were good men.

Sheriff Drew had met his deputies a long time ago, back when they were in their early teens, awkward and uncomfortable, but even then he had known that they were good boys. And this wasn't just a quality that went away when you hit puberty, he knew; no, it was something that was just ingrained in some people, and for whatever reason, Sheriff Drew had an uncanny ability to recognize these types. Over the years, as first a deputy himself and then eventually as the sheriff, he had honed this skill, or *ability* as Deputy Coggins jokingly referred to it. And now he could spot one of the good boys in a crowd. While useful this talent no doubt was, it was much more difficult for him to pick out the *bad* ones—the *bad* boys. This type didn't stick out to him, maybe because his evil meter was usually stuck on yellow. Or maybe it had something to do with the moral ambiguity of the masses, or the Internet, YouTube, or Justin Bieber; he just didn't know. But what he did know was that the good boys, like these two, almost always grew into good men.

Sheriff Drew felt himself nod. They were nimrods some of the time, maybe even most of the time, but they were the *good* kind of nimrods that Askergan County needed.

His thoughts shifted from the deputies to the empty dispatch desk. It was nine-thirty now, and Alice was still nowhere to be found. When he brought the coffee cup to his lips this time, the mug was shaking.

The phone rang loudly, cutting through the silence, and the sheriff snatched it up without thinking.

"Asker—"

"Alice Dehaust, I know your mother, young woman, and if you don't tell that Sheriff Drew that I called, that I have *been* calling, I will go to her and tell her what you done: left an old, lonely widow—"

"Mrs. Wharfburn," Dana interjected, but the woman took no notice.

"—a cold and tired widow—"

"Mrs. Wharfburn," Dana repeated, but the woman was unfazed and prattled on, louder now, as if trying to drown out the sheriff's voice. He felt his head sag.

This was going to be a very long last day.

"The snow is coming down heavy now, and if you want a frozen widow on your—"

He had had enough.

"Mrs. Wharfburn!" Dana shouted, and both deputies looked up from their desks.

At long last, the phone went silent. After a moment of dead air, the woman spoke again, but this time her tone was calm.

"Who is this?" she demanded.

"Sheriff Dana Drew."

There was another pause, and then the whining resumed.

"Sheriff, I have been calling the police station for almost two hours."

Dana grimaced and fought the urge to hang up the phone right then—but he stood fast. Despite her shrill voice and undeniably annoying personality, she too was one of the *good* people. Really, really annoying, hysterical, paranoid, frustrating, and entitled, but *good*.

"What seems to be the problem, Mrs. Wharfburn?" he finally asked.

There was a short pause before the widow continued.

"Well, the snow is coming down heavier now and there are some awful—just *awful*—noises coming from some of the old trees—you know, the massive oak trees out in front of my house?"

Although Dana only nodded, Mrs. Wharfburn either sensed this or simply decided not to wait for an answer.

"They are just creaking and making these terrible noises with every tiny gust of wind. Especially the one by the road, and that one has the most snow on its branches. You know the one?"

Again he nodded, but the ensuing pause suggested that this time she was waiting for an actual response.

"I don't think—"

"The ones I asked to have cut back because I was worried that they would fall on the power lines one day?"

Dana grimaced again, now recalling a conversation they had had what must have been more than a year ago. Come to think about it, that conversation had gone a lot like this one.

"The one that *you* said *you* would come out and look at but never did? Well 'one day' is likely to be today or tomorrow, judging by all of this *snow*," she finished, spitting the last word.

"With all due respect, Mrs. Whar—"

"Don't you 'with all due respect' me, Dana Alexander Drew!"

The sheriff bit his lip.

Good person; she is a good *person.*

"I know your mother, Dana Alex—"

The sheriff took a deep breath.

"Mrs. Wharfburn," he said sternly. "I'm sure that the trees are just fine."

"If the power goes out, I will freeze here. My husband is dead, and I don't know the first thing about driving the snowcat. Heck, the thing has been sitting in the shed for so long now, I doubt it would even start. Just me and Miffy here, and if the power goes out—do you know how cold it is out there?"

The woman's tone suddenly changed again—it was slow and uneven now.

She was terrified, Dana realized, and despite the way she had berated him just moments ago, he couldn't help but feel sorry for her.

People said a lot of things about the woman, as even idyllic Askergan was not immune to the intrinsic magnetism of gossip. In fact, given the rarity of anything of significance happening in the County, Dana was convinced that it was even more rampant.

But what they said about her, about how she just *knew* things that she couldn't possibly know, about how if you got close enough, she could read what's going on in your head... well, those rumors just couldn't be true.

"Do you know how cold it is?" the woman repeated in a near whisper.

Dana remembered the deep chill he had felt just making the short walk from his car to the station.

"I know," he said, trying not to sound too alarmed, "and, to be honest, the snow is supposed to keep on coming and it's only going to get colder."

A thought occurred to him then, as he suddenly remembered seeing Mrs. Wharfburn's late husband, Dicky Wharfburn, a few years back at the only hardware store in town purchasing a big red generator.

Again he found himself rubbing at the deep grooves that ran from the side of his nose to the outer corners of his lips.

I might be getting old, he thought, *but at least my memory is still sharp.*

"Mrs. Wharfburn, do you still have the generator that your husband bought some years back?"

There was a long pause, and if it weren't for the woman's low and slow breathing, Dana would have thought that the line had gone dead, which wasn't completely unexpected given the weather.

"Mrs. Wharf—" he began, but the woman cut him off.

"Big, ugly red thing? With a pull cord, like a lawnmower?"

Dana couldn't help but smile.

"Yeah, that's it."

"I remember Dicky buying the damn thing, and let me tell you, he never used it once. Not once. I told him, too, that it would just sit there, like the chainsaw and the other power tools, getting rusty. I mean, we already have this crank-thingy in the basement that runs the light down there, and—"

Now it was Dana's turn to cut her off.

"Mrs. Wharfburn, do you still have the generator?"

Another pause, shorter this time.

"Yeah, I think so."

Dana was about to say something when the woman on the other end of the line screamed.

The sheriff jumped to his feet so quickly that the base of the heavy black phone lifted off his desk and hovered in the air for a moment before coming crashing back down.

"Mrs. Wharfburn!" he shouted. "Mrs. Wharfburn! Are you all right?"

When there was no answer, he made a move toward his coat that hung on the rack to his left, the phone still pressed to his ear.

"Mrs. Wharfburn!"

At long last, the woman answered.

"A branch just fell through my porch!" she shouted, her voice bordering on hysterical.

Dana felt his diaphragm contract and he slowly lowered himself back into his chair. Looking up, he realized that both his deputies were now hovering over his desk, their expressions grim. He waved them away.

"Sheriff Dana Drew! The next one might come through the roof! Or, even worse, the big branch over the power lines that I told you about last year might hit the lines!"

Again Dana thought about how cold it was outside, and wasn't sure that the latter was *even worse* than the former, but he found himself nodding anyway.

"Do you know how cold it is out there? Miffy and I will freeze—"

Dana realized that he had been holding the receiver tight to his head, and now his ear was hot, throbbing, and sweaty.

"Okay, Mrs. Wharfburn, just calm down. I'll tell you what, one of my deputies—"

A flicker of movement caught his eye and he looked up. Both deputies were leaning on Deputy Coggins' desk, but now they were making dramatic throat-cutting gestures with the blades of their hands. Deputy Coggins had a big, goofy grin on his face, and the sheriff found himself fighting back a smile of his own.

And *these* were the *good* boys.

"I'll tell you what," he repeated slowly, "I'll come out there myself to make sure your generator is ready to go, just in case."

"You better!" the elderly woman on the end of the phone nearly shouted. "Because last time, you said —"

Sheriff Dana Drew hung up.

Even though he knew his deputies were staring at him, their eyes desperate for an explanation, he methodically turned and retrieved his coat from the rack without acknowledging them. With his back turned, a small smile crossed his lips. Finally, after almost a minute of fiddling with his keys in his coat pocket, Deputy Coggins couldn't take it anymore.

"Dana! What the hell happened?"

The sheriff turned.

"What?" he asked, trying to look innocent but unable to completely conceal his smile. "Okay," he said, finally relenting. "A branch crashed through Mrs. Wharfburn's porch and scared her half to death."

Both deputies groaned.

"That's it?"

Dana shrugged.

"She's paranoid that the power is going to cut out, so I am going to head out there to make sure her generator's all set up."

Deputy White chuckled, which was surprising because the big fella hardly ever laughed.

"Good luck with that," the deputy said, and turned back to his desk.

"You bums do some work while I'm gone. And no arguing about hockey, for Christ's sake."

He waited for them to answer, to acknowledge him, but

when it was clear that there was none forthcoming, he shook his head.

The good boys.

Dana adjusted his coat and hat and made his way toward the door, mentally preparing himself for the wind and snow. But before he left, a thought occurred to him and he turned back.

"Paul, see if you can get ahold of Alice, would you?"

"Sure thing."

He turned again, but Deputy Coggins' voice drew him back.

"Hey, Sheriff?"

Coggins' arm was bent up over his head, and when the sheriff turned, he brought it down in front of his face, adding a *whoosh* sound as he simulated a falling branch.

"Dana, get down!" he shouted in a terrible accent.

Sheriff Dana Drew laughed and left the station.

8.

THE SNOW WAS SO thick now, both in the air and on the ground, that Cody Lawrence did not immediately see his brother when he pulled into the small train station parking lot. Then, on his second—and what was to be his *last*—lap around the parking lot, Cody finally saw him.

What the fuck?

Oxford was standing alone, his back against the wall, wearing a fall coat and sporting only a thin wool cap. The man's hands were bare, the digits nearly as white as the surrounding snow, and they were clutching what looked like a magazine and some sort of stuffed animal.

"Corina, please open the door for your uncle."

Corina, who had been staring out the window at the heavy snowfall in near wonderment, did as she was asked. A stinging cold entered the vehicle, and Cody instinctively turned the heat up a few notches.

"Hurry!" Cody shouted at his brother. "Get in!"

The cold air abated momentarily as Oxford first filled the doorway, then awkwardly climbed into the car. To his amazement, Corina, who had been practically manic depressive after having had her phone taken away from her, was smiling broadly. Fully in the vehicle now, Cody's brother pulled the door shut and they were all granted a reprieve from the cold.

"Uncle Ox!" Corina exclaimed loudly.

And then, surprising even the sour-faced Marley, Corina inexplicably turned and hugged her uncle. The embrace was an awkward one given the fact that they were both seated, and it was clear that Oxford had not been expecting this show of affection.

"Hi," he said hesitantly after disengaging from Corina.

"Hi, Ox," Cody said.

Marley followed with a grumbled facsimile of 'hello'.

In the rearview mirror, he caught Oxford's light brown eyebrows rise up his forehead, but Cody spoke quickly before his brother had a chance to address Marley's coldness. If he knew his brother, it was likely that he would have made an ill-timed joke, which, if he knew his wife, would not have gone over well. But given how the latter was acting lately, he was beginning to think that maybe he didn't know her all that well at all.

Fifteen years of marriage, two children separated by nearly a decade, four jobs, two houses, and six months of total time in couples therapy, and he still didn't think he really *knew* Marley.

"That's all you brought?" Cody asked, letting his eyes flick down to the green duffel bag in his brother's lap. "Where's your winter jacket? And your gloves?"

The word 'gloves' reminded Oxford that he was still holding something in each of his numb hands.

"Here," he said to Corina, handing her the magazine.

Corina beamed.

"Thanks!"

Cody turned back to the road, desperately spraying washer fluid to try to clear the icy smudges that streaked the windshield.

"And this is for you, little Henrietta," Oxford said, handing over the stuffed owl.

"Hoooo, hoooo!" Henrietta said excitedly. "Owl!"

She took the toy and held it away from her face by the wings, inspecting it.

"Say thank you," Marley reminded their youngest daughter, not bothering to turn.

"Thank you."

"You're welcome, munchkin."

As Cody pulled back onto the main road, he offered another glance at his brother.

"Is that all you brought?" he asked again.

Oxford smiled, revealing his teeth, which Cody realized all of a sudden almost seemed too crowded. Then he tapped the green bag on his lap.

"All I need," he replied. "Besides, it's not *that* cold out there."

Cody quickly glanced over at Marley to judge her reaction, and was surprised that she was staring back at him, her face still tight as if she had sucked on the juice of a thousand lemons. Cody took a deep breath and decided that he was not going to let Marley ruin his—*their*—Christmas.

Remember the three 'r's: Respect, Resolve, Rekindle.

Earth-shattering philosophical rhetoric, no doubt.

Still, Cody had listened, if only because he thought that *Rekindle* was a euphemism for sex.

And that too had been part of his plan for this weekend: *Rekindle.*

Now, though, it seemed that he would be equally as likely to fuck a polar bear.

He took a deep breath.

"Okay," he began, "look, I'm sorry. The weatherman said that it might blow by us, that this 'polar vortex' or whatever they are calling it might not hit Askergan County."

In the backseat, Oxford turned to Corina and made a comical 'o' face, his eyebrows once again raising high on his stark white forehead.

He's got frostbite.

Corina laughed.

"We are not going to let a little cold air—"

Marley scoffed, but Cody ignored her and continued.

"—we are not going to let a little cold and snow ruin the Lawrence family Christmas, now are we, girls?"

His smile was so fake that it might as well have been drawn on with a pencil.

Re-fucking-kindle.

9.

THIS IS GOING TO be a disaster, Sheriff Dana Drew thought, the corners of his mouth pulled down so far that it looked like he had jowls.

The white wall that met him almost immediately upon leaving the station seemed to only intensify during his drive east to Mrs. Wharfburn's residence. And it was cold—damn cold. In fact, it was so cold that even with the heater of his old Buick cruiser set to high, he still had to keep his gloves on for fear of freezing his hands to the steering wheel.

The sheriff picked up the radio and punched the talk button. It took him three attempts with his thick, cumbersome gloves.

Static.

He clicked the button three more times, and when he was still greeted with only static, he swore under his breath.

"Deputy White? Coggins? Pick up the damn radio," he spat before replacing the handheld back in its holster on the dash.

Off to his right, he saw a car skid and almost swerve into the ditch before the driver managed to right the vehicle.

Fuck. A disaster is right.

As a warning, he flicked on his lights, but kept the sirens off.

The radio crackled.

"Come in, Sheriff."

Dana recognized Paul's deep voice.

"Listen, Paul, the roads are a bloody mess out here—just an absolute disaster." He paused, debating what course of action to take. "I want you and Coggins to be on high alert. Also, give a call to all the plow guys in town; tell them to make their way out to Highway 2 and start clearing."

Dana released the talk button and waited.

"Yeah, ugh, this will be the ninth plow this month and the plow quota has already been met."

Dana grimaced—leave it to Deputy White to be the practical one.

"The guys are going to want double for this one, boss."

Fuck.

Dana pressed the talk button again, shaking his head.

"Doesn't matter—roads are a disaster. We will find the money somewhere."

His mind turned to the vehicle that he had seen swerve moments ago.

"There is no way I want someone to go off the road and freeze to death under four feet of snow while they wait to be rescued."

When Dana let go of the talk button, he heard a click, then dead air, and then another click, as if Deputy White had an inclination to add something before deciding against it.

Dana tried to press the talk button, but his gloves were too clumsy and he dropped the handheld to the floor, the cord snagging on the gearshift.

He jammed the forefinger of his right hand into his mouth and grabbed the fabric between his teeth and pulled. He spat the glove onto the passenger seat and picked the radio off the floor. Dana didn't even bother wiping the layer of slush from the microphone grill.

"And where the hell is Alice?"

*   *   *

Mrs. Wharfburn was standing in the doorway of her large brown estate when Dana pulled up. He hoped, for her sake, that she had seen his lights as he approached, the alternative being that she had been waiting in the doorway ever since he had hung up the phone over an hour ago. Knowing the woman as he did, Sheriff Drew thought either option was equally as likely.

The Wharfburn Estate was ridiculously large for its sole occupant—or *any* sole occupant, for that matter. Although it was technically two stories, the central dining and entertainment areas were on the lower level, and at a whopping four-thousand square feet, he doubted that the arthritic woman that stood in the doorway ever had the need, let alone the will, to go upstairs. In fact, he had heard a rumor that the back part of the house had been completely boarded up, as if she were trying to eliminate those rooms from existence. Out of sight, out of mind, as they say.

Sheriff Drew looked at the woman with the startled expression in the doorway again.

Or maybe in this case it was out of mind, out of sight.

A violent gust of wind suddenly rocked Dana's cruiser.

Jesus!

A loud crack sounded from somewhere in the small, wooded area off to the left of the house. Although Dana didn't see the branch fall, it must have been large to generate the massive cloud of snow. When the air settled, the falling snow seemed to settle with it, as if chasing the wind like a backdraft, and Dana seized this moment to get out of his car.

Even from where he was standing, more than twenty feet from the woman's house, he could hear Mrs. Wharfburn's screechy voice carrying on the tail of the wind.

"See?!" she shouted. "*See*?!"

Dana kept his head down and slowly made his way across the yard, finding it difficult even with his thick black winter boots to traverse the ankle-deep snow. When he was halfway to the door, he paused to catch his breath and finally raised his eyes.

Mrs. Wharfburn was dressed in only a thin white nightgown, her arms crossed over her narrow chest. The woman's hair—rust-colored near her scalp transitioning to black at the ends—was frizzy and unkempt, its height in some places seeming to defy gravity. Her eyes, however, were bright and blue, their penetrating gaze in stark contrast to her almost waif-like appearance.

There was another crack, followed by an equally large crash; this time it didn't come from deep within the woods, though, but near the outer edge.

Dana cautiously turned his gaze upward and eyed the large oak tree with heavy, snow-laden branches that hung ominously above his head. A sudden gust of wind made them sway slowly, almost seductively, like a woman's flirtatious wave. He lowered his eyes again and picked up the pace.

When he stopped next, he realized that the woman's arms weren't laced across her thin chest solely to keep her warm, although judging by the stark white of the broomsticks the woman passed off as legs, it was undoubtedly a welcome byproduct; tucked into the crook of one of her scrawny elbows was a ball of fur.

"See?"

In response to the woman's voice, the fur moved, and Sheriff Drew caught himself staring at beady eyes and the wet, black, wriggling nose of what might have been an overgrown sewer rat.

Miffy.

"Mrs. Wharfburn?" he began, once again turning his eyes downward to make sure of his footing as he took another step forward. He stopped about ten feet from the front door. "Mrs. Wharfburn," he repeated, "where—?"

But he never finished the question. A massive snapping sound erupted overhead and he instinctively jumped backward, covering his head with his gloved hands.

"Fuck!" he cried out as he tripped and landed in the snow.

Breathing heavily, trying to slow his heart rate, he waited for the snow cloud to clear before pulling himself to his feet.

Then his brow furrowed.

What the hell?

Unlike the others, this branch had fallen thick end down and had driven itself into the earth like a spear. In fact, if Dana had arrived five minutes later to Mrs. Wharfburn's Estate and had not seen it fall, he might have thought that this was the most bizarre place to plant a tree. And if he had arrived two minutes earlier, well, said tree might have been sporting a rather fleshy ornament by the name of Sheriff Dana Drew.

The sheriff exhaled and looked past the branch to Mrs. Wharfburn who, surprisingly, hadn't even flinched.

As if she knew *it was going to fall.*

His face twisted even further in response to the stupidity of the thought.

"You okay?" he asked at last, his voice tight.

The cat—*was it a cat?*—yelped, and although Dana had never heard the noise that a sewer rat made, he imagined that this one was fitting.

"Me?" she asked, incredulous. "I told you! Sheriff Dana Drew, don't think that—"

Something in the foreground drew Dana's eyes away from the woman, and he let her prattle on without taking mind.

The area around where the branch had pierced the ground seemed to be devoid of snow. In fact—Dana squinted to get a better look—yes, he could see *grass* around the base of the branch.

What the—?

And then, even more unbelievably, as he watched, the grassy area around the shaft seemed to grow to a diameter of more than a foot.

The snow's... melting? How can this be?

Dana took a step toward the fallen branch.

"Sheriff Drew? Are you listening to me?"

The cat-rat thing yelped again, but the sheriff ignored them both.

The fallen branch seemed to have hit something buried in the ground—something that had long since been covered by feet of earth and grass.

He crouched and tentatively picked up a few sprigs of grass that had now turned as grey as dust. Even though they crumbled between his thumb and forefinger, and felt as much like soot as they looked, they were surprisingly cool to the touch.

Something in the back of his mind chimed like an alarm.

Step back, Dana. Something's not right here—go back to your cruiser, drive back to the station.

But he couldn't; he just *had* to see what was in the ground.

As he leaned over the hole, he picked up the scent of *something*—something thick and indescribable. It was then that Dana realized that he had to breathe deeply through his mouth in order to fill his lungs with the odd, heavy air.

Did the branch puncture the septic tank? No, it would smell—

Come.

The word was so clear, so oddly distinct, amidst the blowing wind that his eyes snapped up and he stared at Mrs. Wharfburn.

Dana didn't know if it had been the wind, or maybe she had been frightened by the falling branch after all, but her hair seemed *taller* somehow. Not wilder or puffier, but *taller*. Even her forehead seemed longer, as if her face had been pulled upward from the crown of her head like taffy.

Even stranger still, was that she didn't look like she had said anything at all.

What the hell?

This time, however, she definitely spoke, but her voice was strange; it was slow and drawn out, as if she were talking underwater, and Dana felt his head begin to spin.

"Sheriffffff Dreeeeeew, whaaaaat's wroooong?"

To top it off, the stupid cat started meowing again, but not like it had been before—not the annoying, high-pitched yelps—but a different sound entirely; something deeper and more guttural.

Dana closed his eyes tightly, trying to clear the strange images and sounds. When he finally opened them again, he found himself staring back into the hole surrounding the branch.

It was then that he saw the streaks of pink liquid—tight, controlled lines of what might have been some sort of bright, viscous paint—slowly migrating up the branch. And there was something else in the hole as well, he realized, a strange, bleach-white shape buried in the dark soil. Something that gleamed the way only bone could.

The sheriff squinted hard.

The white shape was clearly a skull, but it was different; the brow was thicker, more pronounced, and the lower jaw protruded as if the consequence of a severe underbite.

That should have been it. Dana should have stood, backed away from the branch and taken as many breaths of fresh air

that he could manage. But something tugged at him, some sort
of nagging curiosity that he hadn't felt since childhood. Despite
the melted snow, freeze-dried —*burnt?*—grass, and the strange
pink liquid, he found himself leaning even closer, and then,
inexplicably, he reached into the hole with his hand and rubbed
two fingers across the pink fluid.

"Hey!" Mrs. Wharfburn shouted, but her voice sounded far
away, as if the woman were speaking into a tin can and he was
listening at the other end of a mile of string. "Hey, Sheriffffff!
Whaaaaaat the hell are you dooooo-ing?"

The pink liquid was surprising soft, velvety almost, which
was confusing and alarming because it should have only felt
wet. And it was cool, too, almost cold to the touch; based on the
melted snow, he had expected it to be warm. Intrigued by these
undeniably foreign sensations, he leaned forward, deeper into
the hole, with the intent of feeling more of the curious fluid —
was it sap? Some sort of fluid from the bark?—but as he stretched
his arm forward, his forearm nudged the branch, moving it just
a quarter inch to his left.

In a split second that passed so quickly that it didn't fully
register in Sheriff Dana Drew's mind, his entire head was
engulfed in a cloud of pink powder.

Chapter Two
Snowball

1.

OXFORD'S ARM STARTED TO itch even before dinner. The feeling began just above his wrist—a tickling sensation, as if someone were lightly brushing a feather against his pale skin. But as the tickling spread up his forearm, it left a trail of mosquito bites. In a few moments, he found himself having to exercise every ounce of his will to avoid tearing at his skin.

He stood alone, having since excused himself from the family din—which was surprisingly jovial, tongues loosened by the flow of mother's red wine—and stared out one of the large front windows at the white, ubiquitous blanket of snow that smothered the lawn. A crack sounded from somewhere above the house, but the Lawrences had heard so many branches snap and fall in snowy puffs since their arrival a few hours ago that they barely took notice. Instead, Oxford found his mind drifting to earlier that morning, thinking back to the sight of the woman whose name he didn't even know, her pale back riddled with boils staring up at him like the eyes of wild cats at night.

I had been doing so well, he thought begrudgingly.

Oxford shook his head again, trying to stop his journey down the winding highway of self-pity, as he was all too familiar with what lay at the dead end.

Another crack, and this time a giant branch at least three or four inches in diameter hit not more than a foot from his brother's SUV.

Come

"You okay, Oxford?"

Oxford nearly jumped out of his skin, which, given the itching that seemed to now encompass the entire right half of his body, might not have been the worst thing in the world.

He turned slowly and found himself staring into his older brother's pale blue eyes. Then he scratched his wrist, just once, and the sensation of his sharp nails even through his fleece shirt was nearly orgasmic.

"I'm fine," he replied, his voice surprisingly hoarse and dry. He swallowed. "Just listening to the wind."

Cody stared at him for a moment without continuing the conversation. He had noticed the scratch, Oxford knew; the man missed nothing.

"I'm fine," he repeated.

The image of the needle poking out of the once soft but now tough, scarred flesh on the inside of his elbow flashed in his mind, and he forced it away with a deliberate blink.

Come

After another brief silence, his brother finally spoke.

"Yes," Cody said, his voice calm and even, "the wind is loud, even in here."

Oxford stared at the snow for a moment longer, and was reminded of the fat woman from the train station.

Mama says that there is something buried in Askergan, something bad. She says every time the snow comes, she hears it.

Oxford shuddered and hurried after his brother.

2.

JARED LAWRENCE CLEARED HIS throat and brought his half-full glass of red wine to eye level. Even though they were already halfway through their meal, a particularly moist and delicious turkey—*good job, Mom*—the wine had caused his cheeks to redden and made him chatty; so much so, in fact, that he had decided it was time for a toast.

When the clanging forks and conversation continued unabated, Jared cleared his throat again, this time more dramatically.

Heads turned, and when the last Lawrence, little Henrietta, finally looked at him, he spoke.

"I want to propose a toast," Jared began, acutely aware that his words were slurred.

Oxford groaned.

"We already had a toast!" he exclaimed, but he too had been into the wine and was smiling broadly.

"I want to propose a toast," Jared repeated, his own smile growing, "to you guys, for allowing me to bring Seth into our family for the first time."

He turned to look at his partner, who was staring up at him with bright and—*moist? Were his eyes moist?*—glassy eyes. He laid his hand gently on the man's shoulder, and Seth mouthed the words, "*I love you*". Jared quickly looked away, fearing that he too might become overwhelmed with emotion.

There were eight of them at the table, including himself, and all but Corina were staring at him now, their expressions ranging from proud—*Oxford, Cody, and of course Seth*—to slightly uncomfortable—*Mom, Marley*—to completely indifferent—*Henrietta.* When Jared's eyes fell on the empty chair at the head of the table, his smile wavered, but only for a second. Truth be told, he and his father, Gordon—*Gordon, never Gord*—never had the greatest relationship, and he doubted that if the Lawrence patriarch had still been alive that he would have ever mustered the courage to invite Seth to join them. Still, there had been some good times mixed in with the bad and apathetic, and he missed the man. It was their first Christmas without Gordon, after all, which was why they had all insisted on making the trek north despite the impending storm.

But Jared was not naïve enough to believe that a couple of alcohol-induced laughs meant that everything was perfect with the Lawrences.

Far from it.

There was tension here, be it between Cody and Marley, the latter of which refused to meet her husband's gaze, or with Oxford, who was so thin and pale that it was almost impossible to conceive that the man was clean. And himself, Jared Theodore Lawrence? He wasn't fooled by the goofy grins at this table; there was resentment here, resentment directed at him for missing the funeral of the very man they were here to honor.

Jared shook these thoughts from his head before he could be overwhelmed with guilt and made a conscious effort to smile even wider. This was a proud moment for him and Seth, and it would take more than a few memories to sour his mood.

"Thank you," he repeated at long last, realizing that his speech—if you could even call it that—hadn't really amounted to much.

"Hear ye, hear ye," Oxford joked.

Jared watched as the man reached out with his glass and mimed a dramatic cheers gesture. The other Lawrence adults raised their glasses. Even their mother, all seventy-eight years of her, held her glass high and saluted him. Jared beamed, and they all indulged a little more.

*   *   *

Jared couldn't remember who had suggested that they open one gift before bed, but he was excited. It was only fitting; their tradition had been to only open gifts on Christmas morning, but him bringing Seth and this being the first Christmas without their father, it seemed appropriate that their traditions be altered. And he was glad. Change is good. Shit, it was Christmas Eve, and if Mama didn't mind, then he didn't either.

Only Oxford seemed uncomfortable with the idea, and Jared surmised by the way he scratched nervously at his arms that he hadn't brought any gifts. But that was okay. For Jared, the fun was in the giving, and receiving was just a necessary, and occasionally awkward, evil.

There was no Lawrence tree this year—that too had gone to the wayside with Gordon's passing—so Jared corralled the troops around where the tree was usually placed, where he and Cody had piled several colorfully wrapped presents.

Slowly, with Mama still tidying up from dinner, they meandered their way to the various chairs and couches that were scattered throughout the family room.

Jared and Seth took the loveseat, with Seth sitting sideways, his knees pulled up to his chest. Not much of a drinker, the two and half glasses of wine had generously reddened his cheeks, and Jared could tell that the man was buzzed. The thought brought another smile to his lips.

Marley took the chair, what had once been off limits— "Gordon's posterior only", they used to joke—and she had Henrietta in her lap, the little girl's eyelids drooping not unlike

Seth's. Oxford and Cody sat on the other loveseat that kitty-cornered his own, and they too looked a little sleepy. Only Corina was left without a seat, and Jared instinctively slapped at Seth's shins, encouraging him to sit properly. The man's eyes widened and he jumped at the gesture, and Jared felt his smile grow.

"Come sit over here, sweetheart. We can squish," he said to Corina, moving his body as close as he could to the arm of the loveseat and tapping the space between him and Seth.

The young girl—who all of a sudden didn't seem that young anymore—gave him a queer look, her thin, light-colored eyebrows furrowing slightly, the corners of her red lips turning downward. She looked so much like her mother then that it was uncanny.

"No," she said, "I would rather sit on the floor."

Her smallish voice and flat tone seemed petulant and somehow *accusatory*. To prove her point, she moved toward her mother and sister and plopped herself down, pressing her back up against Marley's legs.

"No, thank you," Cody corrected her from Jared's left.

Without turning, his smile never faltering, Jared flicked a hand at his older brother as if to say, *"Don't worry about it"*.

Although times had changed, it had been hard for him growing up as a gay teenager, and he expected that it was hard for her to grow up with a gay uncle, too. She wasn't a cruel person, just bullheaded like her mother.

"That's okay," Jared said, keeping his eyes on Corina. It was Corina who eventually looked away, moments after her eyebrows relaxed and he saw something akin to shame cross her pretty features.

"Ma!" Jared shouted out the corner of his mouth. "Ma, come open a present with us!"

"She'll come," Oxford said. Gifts or no gifts, he was clearly eager to get things started. He made a subtle gesture with his chin at Henrietta, and Jared noticed that with every blink, the girl's lids seemed to open more slowly.

He nodded.

"Corina? You want to help us out?"

The girl, surprised to be called upon, looked up at him.

"Go on," Cody urged, not giving her a chance to respond.

Begrudgingly, Corina rose from the floor and walked briskly to the pile of gifts. After no more than a cursory glance, she grabbed one off the top of the pile, briefly inspected the name tag, and then suddenly flung it at Oxford.

"Corina!" Cody shouted, but Oxford turned in time to catch the present before it struck him square in the chest.

"What?" she replied, a devilish look on her face. "You said get a present."

She paused, meeting her father's stern glare.

"Besides, I knew Uncle Ox would catch it."

Oxford took it in stride.

"'Tis true," he said, raising his chin high in the air. "In my past life, I was Babe Ruth."

Henrietta giggled, as did Seth. Jared turned and saw that his partner had put his knees back to his chest and had turned toward him after Corina had refused their offer of sitting between them.

So damn cute, he thought, observing Seth's rosy cheeks and goofy smile.

This time Marley broke the silence.

"Open it, Oxford, the little ones are fading."

She nodded in Corina's direction, and the soon-to-be teenager rolled her eyes before sitting back down at her mother's feet.

"Sure thing, boss," Oxford joked, and Henrietta laughed again.

"Boss!" she squeaked.

Pinching the red-and-green wrapping paper between thumb and forefinger, the youngest Lawrence brother pulled the paper off in one tear.

"Awesome," he said, holding an object up for everyone to see.

In his pale right hand was a palm-sized sphere of bubble wrap.

"Wow," he continued, pretending to examine the package closely. "I've always wanted one of these!"

Jared glanced over at Corina, who was leaning forward impatiently now, her arms wrapped around her knees. The girl rolled her eyes, and Jared caught her mother doing the same.

"Open it!" Corina demanded.

"Okay, okay," he replied, finally relenting.

The man tore into the package in a way that seemed curiously desperate despite his previous charade. As the bubble wrap fell to the floor, Oxford's eyes widened.

"Is this...?"

Jared craned his neck, trying to see what his brother was holding.

"Oh man, is this real?"

Oxford's voice had turned serious.

Finally, unable to contain himself, Jared asked what it was. Even Seth—more drunk than buzzed, he realized—had turned and was trying to catch a glimpse of the mysterious gift.

Oxford rotated the round object toward the other couch, showing Jared the baseball. There appeared to be writing on the white surface, and although it was nothing more than squiggles from his distance, Jared assumed that it was a signature. Then

Oxford spoke again, and his silent query was answered.

"Mariano Rivera," he said, awe creeping into his voice. He turned to face his brother beside him on the couch. "How?"

Cody was beaming.

"How did you get this?"

"I didn't get it," Cody said, "Corina and Henrietta did." He paused. "See? This is why you always read the card!"

Oxford ignored him and gestured toward his niece.

"Get over here!" he demanded, and again Corina rose and made her way to her uncle. The embrace was tight, and Jared felt his smile returning. Oxford kissed her on the cheek, and the girl made a face before wiping away the wetness with her fingers.

"Thank you!" Oxford exclaimed as his niece retreated back to her spot on the floor in front of her mother.

"Don't sit down," Jared said. "Go get the next one!"

Corina reached for the pile of gifts, digging deeper this time. When she finally pulled her hand out, she was clutching a black case in her hands.

She turned it over, inspecting it, trying to find a name tag.

"Anyone know who this is for?"

When no one answered, she started to unzip the case.

Oxford took his eyes off the baseball and looked up just before Corina pulled it all the way open.

The man immediately jumped to his feet and lunged at her.

"Where did you get that from," he cried. "Don't *fucking* touch it!"

Corina froze and dropped the case to the floor.

Then she started to cry.

3.

CODY WASN'T SURE WHY he had awoken. He lay in the dark for a moment, eyes open, listening to Marley's slow and steady breathing beside him. At first he thought that it had been Henrietta crying again—God knows it had been a nightmare putting her to bed. For some reason, she had awoken following Oxford's outburst during the gift unwrapping in sheer terror, and calming her had been nearly impossible. They had tried everything, and only after two full hours of screaming had she not so much fallen asleep as passed out from sheer exhaustion. It had been strange, and more than a little unnerving, as she had been sleeping well for at least six months. Even though Corina was more than a decade older than her sister, and time, if nothing else, muddled memories, he would have sworn that she had never been as *irate* as her sister had been that evening.

Cody sighed and listened closely.

Nothing.

After listening for a moment longer, he picked up Henrietta's faint snoring in the portable crib by the foot of their bed.

Then he turned his head and glanced at the clock that sat atop the bedside table: 4:07.

Why did I wake?

Marley moaned in her sleep beside him and rolled onto her back. She was wearing a thin night gown, and even in the dimly lit room he could make out her nipples poking through the fabric. Immediately, he felt stirring in his pajamas.

How long has it been since we've had sex? Shit, have we had sex even once since Henrietta's been born?

Cody couldn't remember. He stared at the perfect outline of breasts. They weren't huge by any means, but they were perfectly round and firm. He loved that about them, how they gave just the right amount when squeezed.

Unable to control himself, Cody reached over and tentatively laid his hand on Marley's thigh.

Encouraged by another soft moan, he slowly moved his hand up beneath her nightgown, her bare skin making him even harder. When his fingers reached the soft pubic hair between her legs, he was surprised to find that she was already wet.

Cody's breathing was shallow now, and his pajama bottoms were so tight now that they were borderline uncomfortable.

Rekindle, he thought as he started moving his fingers back and forth. With his other hand, he reached over and started massaging her breast, feeling the nipple harden through her thin nightie.

Marley groaned louder this time, and Cody paused, waiting to see if Henrietta would wake up.

Then he heard it: an audible, if muted, high-pitched *beep* that came from somewhere outside their bedroom door, and he pulled his hand away from Marley's breast.

What the —?

He turned his face skyward, staring into the near darkness for a moment before he heard it again.

Beep.

Marley startled him by swatting his other hand away. He turned back to her, and caught her stern expression staring up at him in the near darkness.

"What the hell are you doing?" she hissed.

Cody gaped.

Rekindling?

The beep sounded again and Marely pulled the covers back up to her chin.

"Go find out where that sound is coming from," she demanded, turning her back to him once more.

Cody couldn't believe it.

What the fuck just happened?

He sat up and stared blankly at the door.

What's happening to us?

The beep from the hallway sounded again, and he gently eased back his side of the covers and slithered out of bed. As soon as his bare feet touched the hardwood, he instinctively drew them back and sat on the bed with his feet hovering; the floor was as cold as a sheet of ice.

Anger slowly started to usurp his confusion.

What right does she have? What right does she have to be so... so fucking mean?

Cody's wandering eyes found the clock again: 4:07—still.

He was nearing tears now.

What the fuck is going on?

With gritted teeth, he slammed both feet on the icy floor and stood.

A second later, he was at the door, grasping at the doorknob. It was nearly as cold as the floor.

Beep.

Cody pulled the door wide and stepped into the pitch-black hallway.

Rekindle my fucking ass. Recycle is more like it.

4.

OXFORD WASN'T SLEEPING. IT wasn't a case of not being tired; on the contrary, he was absolutely exhausted. Although he couldn't remember what time he had gone to sleep the night prior—hell, he couldn't remember much at all about last night—he knew it must have been late. And, besides, he had been drunk and high, meaning whatever sleep he had gotten had not been of good quality. Yet despite his drooping eyelids and almost crippling fatigue, he was unable sleep.

It was the itching. The damn itching would not stop. It felt as if he had taken off his shirt and rolled around on pink fiberglass insulation.

Even though he was in excruciating pain and even more devastating discomfort, Oxford forbade himself from scratching—a sort of demented penance. He only wished that he could exercise the same resolve when it came to other things in his life.

Come

It wasn't the first few beeps that alerted him to the fact that something was wrong, nor was it that the air in his room had gradually cooled—a sensation that his sweating, shivering, itching body would not even register until much later—but rather, it was the *absence* of sound. It took Oxford a few moments to realize that the HVAC fan that usually whirred pleasantly all night like a soft, mechanical lullaby had stopped. When he heard the beep again, he decided to investigate.

The cold floor beneath Oxford's feet was a relief. He stood, pausing only for a brief moment to use a corner of the damp bedsheet to wipe the sweat from his brow, and left his room. As the only bachelor—aside from their newly widowed seventy-eight-year-old mother—he had offered to take the small room in the loft. Besides, it was the only room with an en suite bathroom, which meant—

Stop. Don't even think about it—not today, not with Mom sleeping soundly below. And not after what happened during the gift opening.

That had been difficult even for him to smooth over, to lie his way out of. He had no idea how his case of heroin had found its way into the gifts, but he was just grateful that Corina hadn't opened it completely. He could only imagine what would have happened if a syringe and spoon, let alone yellow powder, had spilled all over the family room floor. He just hoped that the social lubricant of which they had all indulged had rendered them all confused.

And that it helped them forget.

It didn't take a telepath to know that both of his brothers were suspicious of him. And with good reason.

Keep it together, Ox.

The stairway was unusually dark, for which Oxford was grateful; it would not bode well if he ran into any of his family members looking as terrible as he undoubtedly did. He slowly made his way down the staircase, and was again struck by the *completeness* of the darkness in the hallway below. It took but one more beep for him to locate the source of the sound, and when he did, he immediately knew what had happened.

Fuck.

The wind gusted suddenly, rattling the windowpanes above him, and in his hyper-agitated state he nearly leapt back up the stairs.

Come

Come

The wind gusted again, harder this time, and Oxford turned toward the sound, squinting his eyes to peer out the dark windows.

Was that a voice?

He shook his head and squinted even harder, trying to make out anything through the window.

She says every time the snow comes, she hears it—she says she hears it inside."

Oxford shuddered.

It was no use; even though he knew that the entire lawn was blanketed with snow, there were no street lights or lights from other houses to reflect off of it. And tonight, of all nights, the moon had either failed to rise or had decided to remain hidden behind thick clouds.

He heard another sound—not of the howling wind or the obnoxious beeping, but of a door opening. This time, though, he didn't jump, but instead gritted his teeth and tried to stop himself from shaking.

Thankfully, Cody noticed him almost immediately, and although Oxford could see the man's eyes widen even in the near pitch-black darkness, his brother did not cry out.

"The power is out," Oxford whispered, re-clenching his teeth after speaking.

"Fuck."

"Exactly."

A beep sounded, and Oxford saw Cody glance about nervously, trying to identify the source.

"The fire alarm," Oxford said, raising an index finger above his head. "To let us know it's running on batteries."

Cody nodded. His pupils, which had returned to their normal diameter, traveled down Oxford's still raised arm, and he fully observed his brother for the first time. His eyes widened again.

"Why the hell are you half naked? It's freezing in here!"

Oxford hesitated, and that was a mistake. Cody's brow furrowed.

"Are you using again?" he asked in a vehement whisper. "Is that why you couldn't look Mom in the face all night?"

The man missed nothing.

This time Oxford answered instantly.

"No," he lied.

He made a conscious effort to stare into his brother's eyes and not let his gaze wander.

There was an awkward pause, one that Cody threw out like a net, waiting to see what Oxford would say or do to give himself away.

Oxford bore down, refusing to give in.

"We need to get the generator running," Cody finally said, his eyes still squinting, accusatory.

Oxford nodded, and only after his brother turned did he dare swallow the cue ball-sized lump in his throat.

5.

IT TOOK OVER AN hour with both of them shoveling in the dark to finally gain access to the generator. Hell, it took almost twenty minutes for Cody and Oxford to walk the short distance around the house to the generator's approximate location. The snow continued to fall even as they dug, making their efforts nearly as fruitless as digging a hole on the beach too close to shore. The larger drifts already reached Cody's knees. What made it worse, aside from the fact that between them all they had was a crappy, two-dollar flashlight, were the branches: they were everywhere, sitting atop the snow or buried partway into the drifts like sprinkles tossed haphazardly atop a bowl of ice cream. Except these sprinkles were large. And sharp.

"I think I can grab the pull cord now," Oxford said, holding the flashlight close to the exposed top of the generator.

Cody stood up straight, arching his back to alleviate some of the pressure that had built up over the last hour. He should have probably been sweating from exertion, but it was so cold that even this basic physiological function seemed to have shut down.

"Give it a shot—"

A gust of wind tore the words from Cody's mouth, and he tucked his face deep into the collar of his thick down coat to avoid the brunt of it.

Come

Oxford raised one eyebrow.

"You hear that?" he asked his brother.

His fingers finally grasped the plastic end of the starter cord and he tightened his grip.

"Hey," he repeated when his brother failed to answer, "Did you hear that?"

"Hear what?"

"I dunno, it sounded like someone saying, 'Co—'"

A deafening crack sounded from somewhere behind them, and both men instinctively ducked, throwing their arms above their heads protectively.

The crack was followed by a horrible tearing sound, then a soft, almost gentle poof.

"Jesus," Oxford whispered breathlessly.

He swung the flashlight around, but the weak beam had a hard time illuminating the snowflakes a few inches from the bulb, let alone the dark forested area behind the house.

"That was a big one."

Oxford grabbed the pull cord again, and this time he gave it a yank. The motor barely turned over. He pulled again. The generator mustered a faint whirr. He pulled again. And again. With each successive pull, the engine turned over; then, like a man with tuberculosis clearing the mucus from his throat, it finally sputtered and roared.

With a sigh of relief, Oxford stood tall, stretching his aching back. As he did, he peered around in the darkness, feeling the immense weight of it.

We should get inside, he thought suddenly.

The woman at the train station had been right about the cold and the snow, and the longer he stayed outside the more certain he became that she was right about the third thing, too.

There *was* something wrong in Askergan, and he had no desire to find out exactly what.

"About time," he said, trying hard to keep the fear from his voice. "Now let's get back inside before we get raped by one of these falling trees."

6.

WHEN ALICE DEHAUST FIRST opened her eyes, there was only blackness. Confused, she closed them, and then opened them again. Panic began to set in, and a small whimper escaped her lips. Slowly, her visual field began to widen like a reverse pinhole, until her pupils let in too much light and she instinctively closed them for a second time. When she opened them next, her irises finally behaved and she could see again.

Where am I? was her first thought, closely followed by, *How did I get here?*

Alice rolled onto her back, barely noticing that she was topless. Her skin scraped across the—*Jesus, a bare mattress?*—bed as she turned, causing a flare of pain, but the signal crossed with her intense headache and the former was somehow muted.

Well, she thought, grimacing, *whatever I did last night, drinks were involved.*

Alice didn't need to see the rash on her back to tell her that— no, even without seeing the gluten-induced irritation or the fuzz-like coating in her mouth that felt like she had eaten the top of a bulrush, her headache was proof enough that she had indulged.

Alice swore. It had been a good month up until last night, only a few drinks here and there and nothing harder, but now she would have to start all over again.

She felt her nose run and sniffed hard, but when the sensation persisted, she brought a pale finger to her right nostril. When she pulled it away, the pad came back red.

Great, she thought, *drinking wasn't all I did.*

Alice looked around quickly, frowning at the sight of the pale yellow walls that were peeling near the corners of the room, and realized that they were void of paintings, photographs, or even a poster. A poster would have been nice—a poster was all she needed, proof that she wasn't holed up in some sort of crack house. But the only personal item she saw was a photograph on top of the television of a boy of about ten years. At first she thought it was just the photo that had come with the frame, but when she stared harder, she saw a faint pink scar that ran from the outer corner of his right eye and arced down to just below his lips. The boy also had small, dark eyes, eyes that seemed cold, even in the photo.

Alice shuddered.

Disgusted with herself on so many levels, she sat up and looked around for her shirt. Just when her eyes fell on it at the end of the mattress, all wadded up in a ball, a sound from behind her made her heart leap into her throat. Instinctively, she lay an arm across her bare chest and slowly turned.

A door at the back of the room swung open. As Alice watched with an expression that she knew could only be described as pure horror, a man stepped through the doorway. His eyes were so squinted that they were practically closed, and he didn't immediately notice Alice.

What the hell?

The man standing before Alice could not have weighed more than a hundred pounds. His thin, pale chest, marked with uneven patches of dark brown hair, was nearly concave, and she could have counted every single one of his ribs had she been so inclined. Below the man's squinted eyes, which caused a complex network of creases to run from the outer corners before disappearing into his hairline, was a bulbous nose, and below that, chapped lips that could barely be discerned from his scraggly white beard. Unlike his beard, his hair was a stark black—clearly dyed—and although it was messy, Alice could tell that not long ago he had parted it with what might have been a meat cleaver.

Frozen, unsure of what to do next, Alice's gaze slowly traveled down his body, something that she immediately regretted. The man's tight white underwear was stained with brown smudges, and the outline of his semi-erect penis was clearly visible.

Who the fuck?

Desperate now, her eyes drifted back upward, and to her dismay she saw that the man was smiling now, revealing a row of thick yellow teeth. His dark, almost black eyes stared directly at her.

"Oh, hi there, sweetheart."

Sweetheart came out through his mangled teeth like *'shweehaar'*.

Instinctively, Alice's arm tightened across her chest. The man's smile grew.

"I—" Alice turned and put her shirt on as quickly as possible, no longing caring if the man caught a glimpse of her breasts. "—I was just leaving."

She spotted her jeans by the mattress, and in one smooth motion she pulled those on too.

Standing, Alice turned for one last glance and was horrified to see that the bearded man had slipped a hand into his filthy underwear and was fondling himself slowly, rhythmically, as if he were caressing a cat.

"You don't have to go," he said, leering at her. "Not just yet."

Alice backed quickly toward the door.

"Is your boyfriend gone, *shweehaaar*?"

The man took two deliberate steps toward her.

Boyfriend? Brad was here?

Terrified, Alice continued to back up, all the while reaching behind her. When her fingers blindly closed on the doorknob, she allowed herself another breath of the stale apartment air. She turned and pulled, but the door opened only a few inches before it caught again.

The man laughed and took another step.

"No, not just yet," he whispered in a horrible, whistling voice. "You don't have to go just yet."

Juuuust yeehhhht.

Panic began to fill her, but she willed it away, finally risking a glance behind her.

Chain!

The word split her headache in half. She closed the door, unhooked the chain, and then yanked it wide.

"Aw shucks, shweetie."

She dared one more glance at the man and was startled by the fact that he had somehow managed to remove his shitty underwear in the two or three seconds it had taken Alice to open the door. He was standing there, about a foot from the bare, stained mattress, knees slightly bent, stroking his fully erect penis with a thin hand adorned with long yellow fingernails.

Alice ran.

A moment later, she heard the man stumble into the hallway, and when he spoke again his tone had changed, his voice now filled with fury.

"Hey! Where is my case?! Where's my H?! You *fucking cunt*, come back with my H!"

This time, Alice did not turn.

7.

IT WASN'T QUITE SIX, yet every member of the Lawrence clan was wide awake. Even little Henrietta, who normally slept in until almost nine, was awake. And she was crying again — wailing.

What's wrong with you, Henrietta?

But even if his youngest daughter had been acting normally, this in no way a normal day, or even a normal Christmas morning, and the mood was tense bordering on unpleasant.

"Did you make some coffee, Ma?" Jared asked.

Veronica Lawrence nodded. Even though the power was out, more than three feet of snow had accumulated on the ground, and it was pitch black outside, the woman still felt the need to put rollers in her hair. It looked as if she had showered, too, although Cody couldn't see how that was possible without any hot water.

"The pot is almost ready," she replied.

Veronica Lawrence wasn't a small woman, but she wasn't overly large, either. Like an optical illusion, she had an odd *thickness* about her, as if she had extra layers of skin. Not the kind of sagging flesh that obese people were cursed with following substantial weight loss, but it was if she just had more *layers* of it.

She was a tough woman, always had been, but Veronica *cared*. After her husband — the patriarch — had passed, however, her resolve seemed to have softened, for which the Lawrence boys were grateful. But now, given her lack of immediacy, Cody was beginning to wonder if her softening was simply a manifestation of apathy. He took a good look at her face, trying to read the woman. She was pretty, even in her old age, with bright eyes and a small mouth that led to an even smaller cleft in her chin, which all the Lawrence boys shared to some degree or another.

The coffeemaker beeped, distracting Cody.

"Well I made the coffee," his mother said, "but I am not going to put it in your cup for you."

Veronica had softened somewhat, but she had not gone all the way soft.

"Who wants some?" Jared asked.

When his eyes fell on Oxford, he made a face and raised one of his slender palms defensively.

"Forget I asked."

No one spoke until Jared returned with four cups, all jangling together, the black liquid dripping down the sides of the white porcelain.

"I made them the way I like my women," he offered, with a wry smile. "Hot, black, and bitter."

It wasn't the first time he had made this joke, of course, and while it might have been moderately amusing years ago, especially coming from him, no one was smiling now.

Henrietta suddenly appeared at Cody's side and gently tugged at his pant leg. He looked down at her, relieved that whatever night terrors had bled into the early morning seemed to have passed. But his relief was short-lived; the toddler had dark circles around her eyes, and red splotches around her nose and mouth. She looked utterly exhausted.

"Come shopping, Daddy," Henrietta whimpered.

Henrietta was dressed in two sweaters and a pair of snow pants—anything to keep warm.

"Shopping, Daddy," she repeated, tugging his pant leg again. Cody offered a wan smile.

"I can't, sweetheart, the adults are talking."

That was it. Any calm that had passed over her broke, and her face shattered into a wail.

What the hell is wrong with her?

Cody turned to Marley, and caught her looking skyward.

"Corina!" she called across the room.

Corina, white headphones once again jammed in her ears, her eyes fixated on her phone, didn't acknowledge her mother.

"Corina!" Marley shouted again, louder this time, trying to be heard over Henrietta's cries.

Cody cringed.

Corina pulled one of the earbuds out and turned.

"What?"

Pardon, Cody almost said, but decided that tensions were high enough without correcting manners.

"Don't say *what,*" Marley said, and Cody smirked despite himself.

Corina stared at her mother with a blank expression.

"Please take your sister shopping."

"Shopping?" Corina asked, her face twisting. She gestured toward the window. "There is eight feet of snow out there!"

Are, Cody thought, *there* are *eight feet of snow out there.*

There was a momentary break in Henrietta's wails as she turned to look at her sister.

"You take me shopping?" she asked. The toddler was holding two empty grocery bags out to her sister, one in each hand.

Corina rolled her eyes, but she gestured for Henrietta to come to her nevertheless.

"It's Christmas, Corina," Cody said. "Why don't you and Henrietta open a present or two?"

This, at least, seemed to cheer up his eldest daughter.

Obviously, the girl had forgotten about Oxford's outburst the night before.

Cody, on the other hand, hadn't.

"Okay, so, what do we do next?" Oxford asked when the children were out of earshot.

The youngest Lawrence brother looked worse than he had the night before, Cody noted, but aside from Mama, they all looked pretty rough.

"Any extra coffee?"

Cody turned to see Seth, his dark hair a mess atop his head, his eyes red and his thin frame stooped. This visit was the first time that he had met the man, and Cody was less than impressed—Seth hadn't said much at dinner, and had said even less when they had opened the few presents the night prior.

Give him time. He just needs to warm up a bit.

Cody's eyes flicked from Seth to Oxford and back again.

Yeahs, we definitely all look a little rough, he confirmed.

"Call the sheriff," Jared offered, holding out his coffee to Seth, who took it without hesitation and gulped the hot liquid.

Cody nodded. "Yep, probably better to call the sheriff than the power company." He turned his eyes back to the blanket of snow that filled the yard. "Unlikely to get through to anyone there."

There was so much snow that when the wind relented for a moment and the white landscape was revealed, he found it impossible to interpret distance; everything was just one giant, featureless white void. He couldn't even make out where the road stopped, the embankment started, or where the frozen water met the shore. Even the multitude of branches that he had heard come crashing down throughout the night had since been covered with snow.

"Yeah, call the sheriff," Oxford concurred.

"Can't get a signal," Corina replied nonchalantly from somewhere behind them.

Cody looked over at his daughters. Both Henrietta and Corina were picking up coasters from the table, inspecting them, and after Henrietta's approval, put them in their bags. The toddler was more interested in these than the Christmas presents, it appeared, which was all the same to him. If nothing else, it reduced the odds of them coming across whatever was in that black case that Oxford was so desperate to conceal last night.

"How—?"

Even though he had stopped himself, his daughter, as astute as she was, knew what he was going to ask.

"What do you think I was doing on my phone?"

Facebook? Twitter? Instagram?

Cody turned back to Oxford and the other adults.

"Well, let's keep trying anyway. Ma, you check the landline as well. Also, let's turn the heat down a bit; not sure how long the power is going to be out, and the generator won't last more than a day or so if we leave everything on."

A day, Cody knew, remembering the half-empty tank, was an exaggeration.

8.

IT PROBABLY WASN'T THE best idea to go outside and play in the snow, considering that coming back *inside* to warm up afterwards was out of the question. But the Lawrence family could only play so many consecutive games of Scrabble before even those blessed with extreme patience started to become short-tempered. And, at this point, Cody would have done nearly anything to get away from Henrietta's crying—she was *incensed*.

"Holy shit!" Corina said after taking one step outside the house. The smile on her face was enough for Cody to overlook the curse.

His eldest daughter looked like a newborn penguin transitioning from land to water. The snow was up to her waist, and even though Oxford had carved out a small section directly outside the door, Corina could barely move.

"Go on, Corina!" Jared shouted encouragingly.

Both Jared and Cody were behind her, steeling their nerves to eventually brave the elements. Only Marley, Veronica, and Seth, who was still nursing his hangover in the early afternoon, had declined the offer to play in the snow. Even Henrietta, despite her inconsolable crying, had seemed keen, but Marley had quashed that idea before it had gained any traction.

"I can't!" Corina squealed. "I'm stuck!"

But she wasn't stuck, not really, and a couple of breaststroke-style movements later, she was able to walk again, having strayed into where Oxford had displaced some of the snow.

Cody followed his eldest daughter, and almost immediately

the cold air caused him to inhale sharply through his nose. Somehow, though, even coming from the now cool interior of the home, this cold air felt refreshing.

Holding his gloved hands out in front of him, it took but a few seconds before the black leather was first speckled and then covered with white. Cody laughed and belly-flopped into the snow. He raised his face slowly, enjoying the tingling cold on his cheeks as the snow melted. Somewhere, he heard Corina laugh and he smiled again.

"Incoming!" someone suddenly shouted, but before he could react, something hit him hard from behind, and a split second later his face was being forced back into the snow.

With a sharp twist of the torso, Cody managed to flip his body over, tossing Jared from his back. Wiping the snow from his eyes with a gloved hand, he growled.

Cody heard more laughter and pivoted, turning away from Jared to face Corina. Eyes narrowing, he growled again, and in one swift motion he scooped up a wad of snow and began packing it between his palms. It was too fluffy to make a real snowball, but Corina's face elongated in surprise nonetheless.

"Don't you dare!" she yelled, but when she tried to turn and run, she only managed to move a few feet before Cody launched his ammunition.

The snowball was mostly powder, so when it hit Corina in the shoulder, a white puff billowed up and struck her on the side of her exposed cheek. She screamed again, and reached down to scoop up two handfuls of her own.

Cody was about to dive to his right, maybe preemptively bury himself in the snowbank, when he heard a snarl from somewhere behind him.

Jared was on him again, this time hitting him in the lower back with his shoulder, and they both flew forward several feet.

For the third time in less than five minutes, Cody's face was buried in the snow.

Face wash.

His brother pushed his face deeper, then moved the back of his head side to side, ensuring that every pore was packed with snow. Cody struggled, trying to flip Jared off as he had done before, but this time his brother was higher up on his back and his efforts were useless. Just as his lungs demanded that he take a breath, his head was lifted, and like a yeti out of hibernation, he gulped hungrily at the air.

Cody blinked rapidly, trying to get the wet snow that hung from both sets of eyelashes to fall.

"Get off me!" he shouted, spitting snow from his mouth and forcing it from his nose.

Jared laughed.

"Want another face wash?"

Cody tried to turn and look at his brother, but with the pressure on his upper back, he was only able to move his head a few inches. He struggled, wriggled his hips, undulated his lower half, trying anything to break free, but it was no use.

"You are about to go under again," Jared warned, then in a louder voice, "Corina! Get over here and help me bury your father!"

Cody felt hands on the back of his head again and was about to take a deep breath, but as his eyes opened wide in anticipation, the falling snow seemed to part, offering him a clear view across the lawn. Whatever breath he was going to take caught in his throat.

Evidently, Jared had seen it too, as his grip on the back of Cody's head loosened and he slowly peeled himself off his brother.

"What the—?"

Less than twenty yards away from where the two Lawrence brothers lay, a parade of deer—at least seven, by Cody's count—were struggling to gallop through the thick snow. There were plenty of deer around the Lawrence home, of course, especially at this time of year. But never had Cody or Jared, in their fifteen years of coming up to this place, seen this many together, and definitely not a group that consisted of two males, their thick, twisted antlers covered in a thin, reflective layer of ice. As they watched in silence, Cody felt his jaw slacken even more.

It can't be, he thought, blinking hard.

Trailing but a few paces behind the pack of deer, and gaining fast, was a brown bear, his toothy mouth open, tongue lolling, its breath huge puffs of warm air.

The bear should have been hibernating—*had* been hibernating, Cody presumed, based on its thin frame and the loose, hanging brown fur.

What is it doing? Is it… is it hunting the deer?

Cody didn't get a chance to mull the odd question over in his mind before the parade of animals once again distracted him.

Frozen in fear, he watched a pack of wolves come next, their considerably more nimble and lithe bodies making better, albeit not great, progress through the thick snowdrifts. The first of the wolves passed the bear—the much larger animal didn't even seem to notice—and then the entire pack closed in on the deer. There were at least a dozen wolves, moving quickly, determined, more than enough to take down the deer even with the two large bucks. But to Cody's amazement, they ran right past what must have looked to them like a gluttonous meal. And like the bear that they had just overtaken, their thin bodies suggested that they could have done with one. He expected the deer to dart, to spread out as best they could in the deep snow as the wolves approached, but they too seemed not to notice.

"Get inside!" someone yelled, the sound carrying on the wind, which was starting to pick up again.

"Get the fuck inside!"

Oxford—it was Oxford. Cody had forgotten that the youngest Lawrence brother was out there in the white somewhere, brandishing a shovel.

Then there was another sound, one that amidst the heavy breathing and snorting of the wild animals that trudged across the lawn shouldn't have raised much concern. But the sudden crack—a splintering, deafening sound that came from above, followed by a whoosh of displaced air—was equally as terrifying. Somewhere through the layer of cold snow that again covered Cody's face and ears, he heard Corina scream.

Chapter Three
Deep Freeze

1.

FOR ALMOST A DAY and a half now, Deputy White and Deputy Coggins had been trying to contact Sheriff Dana Drew. The sheriff wasn't answering his radio, his cell phone, pager, smoke signals, fucking carrier pigeon—nothing. At first they had thought that he had just cut off early, gone straight home after dealing with the old hag out east—it had been his last day before he was scheduled to take his holidays—but it wasn't like the sheriff not to call. They had heard nothing from Alice or the sheriff's wife, either, and the former had Coggins worried— really worried. It was Christmas Day, and Alice should have stopped by the station; she had promised she would come visit him.

"We have to go out there," Coggins said.

The two deputies had been fielding calls all morning, and now that it was well into the afternoon and the snow still hadn't stopped, the volume was increasing; like an incessant drone, the ringing seemed to never stop. Both deputies wanted to unplug the phones; wanted to block out the ringing and the prattling on the other end of the lines. The only reprieve that Coggins had had was when he had gone home to get a few hours of sleep, and had forced himself—despite all that was going on and all of the people he needed to contact—to shut his cell phone off. And now his reception was sporadic at best. He had extended the same courtesy to Paul, but the big man had declined. A stickler for rules, that one—*never leave the station during a crisis.*

Coggins looked away from Deputy White and stared out the window. Although the plow had come by and cleaned out their lot and most of the streets downtown, based on the calls they had been receiving that was probably the extent of their work. He had thought that most of the townsfolk would have been content with just spending time with their families on Christmas, cuddled and huddled up close like they were supposed to—but no, most of the calls had to do with restoring power, getting their precious television and internet back up and working.

"You think we could get Johnny out here with his pickup to lead the way?" Deputy White asked, his eyes, like Deputy Coggins', trained on the snow that continued to fall.

Paul fought the urge to lick his lips; the cold had started to seep into the station, drying everything out.

"Johnny? You mean Johnny over at Johnny Mech's Autobody?"

Paul nodded.

"He's got a plow?"

Again, Paul nodded.

"Yeah," he replied. "Just a pickup, but it has a plow extension he puts on sometimes. Probably out already, making some extra cash."

"Oh, I wouldn't worry too much about that—if he has a plow, I'll get him to come out here."

Something in Deputy Coggins' voice made Paul turn. The pale man was smiling widely, revealing his small teeth. There was a gleam in his eyes, and staring down his pointy nose, he looked almost sinister.

"I'll call him," Coggins repeated. "Johnny will come."

Paul nodded for a third time and turned back to the snow.

The wind had picked up and the windows started to rattle.

"Who's going out there?"

The answer was immediate.

"Not me."

"Well, fuck, not me either."

There was a pause—an impasse.

"I'll tell you what," Coggins began, breaking the silence, "if you can answer a hockey trivia question, I'll go. If you get it wrong, you go."

Deputy White didn't answer, but in their small, petty world of sports arguments and useless factoids, that was as good as spitting in his palm and shaking hands.

Coggins breathed deeply.

"Which two brothers have the most points in NHL history?"

Coggins saw Paul's reflection in the glass twist as the man's wide nostrils flare.

Then Paul's eyes suddenly widened and he swiveled quickly in his chair to face Askergan County's second deputy.

"Wayne and Brent Gretzky," he said, barely able to squeeze the words through his wide grin.

Deputy Coggins swore.

2.

OXFORD, JARED, AND CODY had been so concerned with Corina's injured leg that it wasn't until much later that they realized that the branch that had smashed her leg had first glanced off the window. Even though the smashed pane was up near the roof, the air that whistled through the broken glass dropped the temperature inside the house, already in the low sixties as it was, even lower.

"It's okay, sweetie," Cody repeated, trying to comfort his crying daughter. "Once we get this boot off, we'll get you all fixed up."

He turned and looked back into the house.

"Ma, get some warm washcloths and some clean towels, okay?"

Corina whimpered.

"Ma!" Cody shouted again.

A moment later, Veronica Lawrence stepped into the mudroom, a large pot of warm water in her hands, two damp washcloths hung over the edge.

Cody grabbed the pot of water from his mother and placed it on the ground beside the bench. Henrietta suddenly appeared in the doorway, squeezing her small body through the tiny space between the frame and Mama Lawrence's wide hips. Her crying had become intermittent as of late, which was at least something positive to hold on to. And it appeared as if the wails were currently in a downswing.

"Wanna see!" the little girl shouted in her high-pitched voice. "Wanna see! Wanna see!"

Instinctively, Cody stood to go to her, to guide her out of the room, but in doing so his hand slipped from behind Corina's calf, and with the support gone, she screamed long and loud. Cody immediately adjusted his hand.

"Wanna see!" Henrietta said again, ignoring her sister's reaction and forcing her way further into the room.

Marley followed closely behind, first-aid kit in hand. There were thick, dark circles around her eyes, and her face, usually soft and round, looked unusually narrow. Neither of them had slept well since the power had gone out, and Henrietta's crying had kept them up ever since they had arrived. At first they had thought that she was getting her molars, but they couldn't see anything cutting through her gums. Her temperature was fine, too, and aside from the mucous generated by her constant crying, she didn't seem to be coming down with anything, either. It was just so odd, and their efforts to calm her so futile, that both Cody and Marley were an emotional wreck.

And now this.

There were six of them in the small mudroom now—Mama, Cody, Jared, Corina, Marley, and Henrietta—and despite the plummeting temperatures, it was suddenly hot and hard to breath.

"Give the first-aid kit to Mama and get Henrietta out of here," Cody instructed Marley.

His wife looked at him then, her hazel eyes blazing, accusatory. But before Cody could say something that he would probably regret later, a hand came to rest on his arm and he turned to see Jared staring back at him.

I've got this, the man's eyes said, and Cody reluctantly yielded.

In a soft, calm voice, Jared took over, saying, "Seth, please come get Henrietta and play with her in the other room."

Henrietta whined in protest and Cody squeezed his eyes

tightly closed.

Please don't start crying again.

He didn't know how much more he could take.

"It's okay, sweetheart," Jared continued, "Seth is going to let you open a few presents—maybe even all of them."

The young girl's face lit up with the word *presents*, her mood changing instantly. A moment later, Seth poked his head into the mudroom and without a word—and consciously avoiding looking anywhere near Corina's injured leg, Cody noted—he scooped up the toddler and whisked her away.

"Mama," Jared said, "see if you can get ahold of Sheriff Drew, or the station, or any of the neighbors—Mrs. Mullheney, maybe."

Mama nodded and also left the room. With her, Seth, and Henrietta gone, the air was suddenly easier to breath.

"Okay," Jared continued, turning his attention to Corina. His voice was soft but direct. "We're going to pick you up now and lay you on the bench."

Corina's wet eyes widened, but she nodded.

Jared turned to Oxford first.

"You grab her left side, under her arm, and I'll take the right."

Jared moved around Cody to prepare himself.

"You take her legs," Jared instructed Cody next. "Keep them as straight as possible."

This time it was Cody who nodded.

"On my count: one, two... three."

On three, they hoisted Corina up as smoothly as they could without a flat board. A small gasp escaped the young girl's lips, but Cody fought the urge to look up, determined to keep his eyes locked on her leg. Although her snow pants were dark from the melted snow, he could see another more viscous liquid starting to stain the material around the girl's shin.

A moment later, Corina was lying on her back, her legs completely stretched out on the length of the bench, her mouth wide in a painful moan.

"Good," Jared said, leaning away from Corina to get a better look. "Ox, see if you can find some ibuprofen or acetaminophen or something stronger." Jared hesitated. "There might be something in—"

Oxford waved him off.

"I'll find something," he replied before rising and leaving the room.

Of course you will, Cody thought, his mind wandering back to the black case, but then Corina whimpered again and he refocused.

"Okay, sweetie, we are going to take off your snow pants now, alright?"

Corina nodded, tears silently spilling down her cheeks.

Her pink snow pants were already pulled down to her waist, and Jared managed to wriggle them down over her hips without much effort. But when they got to about mid-thigh, Corina's breath started to come in short bursts, and when they got to just above her knees, she screamed again.

Jared stopped immediately and exhaled loudly.

"This is not going to work," he said, and Cody nodded in agreement.

When did he become so calm?

Cody and his younger brother had never been very close, something that he attributed to lifestyle differences. And ever since Dad died and Jared had missed the funeral, they had spoken even less. In fact, it must have been nearly a year since the two had exchanged words. Regardless, this man was not the same man that had been prone to losing his temper and yelling until his face went red when he didn't get what he wanted. Nor was this the same man who had fainted when — it couldn't have been more than four or five years ago — Cody had broken his pinky finger in a baseball game and had sent him a picture in a text message. A *picture*, for Christ's sake.

As if reading their thoughts, Mama suddenly returned to the mudroom with a set of cooking sheers, which Jared took from her. The shears made quick work of the pink snow pants, splitting them easily down the leg. Once the fabric had been peeled away, Cody realized that Corina's injury was more serious than he, and probably either of his brothers, had first thought.

The girl was wearing a pair of black tights that stopped just above her ankle. The thick elastic that held them there looked darker than the rest, and it looked tacky as well. Almost immediately, the smell of fresh blood filled the air.

Shit.

Cody gently worked his hand from the bottom of her ankle up her shin, and as he did he could feel Corina's entire body begin to tense. When his hand brushed against something solid and irregular halfway to her knee, she yelped and Cody swallowed hard.

The stiff protrusion could only be one thing.

"We need to get her to the hospital," he said, his voice thin and wavering.

He looked up at Marley, who was still standing in the doorway. Her face was as pale as the blanket of snow outside, her hazel eyes as icy and hard.

"Well, that's not going to happen."

It was Oxford who answered. He had reappeared behind Marley and gently pushed his way by her. In one of his outstretched palms, Cody could see the unmistakable shape of two round white pills.

"Why the hell not?" Cody answered angrily.

Oxford bent down and placed the pills in Corina's mouth, which was open, her lips twisted in silent agony. Somewhere, the wind blew.

Come   *Come*

Oxford brought the glass of water he carried in his other hand to Corina's mouth and the girl swallowed.

"Well, why the hell not?" Cody repeated.

Oxford scratched at his left arm, followed by his neck, which was already red from what Cody assumed was previous scratching.

Jared slowly moved his way down Corina's body, gently guiding Cody away from her injured leg before things got heated.

"Well?" Cody asked again, his anger building.

"Why do you think?"

Cody frowned. He didn't like this game.

"The snow? I thought you shoveled."

"I was—"

"Guys," Jared interjected.

His plea went ignored.

"If you weren't out there shoveling, then what the hell were you doing?"

Oxford opened his mouth to answer, but Cody didn't give him a chance.

"Oh, I think we all know what you were doing out there."

Again, Oxford tried to answer, but he was cut off.

"You have fleas, Ox? Is that why you are scratching yourself all the time like a mangy dog?"

Oxford's calm demeanor vanished, and his face contorted in anger.

"I *was* fucking shoveling, but I can't shovel an entire street or fucking highway!"

"Guys!" Jared interjected again, louder this time.

"And I almost got raped by a fucking brown bear—"

This wasn't entirely true: as frightening as the experience had been, the bear hadn't even noticed him, despite passing within a few feet.

"—or do you not remember the zoo that passed within inches of my lips?"

"Guys!"

Cody put Corina's leg down gently on the bench and stood.

"Why were you shoveling, then?" he shouted angrily. "Trying to find a quiet spot to inject whatever the fuck you're hiding in that black case?"

"Cody!" Jared shouted at the top of his lungs.

Somewhere in the other room, Henrietta started to cry again, and Cody felt himself losing control. He turned to Jared, his face turning a deep crimson.

"Oh, fuck you, Jared," he spat. "You're no angel. Where the fuck were you at Dad's funeral, huh?"

And then Cody completely lost it. He shoved Jared's narrow chest, and the man stumbled backward, tears spilling from his eyes.

"Selfish bastard," he spat, whipping around. "All of you are fucked up. Oxford's a fucking junkie, Mom's fucking depressed... and you?" he stared directly at Marley. "What the hell is wrong with *you*? You can't even... can't even..."

Cody's throat suddenly went dry as he watched Marley's expression change from embarrassment to fear.

"Fuck," he whispered, rubbing his eyes. In the other room, Henrietta's crying intensified.

Everyone was staring at him.

Calm.

The stress of having Marley judge every one of his actions, the evidently poor decision of coming north with the storm on the way, Henrietta's inconsolable nature, and Corina's injury compounded—and he had taken it out on all of them. And there was something else, too—something was wrong here in Askergan, something that Cody couldn't quite place. He knew he wasn't the only one that felt it, either, as they all seemed on edge ever since the wind had started to howl.

Cody shrugged and opened his mouth to apologize when the lights overhead suddenly flickered and the hum of the generator, a noise that they had all become accustomed to, sputtered.

Come

Come

"See?" Oxford said, but the anger and hurt had since fled his voice.

He raised a finger to the lightbulb above, which, while it was again producing steady light, was now emitting a pale yellow glow instead of a bright white.

"That," Oxford paused, "is why I dug out the cars."

3.

EVEN WITH JOHNNY'S PLOW leading the way, Deputy Bradley Coggins' squad car got stuck in a snowdrift not ten miles down Highway 2. The angry deputy slammed his gloved hands against the steering wheel and pumped the gas in frustration.

Then he swore. And swore again.

After punching the steering wheel a second time, he grabbed the radio and clicked the call button rapidly, not bothering to identify himself. There was a brief moment of silence, followed by a burst of static.

"Coggins? That you?" Deputy White asked, and Coggins detected what could have been a hint of satisfaction in the big man's voice.

Goddamn it, why did I ask that stupid question about the Gretzkys?

It had been his cockiness, of course; he knew thousands of obscure NHL trivia facts, but that one was his favorite—his go-to. No one ever got that one right; Wayne had over twenty-eight hundred points, while his brother Brent—who only played thirteen NHL games—had a paltry four points.

Goddamn it.

The radio crackled again.

"Sheriff? That you?"

Deputy Coggins closed his eyes and took a deep breath.

"No, it's me," he said, his voice surprisingly calm. "Got stuck up here on Highway 2."

He honked the horn, and when he saw Johnny's eyes look up at him in his rearview mirror, he made a sweeping arm gesture indicating that the man should get out of his truck and come to him.

"Fucking guy," he muttered, forgetting that the radio was still on. "No, not you, Paul; Johnny—I'm going to see if this miscreant can get me out of here."

He let go of the button and waited.

"Okay," Deputy White replied hesitantly. "Are you going to keep going up to Mrs. Wharfburn's after you're out?"

Coggins brought the radio to his mouth and was about to answer when he changed his mind.

Fuck it, he thought, *better to keep going than head back to the office and field calls all day—again.*

"Hello?" Deputy White asked. As if to reinforce his decision, Coggins heard two phones ring in the background.

"Yeah, I think I'll keep going. The sheriff is probably just stuck inside—snowed in—having tea and talking about the last bowel movement the woman's stupid cat had."

Even though he had meant it as a joke, his words rang hollow. The sheriff had been gone for almost two days, and Coggins had a sinking feeling that something was terribly wrong.

Nevertheless, Deputy White chuckled on the other end of the radio.

"Hey, Coggins?"

"Yeah?"

"Brent Gretzky only had—"

Deputy Coggins reached over and flicked off the radio before the big man could finish his sentence. His mind wandered to how often he needled the much bigger man, and couldn't help but think that he was getting his just deserts, that this was karma coming back around again to kick him in the ass.

A moment later, Johnny managed to clear enough snow to free the squad car and Coggins' finally got moving again.

Just as he put the car back into gear, a jingle—*duh duh duh duh dah, ba badi badi bah*—suddenly erupted in the cab, and Deputy Bradley Coggins was so taken by surprise that he nearly swerved off the road.

"Jesus *fuck*," he swore. His heart was racing so quickly that it took him three tries to grab his phone from the center console.

"Paul? I get it, fucktard. You won." he spat.

There was a breathy pause on the other end of the line, and for a moment Coggins thought that someone—what were the kids calling it again? Bum-dialed?—had rung him by mistake.

"Paul? That you?"

But then a female voice replied.

"It's me, Brad," the woman said, and Deputy Bradley Coggins immediately knew who *me* was.

"Alice?" he gasped. "It's been—" Coggins thought about it or a moment, "—it's been more than two days! Where the hell are you?"

There was another pause, but this time there was no breathing. Instead, Coggins could only hear wind on the other end of the line.

"Alice, are you—?"

"—I—I—it happened again."

There was fear in the woman's voice, fear laced with disappointment and pain.

Coggins' heart fell to the floor.

Fuck.

"Alice—" Coggins began, but stopped himself when he realized that his dismay—his utter disappointment—was going to come off as condescension. He cleared his throat and pulled his foot off the gas pedal. The snow was coming down in a thick blanket, and Coggins could barely make out the back of Johnny the Mechanic's red pickup truck that was but a few car lengths ahead.

"What happened?" he asked, his tone deliberate and direct. Coggins thought for a moment that Alice might misinterpret his question, might think that he wanted her to relive the relapse, and he immediately wished he had used different words.

There was another pause, and the deputy began nervously squeezing the cell phone between thumb and forefinger while he waited for a response.

"I dunno," Alice replied at long last.

Although Coggins was grateful that she had gotten his meaning, he still didn't know what to say. She had been doing so well for so long that he had forgotten how to talk to her about her addiction. In fact, he had almost—not quite, but *almost*—forgotten about it altogether. But now, upon uttering those fateful words, "it happened again", the memory of finding her that night at the police station more than two years ago, a needle still hanging out of her thin arm, blood and vomit covering her mouth and nose like an obscene beauty mask, flooded his mind. He shuddered and decided to try to change the subject... at least for now.

"The sheriff was looking for you," he said softly.

He could almost hear her shake her head.

"I know," Alice replied.

"Where are you now?"

"Driving."

"How far away?"

"Dunno. A few hours, maybe less."

A few hours?

"I don't know what happened this time, Brad, I really don't

remember. I—I remember leaving work, then—"

Her voice hitched and she began to cry.

"It's okay, Alice, it's okay."

"Where are *you*?" she managed between sobs.

Coggins squinted into the white squall before him.

"Highway 2?" he answered uncertainly. "But the roads are bad. Real bad. You probably shouldn't be on the road—no one should."

He squinted hard, trying to make out Johnny's shadow in the truck in front of him. The man appeared to be waving his arm.

"I'm out to meet up with the sheriff at Mrs. Wharfburn's."

Deputy Coggins heard the breath catch in Alice's throat, followed by a thick sniff.

"Why don't you come and meet me there?"

Pause.

"I—I don't think I—"

But the phone beeped twice and went dead before Alice finished her sentence.

Shit.

With only a quick glance down at his phone, nervous about taking his eyes off the road for even a second, he found her number and thumbed send. Nothing happened.

He glanced down a second time and realized that whatever weak signal his phone had grasped when Alice called was long since gone: zero bars.

Goddamn it!

A screech from the road drew his gaze just in time to see Johnny's red truck skid and fishtail wildly. For a brief second, Coggins thought the truck would spin completely around, maybe even smash into the front of his cruiser, but thankfully it butted up hard against the median, stopping its rotation.

Coggins slammed on the brakes, the back end of his own car only tenuously gripping the fluffy snow. He stopped within two feet of Johnny's truck and quickly switched on his cherries.

Moron!

Another noise erupted, less distinct than the cell phone ring, but equally as startling.

"Coggins," his radio hissed, but the word was so peppered with static that he only barely recognized Deputy White's voice.

He tossed his useless cellphone on the passenger seat and snatched the radio.

"Yeah—what is it now?"

More static.

"Speak up, Paul, all I'm getting is static here."

He found himself again thinking of the night that he had found Alice, and another shiver ran up his spine.

"...power out up by... Wharfburn... cell phone..."

There was more static, and Coggins waited.

The power was out by Mrs. Wharfburn's? Well, wouldn't that be ironic.

He thought of the sheriff alone in the dark with the woman.

Ironic and terrifying.

"You hearing me?"

"I am now," Coggins replied, pressing the talk button.

"Power out everywhere north of Mill Road," the deputy repeated, his voice coming through with unexpected clarity.

"10-4. I'm just gonna keep on plugging here. You good to hold down the fort? If you need help, get that cadet—what's his name? Williams?—get him in to give you a hand. Have him take a turn answering the phones."

He paused, but this time there was no static response.

"Paul?" he asked uncertainly.

But the only answer was a gust of wind that struck the side of his squad car with enough force to push the ass end a foot back onto the road.

Fuck.

4.

THE LIGHTS WENT OUT again at almost exactly seven that evening, about an hour after the last tendrils of sunlight stopped licking the horizon. Whether it was some sort of psychosomatic response, or the temperature had somehow instantaneously dropped a handful of degrees, the puffs of moist air that exited Cody's lips and nose grew thicker.

A sudden pang of hunger hit him, reminding him of the fact that he hadn't eaten in almost a day—none of them had.

"Ma, could you put together some sandwiches?" Cody asked, looking over at his mother.

Veronica Lawrence seemed the least disturbed by the afternoon's occurrences, as she had barely acknowledged the situation. Instead, the woman resolved herself to sitting in her chair, slowly rocking back and forth, her hair immaculate, her off-white cashmere sweater wrinkle-free. But it was the strange, flat look on the woman's face that bothered Cody most of all. It was clear that this whole situation was too overwhelming for the woman who, since Gordon had died, usually spent her time alone on the veranda reading or just watching the trees.

Cody couldn't blame her; everything was overwhelming for him too, case in point being him blowing up at his brothers and at Marley. At least Henrietta had stopped crying for the time being, though that was more likely from exhaustion rather than her getting over whatever was irking her.

All he wanted to do was to go home. To round up his family and get the hell out of Askergan.

"Sure, Oxford," Mama said, slowly pulling herself to her feet. "Tuna fish okay?"

Oxford?

"It's Cody, Mom. But, yeah, tuna is fine," Cody answered hesitantly, eyeing his mother as she made her way slowly to the kitchen.

Just a simple mistake caused by stress... this is definitely too much for the poor woman.

All save Seth and Oxford—who were out siphoning gas from the cars and filling the generator—were huddled in the family room again, much like the previous night. But unlike yesterday, there were no smiles or anxious anticipation of gift opening. Instead, the atmosphere was tense bordering on despair.

"We have to get out of here," Marley said suddenly, breaking the silence. Her grief-stricken face made her look at least a decade beyond her thirty and change years.

And you have to stop saying that.

"I know," Cody answered.

Corina turned her head gingerly in Marley's lap at the sound of his voice and stared at him with glazed eyes.

"I know," he repeated.

They had turned the temperature down to fifty-five degrees in the house and had turned off all but one of the lights. But despite their conservative efforts, they had already burned through whatever fuel had been left in the generator.

"Still no signal," Jared said, his eyes transfixed on his phone.

The wind gusted, a high pitched whistle that seemed almost mocking in nature.

> *Come   Come*
> *Come*

It was the third or fourth time that Cody had heard what sounded like a voice carried on the wind, and he cautiously looked around at his family to see if they had heard it too.

I must be losing it, he thought when he realized that none of the other Lawrences had reacted.

But there was something in the way that their glances were all sidelong, as if they were all trying hard *not* to look, that made him think that maybe—just maybe—they had heard it too. He was about to say something to this effect when the back door suddenly flew open and Oxford stepped inside the house, pulling Seth in with him. Oxford quickly closed the door, trying to limit the amount of cold air that followed them over the threshold. Like the rest of them, he looked tired, his eyes sunken into the back of his head so deeply that with his cap pulled low Cody could barely make out the whites. In his mitted hand he held a dark red gas can.

"This is it," he said, his tone flat and even. He shook the can, and Cody could tell by how long it took for the liquid inside to slosh from to one side to the other that it couldn't have been more than half full.

Oxford bent to remove his boots, but he left his jacket, hat, and mitts on. His face was white with frostbite, the tip of his nose so pale that it looked as if he had applied zinc sunblock.

"Aside from this," he said, holding up the gas can, "I put the rest of the gas from the cars in the generator. Got about an eighth full."

He paused, his eyes darting from Corina to Marley before returning to Cody.

"Should give us another two or three hours."

He looked away when he said this, a clear indication to Cody that his estimate was generous.

Seth, who had also removed his boots but left his outer garments on, said nothing. Cody wasn't surprised—the man seemed to have lost the ability to speak, or maybe he'd never acquired it.

"What do we do now?" Cody asked.

Oxford opened his mouth to answer, but before he could, the wind gusted—a long, hard burst that howled for a good minute—and the window high above them shattered and fell inward. Marley and Corina screamed as a massive section of glass crashed to the floor, just missing where Henrietta sat playing with the owl that Oxford had bought her. Cody immediately sprang to his feet, as did Jared, both hopping off their respective seats and lunging at the girl.

Cody reached the frightened child first and quickly scooped her into his arms.

"You okay?" he asked breathlessly, as Jared inspected her legs, arms, and hair for glass or wounds.

Henrietta stared blankly at Cody for a moment before her eyes widened and her lower lip slowly started to tremble. Then she started to cry. Again.

Cody placed his hand on the back of her head and gently pulled her face into his thick wool sweater. It was clear that she had been frightened more by him and Jared hurtling toward her than by the falling glass.

"She's fine," Jared informed him, before retreating to the kitchen to get a broom.

Cody looked over at Oxford, still standing frozen in the doorway. The man's face was gaunt, and the dark circles around his eyes seemed to be etched with charcoal. Desperation clung to his features.

It didn't appear that he had even flinched when the glass fell inward.

Clean for six months?

This almost made him laugh.

"It's going to be okay—everything is going to be okay," Cody said.

His voice wavered slightly, and he looked around to see if anyone had noticed. No one had, except, of course, for Marley. His wife was staring at him, and her hands, although gently cradling Corina's head, seemed tight, as if there was suddenly not enough skin to comfortably cover her fingers. The woman's dark hazel eyes blazed at him—*into* him—and a solitary tear rolled silently down her pale cheek.

Things are going to be okay, Cody thought again, fighting back his own tears. *We can get through this—Respect, Resolve, Rekindle.*

This sounded like a bad joke; even if they managed to get through this, it was clear that things would never be the same between them again. Between *any* of them.

The wind blew again, and this time the bitterly cold air didn't thump the sides of the house with a deep rumbling, but instead it whistled through the sharp remnants that clung to the frame of the smashed window. To Cody, it sounded like a high-pitched laugh.

Coooooome.

"It's okay," he repeated quietly, bouncing Henrietta in his arms. He could barely feel her body beneath all the clothing.

The little girl stopped crying for a brief moment and looked up at him with big, moist blue eyes.

Cody's heart nearly broke.

"I'm 'cared, Daddy."

He looked at her again; he was almost certain that she was going to say that she was cold.

Scared? She can't understand what's going on, can she?

"I know," he replied, barely able to hold back his own tears. *I'm 'cared too, baby girl.*

The little girl's button nose was red, but her cheeks were white and glistening. He would have to cover her face with a scarf soon to avoid frostbite.

"I'm 'cared," she repeated, then started to cry again.

The wind blasted again.

> *Come   Come*
>
> *Cooooooome*

Cody nervously looked around the room.

Do they hear that?

No one spoke or raised their eyes; instead, they were content in burying their faces into the collars of their coats, trying desperately to conserve heat and to ignore what was going on around them.

Did I hear that?

The house went silent for several minutes. Even Oxford seemed to have stopped fidgeting.

"Well," Cody said at long last, "what do we do now?"

What the fuck *do we do now?*

5.

I DON'T THINK I'M in any shape to see him," Alice Dehaust said. *Or you*, she wanted to add, but decided against it. It didn't matter anyway; there was no answer—the connection had been lost. As if to affirm her comment, she looked down at herself. Without a bra, her breasts sagged beneath her black t-shirt, which was ridiculously thin and inadequate for the weather. She recalled finding it wrapped in a ball at the end of a bare mattress and shuddered.

Alice didn't dare look at her reflection in the mirror for fear of what she might find there. Instead, she focused her attention on the road and drove onward, even though she slowly began to suspect that she might be able to walk to Askergan faster than she was able to drive—if walking had been possible in all the damn snow.

Alice had left the creep's house with the intention of heading home, but after falling asleep at the wheel twice, she had decided to check into a small motel.

An hour. I'll stay an hour, she had promised herself, but when she finally woke up—thankfully on a different mattress, one covered with a sheet this time—the entire night and most of the next day had passed. And thus she had left again, not showering, not freshening up, and in pretty much the same shape as she had arrived. Only the rash from the gluten in the alcohol and whatever else she had ingested—*You fucking cunt, come back with my H!*—was nearly gone now, but her mind was still a jumbled mess as she tried fruitlessly to recall exactly when things had gone so wrong.

And, unfortunately, her slow pace gave her ample

opportunity to think—and thinking was the last thing she wanted to do. To force thoughts—*any* thoughts—from her head, she turned on the radio and tried to drown out her ever-wandering mind with the latest Top 40 hits, but the crappy, static-ridden music only served to annoy her further.

Twice she rang Deputy Coggins, but both times it went straight to his voicemail.

In the end, Alice gave up her weak efforts and fell victim to her thoughts. While she hadn't lied to Brad about not remembering last night, she hadn't exactly offered the whole truth, either. Ever since she had escaped from the horrible bearded man with the erect penis, glimpses of the previous evening had come back to her like early morning light through a stained-glass window. She remembered heading into the city for—what? Shopping?—some reason after work, and she also remembered heading to a restaurant when the street lamps had come on. That was when things went fuzzy. The next thing she could remember was talking to a man from Askergan—what were the odds?—about, well, nothing really. The conversation had quickly evolved, however, into one about everything, and she remembered spilling her guts about her life and her addiction. The details of this conversation were a muddy blur, but the rhetoric was well established in her mind.

No, I wasn't abused, or anything like that. Great parents, both of them. And even after I moved away and was still struggling, Dana rescued me, became like a second father in Askergan.

The odd thing was, although she could remember very little about the man that she had met at dinner, other than the fact that he most definitely was not the one who had emerged from the bathroom when she had awoken, she thought that he too had been an addict. Or maybe she was just projecting.

Did I sleep with him?

Her eyes drifted downward as if that would provide the answer; as if she might still have the condom in her lap, or worse, as if it were still hanging out of her.

Her stomach rolled at the thought, and she fought the urge to vomit. The graphic imagery, the drugs clearing her system, and her body desperately wanting more were all a toxic combination.

A gust of wind smashed against the passenger side of the car and was powerful enough to push her into a minor fishtail despite the fact that she couldn't have been going more than fifteen miles an hour.

Christ.

The snow was so thick—blowing and falling were indistinguishable now—that Alice could no longer tell if there were other cars on the road with her.

She pulled her foot completely off the gas and the car slowed to the point of nearly imperceptible movement.

Guilt slowly began to close in on her, and she wondered if she had mentioned Brad to the man in the bar, if she had recounted how important he was for her (failed) recovery, about how great he was to her even before they started dating.

About how he liked to goof around more often than she liked, but he was *nice*. One of the good boys, she often heard the Sheriff call him, a sentiment that she couldn't agree with more.

Even after finding her there, in the goddamn police station of all places, in a comatose-like state high on so many drugs that her tox screen had sounded like the ingredients on the back of a box of Party Mix. And even when their relationship had transitioned from professional, to personal, to *intimate*, he had never judged her.

Brad wasn't the only source of her guilt, either. It was the sheriff, too; he had literally picked her up off her feet and had even gotten her a job—a job at the police station, no less. And what did she do to return the favor? Break his trust again and again; use and abuse, as the saying goes.

Use and abuse.

Alice suddenly wished the heat in the car had another notch—another level. Scalding, perhaps.

Poor Bradley Coggins, with his goofy grin and crowded teeth. Poor Bradley fucking Coggins.

She hated herself then, irrespective of whether she had slept with the strange addict from the bar, and knew as distinctly as she knew it was snowing outside that if she'd had drugs— *Where's my H! You fucking cunt, come back with my H!*—she would use them right now. It didn't matter if the drugs were that pervert's heroin, some cocaine, clonazepam, or Demerol, she would have taken them—all of them, and all at once.

Fuck it, she resigned. *I'll go see Brad, even if he is with the Sheriff.*

Alice Dehaust allowed the toe of her loafer to depress the gas pedal just a fraction of an inch—just enough to cause her body to lurch and her stomach to protest.

As her vehicle slowly began to pick up speed, a blur of motion in her periphery startled her, and she readjusted her two-handed grip on the steering wheel.

What the hell?

She slowed a little and turned to look at what had caught her eye. To her surprise, the wind stopped blowing momentarily, as if consciously deciding to afford her a look.

What. The. Hell.

A whole family of deer, six in total, were galloping through the snow at the side of road; or at least trying to. If the situation hadn't been so surreal, Alice might have considered it comical. The snow was so high in places that the animals couldn't completely clear the banks with their front hoofs and instead ended up lurching forward with their necks, which, once stretched to their limit, slammed down on the snow in front of them. But this demented game of 'whack-a-mole', as bizarre as it was, wasn't even the strangest part—no, that honor was bestowed on the animals' unrelenting resolve; regardless of how hard or frequently they stumbled, they pressed onward, seemingly oblivious to their futility. As she watched, knowing that she should probably pay attention to the road but unable to pry her eyes from the scene, the lead animal—a four-hundred-plus-pound buck—ended up trudging through the snow like a plow, its torso gradually making a slow path through the thick bank. Then, as if that wasn't strange enough, she noticed something else traveling in—*within*—the herd.

Can't be, she thought, eyes wide. *It can't be.*

Alice slumped back in confusion, and in doing so, her arms accidentally pulled the steering wheel to her left; not much, not more than an inch, but her small Camry swerved nonetheless, the back wheels swinging out in a wide arc.

Her body shot forward in panic, and she frantically turned the wheel against the fishtail, her eyes widening to a size reminiscent of the deers' she had just witnessed. It took nearly twenty seconds of skidding before the front tires regained enough traction to respond—and respond did they ever. Fighting the swerve, Alice had pushed the steering all the way to one side, and when the wheels caught, the vehicle suddenly lurched in the opposite direction. A gasp escaped her and the g-forces made her momentarily dizzy. She cranked the wheel in the opposite direction, and this time the tires grabbed the snow-packed road almost immediately, whipping the car back the other way. White-knuckled, Alice wrenched the steering wheel again, but this time her car didn't respond; the violent torque had already sent the vehicle into a deadly spin and Alice screamed.

The last thing she saw before her world went black wasn't the blur of snow or the approaching median, but a glimpse of what she had seen running alongside and within the pack of deer: running between the bodies of their perpetual prey had been three large grey wolves.

Chapter Four
Fragmented

1.

"Jareeed... Jarrrrrrreeeeed."

Jared rolled onto his side and sighed in his sleep.

"*Jared!*"

His eyes snapped open, and his breath caught in his throat.

What the fuck was that?

Heart racing, Jared listened closely, sure he had heard someone say his name; a voice, moaning his name—a voice he knew well.

"Dad?" he whispered.

Jared swallowed hard.

Nothing; he heard nothing.

Somewhere in the room next to his and Seth's, Henrietta started to cry again.

Jared managed a staggered breath, his neck relaxing and his head falling back into his pillow.

What's going on?

He had had a hard time falling asleep; in fact, he had lain there for so long in the icy darkness that he hadn't even realized that he had finally drifted off. It wasn't just the cold or the two pairs of pants that had kept him awake, it was also the weight of their situation. There couldn't be more than a half-gallon of gas left in the generator, and despite what Cody said to placate his wife and ease his children, the roads would *not* be drivable tomorrow. Or the next day. And probably not for a few more after that.

Jarrreeeed.

He could have sworn he heard his name being whispered. Again he shook his head.

Get it together, Jared.

Slowly and inevitably, Jared's thoughts turned to Corina and her brutally broken leg. He had tried to remove the bark and pieces of her tights that had been wedged into the wound, but he hadn't done a great job; the poor girl—not even a teenager yet—was in too much pain for him to do any more rooting in her skin and bone, even hopped up on whatever Oxford had fed her.

Jared was no doctor, but the wound had been hot and red when he had set the primitive dressing, and he knew it wouldn't be long before the infection got serious. And soon thereafter, poor Corina's current ambivalent and numb demeanor would become intractable. No, something had to be done—and soon.

He lay in the dark for a moment, unmoving, wondering if perhaps Seth had said his name in his sleep, or maybe a dream had transformed the beeping fire alarm, warning them that the power had once again gone out, into his name. He listened closely, and this time he actually did hear something, although he wasn't entirely sure what it was. It sounded like several wet, bubbly pops, like someone kneading a wet ball of dough, followed by prolonged silence. He closed his eyes and concentrated, trying hard to pick up more of the strange noise. There was Seth's soft snoring, Henrietta's crying, and—and something else.

The wind struck the house then, and the cardboard covering that Oxford had put up over the broken window flapped loudly.

Come

And there it was, not the wet bubble noise, but the ominous wind that sounded as if it were beckoning to him, *calling* him, and—

Jared heard the other noise again, and he shook the nonsense from his head and shut his eyes, concentrating.

There.

A small smile of satisfaction crossed his lips. Beneath Seth's soft snoring and the roaring wind and Henrietta's crying he could hear someone's labored, hitched breaths.

Corina? Marley?

Cody and Jared had decided that it was best for mother and daughter to stay on the couch; better not to move them again. But this was coming from the other direction; not from the family room, but near the hallway leading to the stairs up to the loft.

Jared cringed; Oxford was staying in the loft.

He slowly rose out of bed, careful not to wake Seth.

It took several moments in the dark hallway before his eyes adjusted to the near pitch blackness. But even then—just standing there listening to the ratchety, wheezy, uneven breathing from the stairway—his heart sank; he had a sneaking suspicion of what had happened.

We should have searched him before entering the house, despite his claims of being clean. Should have forced him to hand over that black case he was so desperate to conceal.

Jared drew a deep breath of his own, wincing when the cold air hit his throat and then his lungs.

Come

He turned his eyes upward, searching; he wasn't even sure that the wind had blown just then.

What the fuck *is that?*

Then he heard the hitched breathing again, and he shook his

head and stepped to action. With careful steps, he made his out the door without waking Seth. Then he walked briskly down the hallway, keeping the fingertips of his right hand in contact with the wall for guidance. When he reached the stairwell, the darkness relented slightly as the moonlight flooded in from the tall windows in the family room.

There, half lying, half sitting on the stairs, was Oxford.

Jared shook his head, but rather than succumb to his disgust, he quickly dropped to one knee and began to strategize how to get his brother back into his room without waking the others.

Looking up at Oxford's pale face, his closed lids so thin that he could almost see the man's pupils through them in the dark, the phlegm rolling around his throat with every uneven breath, he could not fight the thoughts that entered his head.

What happened to you, Ox?

Jared brought his fingers to his temples and closed his eyes, trying to will away Henrietta's wails and think. A moment later, he opened them again and drew a deep breath.

This time it wasn't just the cold that hit his palate and the back of his throat, but there was an underlying funk there, too; the unmistakable thick and raw smell of human feces.

"Jesus, Ox," he whispered, unable to stop himself.

As he reached out for his brother, a flashlight suddenly flicked on from down the hallway and shined directly into Jared's eyes, blinding him. He shielded his face with the palm of his hand the way one might fend off a much taller attacker, and one thought entered his mind: *Please be Seth. Please be Seth. Please be Seth.*

But Seth didn't have the flashlight. Jared's heart sank.

"What the fuck is going on here?" Cody demanded.

2.

CODY FELT HIS ANGER about to bubble over like a tea kettle on the very precipice of boiling.

"You stupid mother—"

Jared hushed him loudly.

"Don't wake anyone else up. Help me get him back to his room."

The demands lacked conviction coming from Jared, who was crouched at the foot of the stairs, his squinted eyes barely visible between his outstretched fingers.

Cody took a step forward.

"Oxford," he started, but he hesitated when Jared stood, blocking his path.

Cody eyed the man and saw that unlike before when he had taken charge with Corina's broken leg, Jared's resolve was no longer there; he was tired, beaten. Cody took another step forward, and as he predicted, Jared bowed his head and backed away from the stairs. Cody felt a flash of guilt seeing the fear on the man's face, clearly remembering how he had pushed him earlier. This seemed to put a damper on Cody's anger and he wondered, not for the first time, what the fuck was going on—with his brothers, with Henrietta's screaming, and with this fucking storm.

And with him. Most of all, he was wondering what the fuck was going on *with him*.

"Oxford," he spat.

His eyes fell on his brother's pale face with his mouth wide and his tongue vibrating with every breath.

Cody leaned in, and almost instantly something caustic hit

his nose and he pulled his head back quickly.

"Oxford! Jesus Christ, Oxford! Did you shit yourself?"

The man moaned in response. Cody turned to Jared, and the younger man averted his gaze, both embarrassed and ashamed of their youngest brother.

Come   *Come*

Cody's eyes narrowed to slits as he turned back to Oxford. To his surprise, Oxford was staring back at him now, and despite the bright light that was shining directly into his face, his pupils were so large that the iridescent green of his irises was invisible.

"Oxford," Cody hissed again, trying his best to ignore the stench.

Then, inexplicably, Oxford chuckled, his tongue flapping about, smacking against the roof of his mouth.

"Oxford," the man repeated, his eyes rolling in his head like loose ball bearings. "I wassss doomed from th' staahrt."

He clucked his tongue.

"What a ssssstupid fucking name, named after a dicthhhhhionary."

His slurred words trailed off.

...or a city, or university, or shirt... Isn't there a shoe named Oxford, too? Cody wondered.

It was such a strange comment, so unexpected, that Cody almost laughed. Ashamed at not being able to maintain his justifiably furious demeanor, he turned quickly, whipping the flashlight around, the light cutting through the darkness like a lightsaber, and saw that Jared was smiling too. Then he heard his eldest daughter moan in pain from the couch not thirty feet behind them, and his anger returned.

Oxford's eyes had closed again, and Cody reached back and slapped him across the face. The sound—an amazingly loud *thwap*—reverberated off the darkness like an echo trapped in a copper pipe.

Oxford's eyes rolled, but failed to open even when his head flung to one side with the force of the blow and smacked against the edge of the stairs. Without thinking, Cody reared back and slapped him again. When his youngest brother still didn't open his eyes or cry out, he reached back and was about to hit him for a third time when he saw a figure pass by both him and his brothers, seemingly not even noticing them.

His hand hung in midair.

"Mom?" he whispered.

Veronica Lawrence just continued to shuffle passed, her feet barely lifting off the floor. She was wearing the same outfit as during the day, which was woefully inadequate in the plunging temperatures.

"Mom?" he repeated, his voice bordering on alarm now.

Yet the woman continued on, slowly making her way to the front door. As Jared and Cody simply stared, dumfounded as the woman reached the doorknob and attempted to pull it wide. It didn't budge; the deadlock was on.

But either she didn't notice this or didn't seem to care, she just continued to turn the knob back and forth, back and forth, her eyes straight ahead.

He felt a cold hand on his wrist and turned to look at Jared. The man's face was a mask of horror.

The creaking sound of the turning knob stopped, drawing Cody's attention back.

Mama Lawrence was looking at her sons, but there was no conceivable way that she was *seeing* them. Her eyes were a milky white, as if cataracts had formed overnight.

Cody felt his heart skip a beat.

"Gordon," she whispered, he lips barely moving. "Gordon

is out there, and he wants me to join him."

Jared squeezed Cody's arm tightly.

And then Veronica Lawrence's eyes cleared moments before rolling back in her head. She collapsed in a heap in the front hallway.

"Mom!" Cody shouted, and ran to her.

3.

DESPITE ALL THE COMMOTION, there was only one sound that mattered to Seth Grudin.

The crying.

It was the little girl's crying that had put everyone on edge, had made him think strange thoughts that didn't seem his own.

The girl—I must stop the girl from crying.

Seth sat up, not even bothering to check if Jared was still lying beside.

His first few steps were odd, as if he were stumbling through the ether, unable to balance himself with any certainty. It dawned on him that he was probably sleepwalking, but this was of little consequence.

The girl—the crying. It needs to stop, to end. If she wasn't crying, then Corina wouldn't have gone out in the cold, wouldn't have broken her leg. If it wasn't for the crying, Jared and his brothers wouldn't be fighting.

If the little shit wasn't crying, I wouldn't be hearing the voices.

Seth sighed and silently slipped into the hallway.

Come.

Somewhere in the back of his mind, he realized that Jared and his brothers were on the stairs, fighting again, but he paid this no heed.

After all, he was on a mission, one that was far more important than whatever inane nonsense they were arguing about.

He was going to the source, to Cody's room. And once he dealt with the crying, their fighting would end.

With his hand pressed against the wall for both balance and

direction, he made it unnoticed to Cody's room and crept through the open door.

Henrietta was standing in her pack-and-play crib, her stark white hands gripping the bars. Her mouth was thrown so wide in a shriek that her eyes had been forced closed by her cherubic cheeks and she didn't immediately notice Seth.

He used surprise to his advantage, and by the time she needed to pause to take a breath, he was already directly in front of her. Cooing softly, Seth placed his hand gently behind her head, while apply pressure with his other to her lower back at the same time. Surprisingly, when Henrietta looked at him, she calmed, her large blue eyes staring up at him in confusion.

"Shhhh," he whispered as he carefully laid the child on her back.

Those eyes — so deep, so blue. You knew something was wrong here all along, didn't you? You knew that something in Askergan is just not right.

Then Henrietta appeared to smile.

But this was no friendly smile; it was more of a sneer.

Her mouth opened and she started to speak in a voice that was not of a three-year-old girl, but of someone much older, someone with a harsh, gruff tone.

One that he knew well.

"You ain't worth nothing, fagot. Just a queer, sucking dick like a woman. That's all you are — a queer. Ain't worth nothing."

Seth continued to shush the girl, even as the tears spilled down his cheeks. He rested a hand on her forehead as he reached with his other for the girl's pillow.

"Yes, Dad," he said as he lowered the pillow onto her face. "I'm not worth anything... but don't worry about that now — now you must sleep."

He pushed harder, and her tiny arms reached up and

grasped at his hands, trying desperately to pull them away.

But Seth held the pillow firm, even as she started to kick her legs and her body began to twist and writhe.

"Mom!"

The shout rang through the hallway and echoed in Cody's room.

Seth snapped out of his stupor, pulling the pillow away from Henrietta's face.

Jesus Christ! What am I doing?!?

Henrietta took a massive gulp of air, and then let out a wail that nearly deafened him.

What the fuck *am I doing?*

Seth's expression, previously deadpan, convoluted into sheer horror. The pillow slipped from between his fingers and fell to the floor.

He swallowed hard and swiveled on his heels, unable to even look at the little girl in the crib.

Heart racing, sweat and tears streaking his pale face, Seth fled from the room, promising himself that he didn't mean it, that it wasn't him.

That it hadn't happened.

That he hadn't just tried to smother an innocent, beautiful three-year-old girl.

4.

IT WAS THE DAMN voices. Or maybe the *damned* voices. Oxford did not—could not—know. They were always there, of course, the clichéd angel and devil, guiding—or misguiding, as the case were—his jilted morality. But now they seemed different, somehow. They'd been different ever since he had arrived at his mother's place on Cedar Landing.

I'm sorry, Mom. I'm so sorry. Just one more chance, that's all I need. Just one more chance.

Come   Come   Come
Come   Come

Oxford clenched his teeth.

Get the fuck out of my head!

The voices were more insistent, and the incessant nattering had recently become far more devil than angel. But it didn't matter—he had silenced them, silenced them the only way he knew how. And it had felt good, so damn good, in the way that a stolen cookie was always sweeter and more tender than one bought or made.

Had.

Past tense; *had* felt good. But that was very different than how he felt now—very, very different.

Oxford coughed harshly, then winced at the acrid bile that rose up in the back of his throat like devil's fingers trying to claw their way out of his esophagus.

An image of the woman at the train station flashed in his mind, only this time, she wasn't pointing a chubby finger at her temple, but a gun.

Mama says something ain't right in Askergan. Mama says the voice are inside.

A wave of nausea hit him so suddenly that it was all he could do to prevent from vomiting. He thought it was a losing battle, and rolled over onto one side to avoid puking on himself, but he managed with deep breaths to stay the course.

And then he almost lost it again when he smelled shit.

Oxford groaned and with great effort he took his left hand — not the right; the crook of his elbow felt heavy and sore on that side — and snaked his swollen fingers down his side and to his boxers.

What the — ?

Something rough brushed against his fingers. Momentarily forgetting his swollen head and burning throat, he sat up awkwardly, fighting the spins. He felt around his boxers again and although he was able to identify the material, he was no less confused.

Toilet paper? Did I go to the bathroom and forget to remove the toilet paper after taking a dump?

But as he moved his hand around down there, it become as obvious as the increasingly pungent odor of human feces that his situation was far, far worse.

Disgusted with himself, he frantically searched the dark room for something to clean himself with. Finding nothing, he turned his attention to the toilet paper that was jammed into his underwear. Oxford shook his head again and looked away, the spins picking up in intensity. He felt hopelessly stranded on a teacup carnival ride, every movement making his head spin. No, the soiled strips of two-ply could not be used to clean up *this* mess. But he had to find something, because if Jared, or worse, if Cody, discovered him like this — well, he wasn't sure what they would do.

Towel—where the fuck is my towel?

"Looking for this?" a voice to his right asked, and Oxford's heart replaced the puke in his throat.

He turned slowly and faced Cody, who was sitting in a chair in the corner of his room, blanketed in shadows. In the brief moment that their eyes met before Oxford looked away in shame, he caught anger in his brother's stare.

Anger and disdain.

Cody tossed the small black case at Oxford, and unlike the wrapped baseball that Corina had thrown at him what seemed like weeks ago, he failed to react in time. The leather bag struck him in the collarbone and he winced. Instinctively, his left hand, fingers brown with shit, reached out and tucked it in close to his hip. Then he glared at his brother.

I hate you, he thought, trying to convey the message with only his rheumy eyes. *I hate you for judging me. You aren't perfect... I see the way Marley stares at you. You aren't perfect.*

But Oxford found it difficult to keep this face—this expression. Not because he didn't mean it, but because he hated himself more.

"I want you gone. Go do your fucking drugs as far away from me and my kids as you can, junkie," Cody said.

Message received.

It might have been the shock of the bluntness of his brother's words, or maybe the final, lingering haze of the heroin wearing off, but all of a sudden Oxford felt cold—freezing, in fact. His brother was wearing his cap and snow jacket, and his breath was coming out in puffs from between tight lips. Oxford, on the other hand, was clad only in his boxers, although the backs of his legs were covered in shit, which he guessed offered him some insulation.

The thought made his stomach flip again.

Cody's lower lip curled in utter disgust, his eyes fixating on Oxford's shitty lower half.

"I—I—I think the tuna was bad," Oxford remarked, but Cody didn't laugh—he didn't even crack a smile.

"Jared and Seth are going to get help, and I don't trust you here with my family," Cody said flatly as he stood. "I want you gone."

Oxford looked away and stared out the loft window. White—he saw only white.

Gone? Where am I supposed to go?

The wind howled again.

Come   *Come*   *Come*
       Come   *Come*

              Come

Oxford closed his eyes tightly. Clearly, his attempts to silence the voices—and that one in particular—had been a miserable failure. The idea of going out there with whatever was calling him made his fingertips tingle.

Leave me alone! Get the fuck out of my head!

5.

DEPUTY BRADLEY COGGINS ALMOST made it to Mrs. Wharfburn's house. At least he thought he was almost there; the blowing snow had transformed Highway 2 into a blanket of white. In fact, visibility was so poor that when Johnny braked suddenly, Coggins only barely managed to prevent his car from plowing into the back of him.

A minute or so later, a man's face appeared at his window, a round pink sphere breaking the monotonous, snowy scene, trails of congealed snot hanging from each nostril. Johnny's fur-lined hat was pulled down so low that it hid what Coggins knew to be thick, wiry eyebrows.

No heat in your piece of shit truck, Johnny?

Despite the man's obvious discomfort—he was now bobbing up and down, blowing air into his thinly gloved fists— Coggins turned to the radio and fiddled with the dial. It had been more than a half hour since he had been able to capture any signal, but he tried anyway—as before, the entire AM dial was dead.

A blast of wind struck his car, startling him our of the charade.

Come

It sounded as if Johnny were in the car with him.

Coggins turned to the window and lowered it half an inch.

"What'd you say?"

"Can't go any further on the highway," Johnny huffed. The man's round face reddened when he spoke, and Coggins wondered briefly how and when the man had gotten so fat.

Twice, Coggins had arrested Johnny for pushing pills, and

both times the man had displayed all the telltale signs of being a user: mottled skin, flesh that seemed too small—too taut—for the bones beneath, and a discomforting way of darting his eyes when he spoke. Now, however, loose flesh hung from Johnny's round cheeks, and his eyes were wide and frightened.

"Plow keeps getting jammed on—"

Coggins nodded briskly and closed the window before the man had a chance to finish. The wind howled, muddying whatever Johnny was saying from beyond the glass.

"...gas...wind...thick..."

It all sounded like descriptions of the man's last bowel movement to Deputy Coggins, but he didn't care; he had heard all that he needed to hear.

He turned back to Johnny once more, who was still flapping his pale lips, and Coggins nodded again.

Okay, I get it. Now get lost.

Johnny stopped talking, resigning himself to just standing there in the blowing snow. They locked eyes; then Johnny bowed his head, turned, and took two steps before being swallowed by the white.

A moment later, Coggins heard the man's engine fire—*remind me to get his emissions checked*—and then he spotted his taillights, oddly pink and diffuse in the blowing snow. The two vehicles slowly inched forward in single file, Coggins following the plow onto the off ramp that he hadn't even known was there. When they reached the stop sign, Johnny honked twice, a muffled sound that was barely audible through the wind, and turned right. Coggins watched him go.

When Johnny's truck was out of sight, he turned his head in the opposite direction. The road was so covered in snow that it was indiscernible from the shoulder or lawn or whatever the hell was around these parts.

He looked back in the direction that Johnny had just driven, and was amazed to see that the trail that the man had made was almost already starting to disappear beneath blowing snow. In a few minutes, he knew, it would be all but gone.

I should follow him, go back to the station.

But something was drawing him the other way, pulling him toward the sheriff and Mrs. Wharfburn's house.

Deputy Coggins pulled his car as far as possible onto the shoulder, which was a task in and of itself because he had no idea where the road ended and the shoulder began.

Annoyed, he crouched down and looked upward, trying to make out the green street sign. He thought it said Cedar Landing, but with the snow covering more than the top half of the letters, it could have just as easily been Seton Lane. Instinctively, he reached for his phone, but then remembered that the signal had been lost some time ago. He checked anyway.

Fuck.

Coggins sighed and picked up the radio.

"Whitey, don't know if you can hear me, but I think—" He squinted up at the road sign again. "—I think I'm at Cedar Landing. Gonna have to continue on foot."

What were the odds? The fool took me exactly where I need to go.

Coggins paused, listening for a moment to the static that answered him. He pressed the talk button again.

"If I'm at Cedar Landing, should only be an hour or two to hoof it out to the Wharfburns', even in this snow. Just don't wait up, sweetie-pie."

Deputy Bradley Coggins put the radio back on its hook, pulled the keys out of the ignition, and took a deep breath. Then he adjusted his hat, zipped his coat up to his chin, and stepped out into the cold.

6.

"JUST FUCKING GO!" MARLEY shouted, her voice bordering on hysteria. "Her leg is getting gangrene! Just. Fucking. Go!"

Jared looked over at the couch and at Corina's leg. She was being dramatic, of course, but the wound did appear darker even through the bandages—and this was from more than ten feet away.

"Marley," Jared said slowly, staring into her wild eyes, "I don't think—"

Marley stepped forward, and although she was a small woman, barely more than a hundred pounds, her hands struck Jared's narrow chest with enough force that he stumbled backward and nearly fell.

Cody quickly stepped between them.

What the hell is wrong with her?

But he was acutely aware of the fact he had done nearly the same thing less than a day ago.

She was losing it; they all were. Including Mama.

Remembering his mother with milked over eyes sent a tremor up his spine.

"Marley, we're all just—"

"It's okay," Jared interrupted, but it was clear that he was no longer the focus of the discussion. Probably never had been, despite the anger that she had directed toward him.

"*You* should be going," Marley said, turning to Cody.

Cody shrugged and opened his mouth to say something, but Marley shouted again before he could speak.

"*You* should be fucking going!" she repeated.

Then, after a deep, hitching breath, she added in a much

smaller voice, "We need to get out of here."

Somewhere in the loft—*why the hell are they up there?*—Henrietta, who had been playing calmly with Mama Lawrence most of that morning, started to cry again.

Silence fell over the three of them, the little girl's cries suddenly bringing them back, making them all acutely aware of the gravity of their situation—that it wasn't just about them or their petty arguments anymore. Marley was right; they needed to get out of here. Something was very, very wrong in Askergan, something that had nothing to do with the power going out or the cold—something to do with the wind, and that nagging sound—

"I'll go," a thin voice suddenly announced from behind Jared and Cody.

Cody turned and examined his younger brother. Oxford was pale and exhausted, his cheeks a prominent, bony white, his eyes so sunken that they were barely visible. At some point during the half hour that Jared and Cody had left him to his own devices, he had cleaned himself—which must have been difficult given that the generator had been dry for several hours—and had dressed.

"I'll go," Oxford repeated.

"You need to get out of here," Cody said, scowling. "You need to get far away from here."

Oxford shrugged as if to say, *That's what I'm proposing.*

An awkward silence ensued, and Jared took this time to think. It made sense, Oxford coming with him instead of Seth. That way Oxford would be away from Cody and his family, but he wouldn't be left to wander in the white desert by himself, either.

It would suck to go without Seth, but the man should be able to keep it together without him... shouldn't he?

The thought made Jared wonder. Seth had been acting strange ever since they had arrived.

What the hell is his problem?

Jared shook his head.

"Okay," he said at last. "You come with me—Seth, you stay here with Cody and Marley and help with the kids."

As if in response to being referenced, Corina, still lying on the couch, eyes fluttering, moaned low and slow. The sound was unnerving, like vibrating sheet metal, and Jared was surprised when, out of the corner of his eye, he saw Seth's eyes suddenly go wide.

Jared squinted at him.

"No, no, I think I should—"

"Please, Seth, please stay with the kids."

Please.

He didn't have the energy to argue. But then Marley spoke up again, and he didn't have to.

"*You* should be going," she ordered Cody for what must have been the fifth or sixth time in the last ten minutes. But this time her voice lacked conviction.

No, Jared felt like saying. *No, he should be staying here with you, with his family.*

But when he looked over at his brother, he could see the man was torn; it was as if Cody knew he should stay, that Jared was right, but at the same time, something was pulling him away. Jared thought he understood, because he felt that same strange desire to leave this place.

Jarrrreeeeedddd.

Jared's heart skipped a beat, but he refocused when Seth finally relented and made his way to the windows at the front of the house.

I said, 'help with the kids', not stare out the fucking windows.

Cody's voice drew him back.

"So long as you don't stay here, I don't gave a rat—" Cody looked around briefly, and then lowered his voice. "I don't give a rat's ass where you go."

For a brief moment, Oxford's face contorted and it looked as if he might break into tears. Jared felt bad for him then, and wished that he had been the one that Cody was directing his anger at—God knows, he deserved the wrath as well. But then reality took over.

You did this to yourself, Oxford, Jared thought. Yet, despite the admonition, he found himself fighting his own tears.

"C'mon," he urged Oxford in a low whisper, trying hard not to let his voice waver. "Let's get ready."

*   *   *

Roughly fifteen minutes later, Jared and Oxford stood at the front door, bundled in so many layers of clothing that they looked like cheap airline passengers trying to avoid paying baggage fees. They stood side by side a few feet apart, each holding one strap of a large black duffel bag that hung open. Jared took one last opportunity to look inside to make sure they had everything, which was ironic, because aside from the extreme cold, they had no idea what they were preparing for.

Inside the bag were four bottles of spring water, three granola bars, two apples, a roll of duct tape, a pair of scissors, a large knife, the baseball that the girls had given Oxford, rubber tubing, and a funnel. To Jared, the eclectic mix of food and other materials looked like they were preparing for a prolonged kidnapping.

"You should be going," Marley said again. Although she was staring at Cody when she said this, it was clear that she meant all of them—herself included.

He saw Cody open his mouth to say something, but then he apparently decided better and closed it again. Jared glanced at Oxford and then back to Cody.

We better hurry. Shit is going to hit the fan.

Shit.

The word resonated with Jared, and he found himself suddenly wracked with sobs.

What happened to us? What the fuck happened to us?

He felt someone reach out to him then, and when their arms wrapped around his shoulders, he let out a barrage of tears. Through blurred vision, he recognized Seth's pale face and he hugged the man back.

Then Seth leaned down and whispered something in his ear.

"Please, Jared, please let me come with you," his voice hitched. "Please, I can't—I can't stay here, not with *them.*"

Jared quickly sobered and brushed the tears away. Seth looked so terrified, his eyes so wide, that at first he didn't know how to react.

"Jared, you okay?"

It was Oxford, and he seemed to have not heard Seth's pleas.

"I love you," he said, surprising himself with the words. Then he kissed Seth gently on the lips and guided him away. "Stay and help with the kids. *Please.*"

There was nothing else he could say. Jared didn't understand much of what was happening, but what he did know was that dealing with Seth's strange aversion to his nieces was far from the most pressing issue.

Please Seth.

The wind suddenly gusted and the cardboard covering the smashed window flapped. Jared looked up to see the final piece of duct tape holding it to the window frame stretch—it wouldn't hold for much longer.

Come

Mama Lawrence appeared next, which was surprising given the fact that not only had she not said much in the last day or so, but Jared couldn't even remember her acknowledging the situation. If he didn't know better, he would have thought that her age was catching up with her; that this debacle, combined with the recent death of her husband, had triggered the onset of some sort of affect—or worse, dementia.

And then there was the *episode* in the middle of the night, her babbling about Gordon and wanting to go outside for Christ's sake.

It's being snowed in, it does something to the human psyche.

This was probably true, but Jared didn't think that this was all it was.

There was something else, too. Something far more insidious was at play.

Mama just stood there for a moment, staring at her middle son before passing the now whimpering Henrietta to Marley. Then she reached in and hugged him tightly, craning her neck upward, while at the same time whispering into his ear. Jared's fears of his mother having lost it vanished temporarily.

"Look after him," she instructed, clearly indicating Oxford. "He needs you."

Jared squeezed his mother's back gently to let her know that he understood.

He needs a lot more than just me, Ma. A lot more.

Mama Lawrence hugged Oxford next and, curiously, Jared caught her whispering something into his ear as well, but he couldn't make out the words. He made a mental note to ask Oxford about it later.

Jared turned to Cody and his older brother nodded at him,

which, for them, was enough. It appeared that whatever disdain Cody harbored for him—

You're no angel. Where the fuck were you at Dad's funeral?

—ran deep; he didn't blame him.

"I'll see you when we get back," Jared said, returning the nod.

Although Cody didn't reply, Jared caught a subtle head tilt. *And if you don't?* the tilt asked. *If you don't come back?*

Jared's gaze fell on Corina lying on the couch, her injured leg elevated by two pillows, her breathing shallow.

He shook his head.

I'll be back.

"Goodbye, everyone," he said, then turned, not wanting the ordeal to be drawn out. Oxford took the duffel bag from him, zipped it, and fell in behind his older brother. Then Jared pulled open the door and stepped out into the blinding white, the freezing wind blasting him in the face like ice pellets.

Come

Come   Come

Come   Cooooooooooooooome

I hope to God that I come back.

Chapter Five
Meeting Mrs. Wharfburn

1.

Please, don't let them see me like this—please don't let my children see me like this.

Veronica Lawrence turned away from her two sons the moment they were engulfed by the cold.

Come.

Tears welled in her eyes, but she forced them away by blinking rapidly and pretending that they were just the result of the icy wind that had spilled in through the open doorway. But this was a lie, and when her vision cleared, what she saw reaffirmed her emotional state.

The scene before her was languid, pathetic.

Although different in so many ways, it reminded Veronica of her husband's final days as he lay motionless, dying on the hospital bed; it was different then, but the same.

They had all been stuck in a sort of glue, waiting for Gordon to die.

And that was what it felt like now; waiting to die.

Her daughter-in-law had slowly made her way back to the couch and was trying to lift Corina's head and slide back into the groove that she had formed in the cushions over the past day or so. Her eldest granddaughter, thirteen years young, had the face of a much older woman—complete with a sickly sheen on her porcelain features that reminded Veronica of some sort of creepy doll.

And then there was Cody and little Henrietta.

Although she didn't see her grandchildren that often, and even less frequently now that Gordon was gone, from all accounts the toddler had a generally joyous disposition. But ever since she had arrived, the little girl had been irate. It was as if Henrietta was the only one brave enough to voice her unease—to acknowledge that there was something out in the snow.

And there *was* something out there—Veronica was positive about that. And whatever was out there in the blinding white was far more deadly than snow and ice and wind.

There was something out there that knew about Gordon.

Something that *was* Gordon.

A bout of dizziness flashed over Veronica, a spinning that she was only capable of righting by focussing on her eldest boy.

The look in Cody's eyes as he watched his brothers' leave had softened. He was furious at Oxford, and had every right to be, but he was too scared to remain angry.

And he had every right to be scared, too.

Cody had always been her favorite son, even if having a favorite son was something that was inexcusably taboo. He was her favorite son not because she had the most in common with him—truth be told, she had more in common with Oxford than Jared or Cody—and not because she was closest with him. Rather, it was because Cody somehow made the most *sense* of the three of her sons. He was just a straightforward, mostly rational man. A quality that often eluded her other two sons.

And she could read him, too; read him as easily and quickly as she completed the crosswords every Sunday morning.

"Mother?"

Veronica blinked again and emerged from her thoughts.

"Hmm?"

Cody had a queer expression on his face.

"What did you say to them?" he asked.

Veronica could read him like a book, but she doubted that the reciprocal was true. Like Gordon, she was guarded with her own thoughts.

"Nothing," she replied sternly. But what she really meant and conveyed was, *'none of your business.'*

Cody continued to stare at her as Henrietta finally calmed and nuzzled into his shoulder.

"Aren't you cold, Ma?"

Veronica shrugged.

Of course she was cold, but she was so tired that this usurped all other sensations. It was as if the weight of the world had descended on her when the blizzard had fallen, a weight that had compressed her spine like a Slinky.

And now *Gordon;* her late husband was somehow calling to her, begging for her to join him out in the snow. Which made no sense, because—

Come.

Cody's eyes flicked upward.

He had heard it too, of course, she could see it in his face.

Why doesn't he say something? Doesn't he want to see Gordon, too?

There was no denying it, Gordon was a hardworking man that rarely expressed his feelings. But he had loved his children, and even though he had had a difficult time showing it, Jared, Cody, and Oxford *must* have known that.

They *must* have known.

Then why isn't he going to him? Why isn't Cody going to Gordon, when the poor man is trapped out there all alone in the snow?

Tears welled in her eyes, but she ground her teeth and forced them back.

No. I need to be strong. Gordon can't be out there.

Gordon's dead.

Veronica's eyes again darted to Corina's smooth, pale face.

I need to be strong for her—for all of the Lawrences.

"Mom?"

Veronica closed her eyes, and kept them shut for several seconds before opening them again.

"Hmm?"

"I asked if you are cold, Ma."

Didn't I answer that question already?

Veronica Lawrence shrugged.

He isn't going to greet Gordon because Gordon is dead.

"No, I'm fine," she answered, pressing her lips together.

Despite her words, Veronica shivered violently.

She looked up at Cody then, and saw an unexpected expression of understanding on her eldest son's face.

Whatever's out there is not Gordon.

"...and I don't want to find out what it is," she whispered, her eyes slowly turning upward to the bathroom in the loft above.

"'Ma?'"

You are not Gordon. Whoever or whatever you are, you will not have me.

For what seemed like the first time since her sons had arrived, Veronica Lawrence felt as if she could stand up straight; as if whatever impossible weight had fallen on her ever since she had first heard her late husband's voice on the wind had suddenly vanished.

And she knew how to make it stay that way—which was something that she hadn't learned from Cody, but from Oxford. Poor, addicted Oxford.

"Ma? You okay, Ma?"

2.

THIS TIME, JARED COULDN'T help himself.

"Did you hear that?" he asked Oxford, turning to face his brother.

Oxford was dressed in a thick red lumberjack jacket, the snaps of which were stressed nearly to the point of breaking, the black puff of another jacket forcing its way through the spaces between. The black hood of the base layer was pulled up over a blue-and-yellow cap, and his face was covered up to his eyes with a green turtleneck that somehow squeezed up from beneath the two jackets. Oxford's legs—what Jared could see of them, given that snow came up to his knees—were almost comically thick from the sweatpants that were stretched by the layers beneath. The duffel bag was still slung over one shoulder, the strap hooked through gloved fingers that were also stretched. In a word, he looked ridiculous.

"What?" Oxford said when he finally noticed that Jared had stopped inching along ahead of him.

Jared opened his mouth to repeat the question, but the wind gusted again and he was forced to shut his eyes and tuck his chin into his scarf to avoid the full brunt of the blast.

Come Come

             Come   *Come*

When the wind finally stopped, Jared pulled his face out of his scarf.

"That," he said simply, gazing upward.

Oxford stared at him.

"That?"

Jared nodded.

After a brief pause, Oxford's eyes went wide.

"I thought... I thought... Wait, *you* heard that?"

Jarrreeeeed.

Like Oxford, Jared didn't answer right away. Instead, he just stared at his younger brother for a moment, trying to remember the way he had been before his addiction had taken hold. The man had always been thin, but where he had once been lean, he was now wiry and taut. His eyes, small and dark like raisins pushed deep into soft dough, had once been vibrant, but any clichéd glint had since been rubbed away. The shallow cleft in his chin, the one that all three Lawrence brothers shared, once but a mere dimple, was now like a bullet hole in the bottom of his narrow face. Before Jared's memory become a full-fledged reverie, a vision of his brother lying on the stairs at Mama's house took hold: lids open but slits, mouth slack, and the stink of feces filling the stairwell. And, not surprisingly, this most recent vision was more powerful and resonant.

"Yes," he answered at long last, nodding his head as much as his own hood would allow. "At first I thought it was just the wind—someone trapped out in the snow, maybe—but..." He allowed the sentence to trail off.

The shock in Oxford's eyes was quickly usurped by another emotion: relief.

"...but," Jared continued, "as soon as the tree broke the window, I knew it wasn't just the wind."

"And—and since we left?" Oxford stammered.

Jared nodded slowly.

"It has gotten louder. But, it also seems more, I dunno— more *persistent*. Content, maybe, too. Is that weird?"

It was a stupid question; weird was the wrong adjective—it was bizarre, it was insane, and it was really, really fucking scary.

A large puff of fog exited Oxford's mouth through his turtleneck, as if he had been holding his breath ever since Jared first mentioned the wind. His eyes started to water, and if there hadn't been a barrier of snow between them, Jared would have gone to his brother then.

"Man, you don't know—" Oxford paused, his breath hitching, eyes downcast. He cleared his throat, then looked directly at Jared. "You don't know what I thought—"

Jared raised a gloved hand. The fact was, he thought he *did* know; it was obvious. For a second, he considered that maybe it had been the wind that had driven Oxford to relapse, as bizarre as that sounded.

"Jared? What the fuck is that? Is there someone out here— out here in the snow with us?"

As if angered by the fact that they were talking about it, the wind suddenly gusted long and hard, bombarding them with frozen snow swept from the ground. This icy blast lasted so long that Jared had to not only tuck his face into his scarf, but he was also forced to crouch and turn his back to the wind. Even still, the cold penetrated his many layers of clothing and numbed his body like an ice water epidural.

Cooooooooooooooooooooooooome

Jared thought briefly of poor Corina, her leg shattered, and the six of them—Marley, Mama, Corina, Seth, Henrietta, and Cody—all sitting huddled together in the cold, dark house, trying their best to stay warm—to stay sane.

He looked back at Oxford. The man was clearly scared— scared and sick.

No, not out here, Jared felt like saying, before pointing at his head. *In here—inside.*

But he couldn't say that—he couldn't say what he felt. He couldn't risk Oxford breaking down—not here, not now.

"I don't know," Jared replied honestly once the wind finally stopped. "I really don't know."

An image of Corina's broken leg passed through his mind.

Gangrene.

"But what I do know," Jared said, turning away from Oxford, "is that we should hurry."

Oxford might have been thinking the same thing, as he nodded briskly and immediately trod forward, driving his knee into the thick snow.

Alright, Jared thought, *we're coming, who—or what—ever you are.*

3.

DEPUTY BRADLEY COGGINS SERIOUSLY questioned what the hell he was doing. Even though the snow had stopped falling, the wind was relentless, and the snow that hugged the terrain like some sort of sadistic blanket made moving forward nearly impossible. Even with the snowshoes—*police issue, ha!*—the going was difficult, and he found himself having to stop and catch his breath every sixty or so meters. He, Deputy Bradley Coggins, he of the sub-three thirty marathon time, he of but skin and sinew, was tired from *walking.* But it was an awkward movement: lifting his foot higher and stretching it longer than a normal stride before trying to place the saucer-like snowshoe down flat. Flat, mid-foot strike, instead of the heel-to-toe he was accustomed to.

With his first few steps, his heel had caught in the snow on footfall and he had gone down hard. Several curses and one furious fist-filled encounter with a snowdrift later, he had gotten the hang of it. But now, less than a half hour later, his shins were burning from all the toe lifting. And to top it off, the strap of his bag, which was filled with a whole bunch of crap that he was positive was completely unnecessary, was biting into his shoulder despite being cushioned by his thick coat.

After a while, the monotony of the matte white stretching out before him caused his mind to drift. He thought first of Alice's setback; then his mind shifted to Deputy White, sitting alone in the office, undoubtedly fielding dozens of calls all of the same theme and temperament: icy, both. A smile formed on his cold, dry lips. Despite his own ridiculous situation—*fucking snowshoes*—the image of the hulking Deputy White gripping the small telephone receiver so tightly that his fingers were as white as Coggins' own, trying desperately to remain calm, made him thankful that the man had somehow known the answer to his trivia question.

Oh, he is going to be ripe for some teasing when I get back, Deputy Coggins thought with a chuckle. *Primed and ready.*

In an instant, the weather, which had eased slightly over the last ten minutes, suddenly changed. A gust of wind unexpectedly hit Deputy Coggins in the back with such force that he lurched forward, and had it not been for the wide base of his snowshoes, he would have undoubtedly taken another bite out of the snow in front of him. He heard something trailing on the wind, a voice or something of the like, but before he could offer this any contemplation, a massive crash sounded from the tree line to his left. Deputy Coggins had been a police officer for more than a decade, and a deputy for a little over a year, and although pulling Johnny the Mechanic types in for drug-related questioning were often the highlight of his week or even month, his police instincts were *ingrained.* And now, despite nearly being pushed face first into the snow by a mysterious, verbal wind, his instincts took over.

Deputy Coggins spun toward the sound from the woods — at least, that was what he *intended* to do. But his snowshoes remained rooted, and when he twisted, he fell onto his back and found himself staring at nothing but the puff of snow from a fallen branch. It must have been the cold or the snow, or maybe it was the sudden break in the monotony of the white landscape before him, but for some reason he had drawn his gun on the way down.

Jesus Christ, he thought, and was about to holster his weapon when a moist, breathy sound exploded in his right ear. In a split second, he forced his back deeper into the snow, shifted his shoulders, and fired two shots.

A spray of blood—hot and steamy, like vapor collecting on the inside of a lid of boiling water—spotted Coggins' eyes and mouth.

There was a deep, guttural groan, and then a form collapsed a few feet from him, causing another puff of snow to rise into the air.

Oh my God.

Coggins quickly rolled over, trying desperately to make out who or what he had just shot, but the wind gusted again, picking up the airborne snow and swirling it around his fallen body, obscuring his vision.

Coggins! What the fuck! What have you done?

Deputy Bradley Coggins squatted for a moment, motionless. Then, something answered.

Come.

4.

THEY WERE COLD AND exhausted, but their nerves were nevertheless primed. Even Oxford, whose inner turmoil was bubbling like a witch's cauldron—a torrid mix of emptiness and heroin gut—was somehow ready.

It's one of two things, Oxford thought, knowing that Jared was thinking the same. *Either we are sharing one delusion, or somebody is definitely calling—begging—for us to* come *somewhere.*

Both possibilities sounded equally dubious, but one thing was certain: the closer they got to Mrs. Wharfburn's house, the more desperate—no, desperate was the wrong word; excited, maybe, or aroused—the voice or delusion became.

Every time Oxford heard the voice, he thought of the leather case in the breast pocket of his inner jacket, buried under what felt like several tons of clothing. Somehow, that inert black case seemed to be radiating heat, and considering that it was placed just above his heart, it felt like it was powering him. Unlike the uncertainty of the voice, however, he knew *that* was a delusion.

"Look," Jared whispered, drawing Oxford out of his own head.

He raised his eyes and followed the imaginary line from Jared's outstretched finger. There, only a couple hundred yards ahead of them, was the unmistakable outline of a police cruiser.

"Police?"

At first glance, the police car seemed a blessing; surely the sheriff or one of the deputies could get some help out to the Lawrence home. But there was something odd about the way it was parked, just a little sideways on the road, and the fact that there were no tire tracks in the snow was not promising.

Clearly, the car had been there for some time, and on a hellish day like today, the police department must have been overwhelmed; no, something *definitely* wasn't right.

Jared must have thought so as well, as aside from the ominous *"Look"*, he said nothing further.

When they got closer, they noticed a thick layer of snow on the rear windshield and at least three inches of powder on the bumper. Either the police officer to whom this car belonged had decided to take a long nap or... or... or what?

Oxford didn't know.

"Look," Jared said again, and this time he pointed beyond the cruiser.

The snow-covered lawn was littered with branches, most likely having fallen from the two large oak trees that overhung it, their remaining limbs so icy that they reflected the fading sunlight like quartz. Much like on Mama Lawrence's lawn, most of the fallen branches stood on end like newly planted saplings, their frozen tips so heavy that they had plunged like javelins. But no, Oxford knew that no matter how bizarre, Jared's whispered instruction was not meant to indicate the maze of sticks that peppered the lawn; no, he was focused on something beyond.

The door to Mrs. Wharfburn's Estate was wide open.

What the hell?

If the officer was taking a nap, or worse, if he was for some reason *engaging* with the stubborn Mrs. Wharfburn, they were doing so in the cold — the bitter, bitter cold.

Was that it? Was a police officer trapped inside? Calling for help? Moaning for someone to come and help? Come... come help me?

A blast of wind hit Oxford square in the face, and he instinctively buried himself up to his eyebrows in the thick collar of his jacket.

Come

The voice was louder now. So loud, in fact, that it shocked Oxford into raising his eyes out of his coat to look around. Even with the wind swirling about them, picking up the snow that was layered on the lawn and obscuring nearly every one of his senses, somehow he knew—he just *knew*—that the words had originated from that open doorway.

Please be the sheriff.

But somehow, he thought not.

Oxford lowered his face back into his collar. Three deep breaths later, he raised his eyes from his shell again and looked at Jared. The man's wide brown eyes said enough.

"I know," Oxford said, swallowing hard. "I don't want to go either."

Both men's gazes drifted back toward the house. As Oxford watched, the doily that hung in the oval window above the frame slipping downward, slowly transforming into a set of massive cream-colored teeth, and the doormat, black and red, extending outward like a tongue, slimy and wet as it lapped at the snow on the porch.

Mama says that there is something bad in Askergan—something wrong. She says every time the snow comes, she hears it. And now you hear it, Oxford. Now it's in your head, too. Coooome.

The mouth laughed, a horrible, grating sound.

Come inside!

Oxford squeezed his eyes shut, and his hand instinctively went to the spot over his heart. It wasn't that he felt the urge to use again just then, but it was more to see if the case was still there and to make sure that he wasn't high already.

He opened his eyes again and the doorway had thankfully returned to its benign, inanimate self: just wood and aluminum and fabric. Then he turned to Jared, who was staring at him with a queer expression showing on the small exposed section of his face. He pulled his gloved hand away from his chest slowly, trying not to draw attention to the spot. Jared's eyes remained fixed on his.

"I don't want to go in either," Oxford repeated. "But we have to."

We have to because of Corina.

Jared nodded slowly.

"We *have* to."

Jared took the first step toward the open door, and Oxford adjusted the duffel bag on his shoulder before he followed.

We have to, he repeated in his mind like a mantra. *We have to. We have to. We have to.*

The image of the doorway as a mouth flashed in his mind again, and a single tear rolled down his cheek.

There *was* something evil buried in Askergan, just as the woman in the train station had said. And Oxford was certain that the evil was buried *here*, in this place.

5.

Alice Opened One Eye and cautiously looked around, making sure not to move her neck in case something was broken.

It was strangely bright in the vehicle as the setting sun reflected off the broken glass that was scattered across the dash. Confused, she tried to open her other eye, but the lids held fast. Instinctively, she brought her left hand up to her head and her fingers met a tacky substance that could only be one thing: blood. Her breath caught in her throat, but she relaxed when her probing fingers found only a small cut about an inch and half above her right eye. She did her best to wipe the blood away from her eye with her hand, and was further comforted by the fact that she could see just fine—aside from the bright light that pierced her retinas.

Alice used both hands to quickly search the rest of her body for injuries, starting from her neck and working her way downward. Her right side was tender, as if she had fielded a stiff kick to her ribs, but she didn't think anything was broken. A little further down, she found that her left shin was also sore, but it was nothing serious, either. Content that she was physically okay, Alice shifted her attention to the inside of the vehicle.

The cabin seemed to be in pretty good shape, which was not unexpected considering that she mustn't have been driving very fast. Too fast for the conditions, no doubt, but not fast on any global scale. Alice had, however, been traveling fast enough for the airbag to deploy, and now it hung limply from the steering wheel like a giant condom, a thin streak of blood from the cut on her forehead tracing a line down one side of the spent nylon. The windshield had also been smashed, but she could see no other obvious damage.

It took her a few moments more to realize that she was squinting, and only an instant more to notice that she was shivering. A gust of wind blasted the car, spraying the fragments of shatterproof glass across the dashboard and onto her lap. Confused and disoriented, Alice, clad only in a thin black t-shirt, immediately started to panic. She twisted against her seatbelt, trying to open the door and rise all in one motion. A searing jolt of pain shot up her bruised ribs, and she slumped back into the driver seat, wincing. She was going to freeze to death.

Think, Alice.

She calmed herself with three deep breaths.

Think, goddamn it. Think!

She squinted against the bright light flooding the car.

Why is it so bright in —

Then a foggy memory of yesterday, or maybe it was the day before that, came to her. Blurry patches of having gone to work and fielding calls from desperate old ladies worried that the power would cut out if the storm amounted to anything near what the weatherman predicted. But when she again looked down at what she was wearing—just a thin black shirt and a pair of jeans—it hit her.

Slowly and methodically, Alice unclicked her seatbelt and then unlocked the door. Thankfully, whatever she had struck had not damaged the door, and it swung open with ease. Before stepping outside, she reached down the side of the seat and popped the trunk. Then she slowly slid her body out of the car, wincing again with the pain that wrapped her right side. The cold slapped her in the face, and her shoes—thin loafers—were immediately engulfed by the snow. Her feet, which she thought had been numb in the cold car, suddenly came to life as if thousands of tiny tacks were embedded in her flesh.

"Fuck!"

Quickly, trying to hop her way through the thick snow, Alice moved to the rear of the car and flung the trunk open. Inside was a duffel bag, unzipped, one leg of a pair of slacks hanging out like a black tongue.

Yes!

Alice reached into the bag and rifled through the contents: her black slacks, a long-sleeved dark blue cotton shirt with the words "Property of Askergan County PD", and a small black pouch.

Her smile vanished when she saw the pouch and she swallowed hard, images of the nude man with the beard stroking himself coming back to her with horrifying clarity.

Where is my case! Where's my H!

Had she...?

Her hand shot out and she snatched the small black case, keeping it at arm's length as she squeezed the fake leather once, then again. Then she brought the bag closer to her face and relief washed over her; it wasn't the pervert's heroin after all, but just her makeup case.

The wind blew, and this time she shivered violently. Pushing the duffel bag to one side, she caught a glimpse of her Canada Goose down coat, and inside the sleeve she found her mitts and hat. As she put her clothes and jacket on, she glanced around and, for the second time in less than a minute, her body seized.

Oh my God.

The strange bright light flooding her car wasn't the sun's reflection off the snow or the shattered windshield, but the headlight of another vehicle.

I hit another car?

Her heart was pounding in her throat as she quickly finished dressing.

She didn't remember hitting a car; she remembered speeding up a tad before going into a spin and then jolting against a median. Had it been a *car* that she had struck and not the median?

Alice didn't even bother tying the laces of her large and rather ill-fitting work boots—police issue, even though a policeman she was not—and tossed her loafers into the trunk before slamming it closed. Then she ran to the other car.

The other vehicle was angled thirty degrees to her own so that one of the headlights, the protective cover of which lay smashed in tiny glittering pieces on the snow, shone directly onto the driver's seat of her car.

The driver's side door of the other car was open wide and the chime was going off, a *ping ping ping ping* that was barely audible over the blowing wind.

Fuck, it's cold.

She leaned into the car, quickly scanning for any passengers. There was a car seat in the back, but like the rest of the vehicle, it was empty.

Unlike her own car, the windshield of this vehicle was still intact, and she instinctively reached over and turned the key that still hung from the ignition. The car sputtered, but didn't start. She tried again, and there was a sudden hiss and a sharp pop that was quickly swallowed up by the wind, and she decided that it was probably best not to try a third time.

Where the hell did the driver go?

She would be lying if she said it didn't bother her that while she was wasting time looking around this car in the freezing cold, the other driver had not extended her the same courtesy.

Maybe he had been drinking? After all, it was Christmas.

Or maybe the car was abandoned?

But *she* had caused the accident, of that she was sure; *her* car had spun out.

The wind gusted again, and she pushed more of her body into the car to shield herself.

Come

Alice whipped her head around.

"Hey!" she shouted. "Anyone out there?"

She waited for a moment, listening for the sound again, but when all she heard was the wind, she chalked it up to her imagination and turned her attention back to the car. Only then did her eyes slowly begin to focus on something on the steering wheel just mere inches from where she gripped it. Instantly, her hand recoiled and her body stiffened, causing the back of her head to smack painfully against the roof of the car.

It wasn't the blood that bothered her—Lord knows she had seen plenty of that at the station, usually in the form of men with broken and bloody noses that Sheriff Drew dragged in after a bar fight—but it was what was *in* the blood, stuck to it, like the body of a miniscule rat, that gave her pause: a tuft of grey hair.

Jesus.

Alice pulled back further, looking around frantically for more blood. There was a splash on the edge of the seat, so dark that it was almost black, and a larger puddle on the floor mat.

How did I not see this before?

The wind slapped against her exposed body and she whipped around, having thought she heard a voice again. She half expected to see a man with a head injury stumbling towards her—perhaps a man in a grey suit and a loose dark blue tie who had been stuck in the storm and was trying to get home to his suburban wife and kids—but instead she saw nothing. Nothing except for the blanket of white broken only by the dark impressions her car tires had made when she had spun out, and even those were starting to fade.

"Hello?" Alice shouted, but her words were seized by the wind and dissolved like snowflakes on a warm kettle.

She cupped her hands around her mouth and shouted again, but her efforts were fruitless; it seemed the louder she yelled, the harder the wind blew and the colder it got.

Shaking her head in frustration, she looked down and realized that between her feet was a trail of blood, but unlike the dark stain on the driver's seat, this blood was bright red. Alice allowed her gaze to follow the trail for maybe ten or fifteen feet into the distance before it disappeared into the blowing snow. Then, as if clearing a path, the wind suddenly stopped and she noticed a green roadside sign not a quarter a mile back indicating an off ramp. She couldn't remember passing an exit for some time; in fact, she couldn't remember seeing much of anything since talking to Deputy Coggins—just the blinding white. She looked back at her car and tried to determine how far she had skidded. Unbelievably, the snow had already started to fill her tire grooves to the point that they were nearly indistinguishable from the rest of the road. The wind picked up again, and as Alice watched, the tracks disappeared entirely.

Come

She turned her head downward again and stared at the splattered blood for a moment.

Then the wind gusted again, and Alice made up her mind.

Come.

6.

OXFORD LET JARED ENTER Mrs. Wharfburn's house first before following, bag over one shoulder, gas can clutched in the opposite hand, even though every fiber of his being was screaming for him to turn and leave. It wasn't so much that he walked over the threshold, but rather like he was *guided* inside the house, as if the voice, which had slowly but consistently escalated in both volume and frequency inside his head—*Come, Come, Come, Come, Cooooooooooooome*—was a vortex or tractor beam, and Oxford was helpless to resist.

He was only two steps into the house before Jared stopped abruptly, causing Oxford to bump into his back, and he almost slipped on the dark red tongue of an entrance mat.

"Keep moving, Jared," Oxford muttered, adjusting his cap, which had been knocked low on his brow.

"You feel that?" Jared whispered over his shoulder.

"Feel wha—?"

But then he paused—he *did* feel something. Oxford gently nudged Jared forward, and his brother took two more steps so that he could fully enter the house. And then it hit him like a wall.

It was *warm* inside Mrs. Wharfburn's house, warm and humid.

Oxford's skin, which had stopped bothering him on their trek from Mama Lawrence's house due to the cold, suddenly became unbearably itchy again. It was all he could do to resist stripping down to his bare skin and tear at it with his fingernails. Instead, fighting the urge, he slowly and methodically reached up and pulled the turtleneck from his nose and mouth, hoping that the deliberateness of his actions would prevent him from succumbing to his desire to scratch. Immediately, a sickly-sweet smell like overripe fruit filled his mouth and throat and he gagged.

What the fuck?

Oxford quickly pulled his turtleneck back up.

"Why is it so warm in here?" Jared asked.

"Don't know," Oxford answered, his voice muffled through the fabric. He gulped hard, trying to keep whatever little food still rested partially digested in his stomach where it lay.

"Generator, maybe? Better yet, what the fuck is that smell? It smells like baby dia—"

Jared held a finger up to his still covered mouth and Oxford hushed.

After a brief moment, he lowered it.

"I don't hear a generator," Jared said matter-of-factly.

Neither did Oxford, and given the fact that the door had been left open when they had arrived, the residual heat inside the house was more than disconcerting—and that said nothing of the humidity. Oxford reached up and pulled off his hood and then removed his hat. He had been standing in the doorway, the cool air at his back, for less than three minutes, and already sweat had begun to form on his forehead. He watched as Jared started to remove his scarf, but one whiff of the sweet air and he quickly pulled it back up again.

Oxford removed a glove cautiously, hesitantly, as if not truly believing the warmth that enveloped his hand. Satisfied that the heat was indeed real, he quickly removed the other glove and then clenched his fist, trying to squeeze the frosty tightness away. After a few contractions in the warm air, he managed to regain enough dexterity to undo the first few buttons of his outer coat.

Jared disrobed similarly, then nodded at the duffel bag that hung on Oxford's shoulder. Oxford obliged, laying it on the floor. They tossed their hats and gloves inside and Oxford pulled out a bottle of water. Holding his breath, he lowered his turtleneck and took a large gulp. The liquid felt good, cold and clean, as it made its way down to his stomach. He pulled the turtleneck back over his mouth and offered the bottle to Jared. His brother declined.

"Mrs. Wharfburn?" Jared shouted. Then he turned toward the interior of the house and yelled again. "Mrs. Wharfburn?"

Oxford, so shocked by the sudden change in volume, dropped the plastic water bottle, and its contents spilled across the hardwood floor.

"What the fuck, Jared?"

He bent and picked up the bottle, trying to save however much of the liquid he could. Again, his brother ignored him.

"Mrs. Wharfburn? Sheriff? Deputy?"

No answer.

As Oxford screwed the cap back on the water bottle, he slowly raised his head and looked around. From his squatting vantage point he noticed something—a shape, a form—not ten paces from where he stood, lying on the floor by the base of a staircase off to the right.

Putting the bottle back into his open bag, he slowly strode over to the object, subconsciously aware that the further he moved into the house, the warmer it got.

"Mrs. Wharfburn!" Jared shouted again, this time from behind him.

When Oxford came up to the wrinkled form on the hardwood, he immediately recognized it as an animal pelt.

But that didn't make sense.

Not only was it strange that Mrs. Wharfburn, who every

year would head down to the water and scold any and all of the duck hunters for what she called "sport murder", would have such an item in her home, but the type of animal was odd, too. It looked like—Oxford squatted again and used one hand to flatten some of the folded grey fur—it looked like a wolf, and a big one at that. He leaned down even lower to get a better look in the dimly lit house, as whatever was heating the home, generator or not, didn't seem to be powering the lights.

It was indeed a wolf pelt, a large grey wolf that, judging by the size, had likely been over a hundred pounds before it had been killed. He cautiously extended a finger and prodded the pelt. The fur gave slightly, and when he withdrew his hand, it rebounded. His brow furrowed. It felt wet somehow—the fur itself was dry, but the underside felt moist; it felt fresh.

"Sheriff? We need help! Sheriff!" Jared yelled.

Oxford grabbed the wolf's flank and in one motion flipped it over. When his eyes flashed on the glistening underside, he bolted upright and froze. It wasn't a wolf fur or pelt, meticulously removed and dried, he realized in horror, but a wolf *skin*—all of the layers, at least a full inch thick. And it was still wet with blood.

He swallowed hard.

"Jared," Oxford whispered.

"Sheriff? Wharfburn?"

"Jared," he whispered again.

When his brother still didn't respond, he raised his voice.

"Jared, we have to get out of here."

His brother finally turned and looked at him.

"What?"

Oxford scratched furiously at his left arm, trying unsuccessfully to reach his skin through all his layers of clothing. Jared looked down at the grey form at his feet.

"Wolf pelt?"

The immediacy of his response caught Oxford by surprise, and he shook his head.

"Well? What is it? A dog?"

When Oxford didn't answer, Jared took two large steps toward him. Then the man's foot hit something, what Oxford had initially thought was a tablecloth or blanket, and he nearly fell.

"What the fuck!" Jared shouted, clearly frustrated as he regained his balance. "Oxford, stop fucking around! What is it?"

Oxford looked over at his brother, his gaze lowering and slowly focusing on the fabric that Jared had stumbled upon.

"No," he moaned.

Warmth slowly spread from his crotch and down both legs, before being eagerly lapped up by his first layer of pants and then by the second.

"No, no, no, no,"

Please, dear Jesus, no.

"Oxford?" Jared no longer sounded angry. Instead, his voice, like his lower lip, was trembling. "What's wrong, Oxford?"

Oxford tried to backpedal, but his legs refused to respond and he fell on his ass. Tears burst from his eyes and ran down his cheeks.

"No, please, no."

Jared took a hesitant step toward his brother. This time when he spoke, it was a mere whisper.

"Oxford?"

Oxford didn't even acknowledge him; he couldn't take his eyes off what he had first thought was a towel.

Mama says there's something bad in Askergan—something

wrong.

It wasn't a towel or a cloth; no fabric that he knew of had the texture of beef jerky.

No, this was no fabric.

His eyes fell on a tuft of rust-colored hair affixed to the top of a flat, leathery oval. When he recognized two ragged holes, he screamed.

He hadn't meant to, didn't *want* to, but he had long since lost control of his body.

It wasn't a towel.

It wasn't a table cloth or a sheet.

Even though the features were flattened and stretched out, the resemblance was unmistakable: Oxford was staring into the eye sockets of Mrs. Wharfburn's hollow skin.

Chapter Six
Three's Company

1.

"UMM, MARLEY? I—I think you should come look at this." Cody blew on the window and then wiped the moisture away with his jacket sleeve.

"Marley?" he said again, not taking his eyes away from the scene unfolding outside.

Marley surprised him by actually answering.

"What? I am not going to get up and go to the window to see another goddamn wolf or bear or fish or whatever other animal is crossing the lawn," she snapped.

Cody turned and looked at his wife, who was still on the couch, Corina's injured leg propped on a pillow in her lap. She stared daggers at him, her mouth a thin, tight line.

"It's not an animal," Cody replied flatly. "It's a man."

Something flashed across Marley's face and Cody nodded as if she had asked a question.

"And he looks—" He paused. "He looks hurt."

Cody turned back to the window and stared at the man, clad only in a thin jacket without a hat or gloves, who was hunched over trying to limp his way through the heavy snow.

Cody suddenly felt someone beside him, and was surprised that Marley had somehow disengaged from Corina so quickly. But when he turned, his heart sank: it wasn't Marley, but Seth. Jared's boyfriend's dark eyes were wide, and he smelled of sweat.

The two men stood there for a moment, neither saying a

word, their eyes transfixed on the wounded man lurching his way through thigh-high snowdrifts.

Where the hell is he going?

It was Seth who spoke first.

"We should help him," he said, but his voice lacked conviction.

Cody glanced at his wife, who remained seated, her face now trained on their sleeping daughter. When he turned back to Seth, the man had tears in his eyes.

"I'll go," he said, his voice trembling. It was an odd response, given that a question hadn't been asked. In fact, now that Cody thought about it, Seth had been acting odd pretty much since the power had gone out—twice, he had caught the man talking to himself while trying his best to stay *away* from Henrietta. And he was supposed to be helping.

Cody turned to face Henrietta, who was sound asleep curled up on the sofa chair across from his wife, thankfully offering them a reprieve from her crying. Only the toddler's nose and closed eyes were visible, a thin line of pale flesh peeking out from between a cap and a thick scarf.

Hurry, Jared.

He turned back to Seth and nodded. Without another word, Seth whisked up an extra pair of gloves from the coffee table, then grabbed one of the two remaining bottles of water off the counter.

Cody heard a rustling sound from the mudroom, then the door opened and he watched as his brother's boyfriend waded his way down the driveway, following the path that they had dug out while playing in the snow what seemed like months ago.

How long can we stay here?

It had been more than three hours since he had looked

beneath Corina's bandages. He had convinced himself that he was waiting so long to look because seeing the wound would make no difference, because there wasn't anything they could do anyway. But the truth was, he was just scared—just plain scared. Terrified, even.

One more day? Two?

Lost in thought, Cody barely noticed Seth make his way to the bottom of the driveway, but when he reached the road and turned right—the exact *opposite* direction of the wounded man—Cody's mind snapped into focus.

What the—?

He knocked on the glass, three hard raps that were muted by his thick gloves.

When Seth failed to turn, he knocked again.

"Hey! You're going the wrong way!"

Cody realized he had been holding his breath, and when he finally let it out, the window in front of his face fogged.

What the fuck is going on? Where the fuck is he going?

When the fog cleared, Seth was gone.

Cody could only stare at the disturbed snow that the two men, heading in opposite directions, had made. Eyes wide, he turned back to his wife and eldest daughter, who remained in the same position they had been five minutes ago when Seth had still been with them. He looked at Henrietta again, who whined but thankfully remained asleep, and then he briefly wondered where his mother had gone—he couldn't remember seeing her since she had given him the pills. Was she sleeping, maybe? How could she sleep at a time like this?

"Fuck," he said out loud. It was too much—too many fucking layers to this onion, too much shit going wrong.

Seth, where did you go? And who the fuck was the other man?

He blinked hard several times, trying to get the men to

reappear on the lawn, but it was no use. They, like Jared and Oxford, were gone.

One day, he thought again, turning his attention back to Corina, his mouth twisting in anguish at the sight of her slack jaw and swollen eyes. *We can maybe make it one more day.*

Cody breathed deeply.

Come   Come   Come

Instinctively, he glanced up at the cardboard window covering to watch it rattle with the voice on the wind, but it didn't move. It took him a moment to realize that the wind hadn't blown just then—the voice had been in his head.

Cody looked to his right, pressing his face against the cold glass, but the limping, injured man was gone. All that was left to convince Cody that he hadn't imagined the entire thing was the shadow of the tracks he had made in the snow. And even those wouldn't be visible for much longer.

One day. I—we can survive one more day.

2.

A DOG. JESUS H. Christ, it was only a dog.

Deputy Coggins stood over the dead animal, watching in disbelief as its warm blood first stained then melted small pockmarks in the white snow. It was a boxer, long and lean, its long red tongue hanging almost goofily out of the corner of its mouth. Coggins tore his gaze away from the creepy, frozen grin and focused on a hole in the dog's neck just above a green collar with a heart-shaped tag, and another one about eight inches below that, squarely between its ribs. Vapor rose from the red holes like steam rising from warm soup in a thimble.

Coggins shook his head.

Why was there a dog out here?

Aside from the forest—the source of the falling branches— he could see nothing; just a sea of white. Even the tracks his snowshoes and the impression his body had made in the snow when he had fallen were already fading. Something else was nagging him, though, and it wasn't just the snow or the cold or the dead dog at his feet. It was that he had fired; that he had shot his gun at a noise—a wet, moist breathing sound.

Why the hell did I just turn and fire?

He pushed away thoughts about what might have happened had it been a man or woman, or worse, a child that had snuck up on him. He looked around again, his eyes wide.

No, they wouldn't be out in weather like this. Only me and—and this stupid fucking dog.

Coggins looked down at the animal's frozen grin and frowned.

Why the hell did I shoot?

Frustrated, he kicked snow onto the dog's still warm body, then immediately regretted the cowardly act.

Fuck.

Coggins wondered how he would explain this to the dog's owner.

'Sorry, ma'am; sorry about your pooch. But—but I heard a wet, slobbery noise and, thinking that it might be an attacking vagina, I turned and fired. I am sorry, but it just wasn't my fault.'

The ridiculous imaginary conversation did nothing to lighten his mood.

What's wrong with me?

Ever since he had left his car he had been on edge, his body primed for action, as if he were expecting to encounter something out here in the snow. It was so unlike him— normally he was calm and calculating.

As he bent down to inspect the details on the dog tag, he saw more blood, a few droplets accompanied by a thin red line *ahead* of the dog. Deputy Coggins' brow furrowed beneath his wool cap.

Behind the animal, he saw two individual sprays of blood about ten inches long extending from its back legs and toward the forest; one for each shot fired.

But how is there blood in front *of the dog?*

Coggins took two steps forward and crouched. This blood was older, darker, some spots only recognizable by the indentations that they had made in the snow, their color having since been washed away.

Coggins' head shot up. This was not the dog's blood.

His gaze followed the direction that the animal had been headed, the same direction *he* was headed, and he noticed that if he stared long enough, he could just barely make out what looked like a faded track through the snow.

Still on his haunches, Coggins shuffled forward, investigating what he now realized was a trail of blood and a path cut through the snow. The sheer height of the drifts made it impossible to determine if it had been made by a dog or something larger.

A deer, maybe?

But somehow —*come*—he didn't think so. Somehow, he just knew that a man had made this path.

Sorry, pooch, he thought again, his eyes following the path into the distance. *I'll come back for you later.*

Deputy Bradley Coggins picked himself up, kicking snow from the tops of his snowshoes. After stretching his back and legs, he began to walk, the awkward, stiff-ankle gait imposed by the snowshoes, following as best he could the track before him. It wasn't until much later that he realized he had forgotten his bag with the dog.

*   *   *

Coggins had been tracking the man for nearly a mile now. He had first seen the hunched figure at the edge of the clearing near where he had shot the dog, struggling to make his way through a line of bare trees.

He must be drunk, Coggins thought initially, watching the man stumble forward, nearly falling with each and every step. A few times the man did actually fall, but he picked himself up with barely a hesitation and continued on his determined path.

Drunk. Or maybe high.

As he watched, the man stumbled again, but he bore onward without even bothering to brush the snow from his—*bare!*—hands.

Really, really fucking high.

He thought of Alice then, and a wave of disappointment washed over him. He wasn't really sure why he had told her to come meet him and the sheriff at Mrs. Wharfburn's—maybe it was to make sure that she didn't fall even deeper into the rabbit hole, or maybe it was for the same ridiculous reason he was out in the snow; a strange *nagging* or *tugging* that just wouldn't let go. Alice would have been much better off at home, of course, in bed recovering, than out here—driving, of all things—in this weather. But that *pull*—

The man tripped again, and Deputy Coggins was brought back to reality. Even though he had first seen him more than ten minutes ago, Coggins hadn't been able to catch him despite the fact that he was wearing his police issue snowshoes and the man was wearing what looked like small boots or maybe even dress shoes. The thing was, the man he followed paid no attention to his surroundings or even his wellbeing, trudging through small shrubs and the thin forested areas without any consideration. Coggins knew that something just wasn't right about the man—high or drunk or not. This entire situation—the dead dog, the man walking less than two hundred meters in front of him, the strange wind that blew and sounded like a man's voice—everything was somehow related. He could just feel it.

But it didn't matter, not now—Coggins wasn't in much of a hurry. Instead, he was content with just following after the numb man ahead of him, convinced that he would lead him to the source, or in the very least, to some clues, to unlock this mystery.

He scolded himself.

Clues. Okay, Columbo.

Then he saw it and his heart skipped a beat: Sheriff Drew's cruiser, unmistakable despite the thick layer of snow covering it like a plush comforter. The man, who must have seen the vehicle too—it was impossible to miss the obvious silhouette—unsurprisingly took no notice; he just kept stumbling along his merry little way. Coggins realized that there were more prints—not so much prints as *imprints*—near the vehicle. And judging by the fact that the still blowing snow had yet to completely fill these indentations, they must have been recent.

What the fuck is going on here? Where are you, Dana?

All of the excitement of following the drunken man suddenly started to wear off and exhaustion set in. He didn't know exactly how many miles he had walked, but hiking through the snow and lifting the damn snowshoes high with every step had sapped any energy he might have had left. And this energy void was slowly being replaced by something else: the cold.

Deputy Coggins watched in bewilderment as the injured man stumbled up the porch and into the gaping—*open? Why the hell is the door open?*—doorway of Mrs. Wharfburn's estate.

A knot formed in his stomach when he saw the house.

All paths lead here, Columbo.

He suddenly wished that he was at home, lying in his bed, maybe with Alice curled up beside her.

Anywhere but here.

Bradley Coggins was not a religious man by any stretch, but he felt his eyes drifting upward to the dark grey sky above nonetheless.

Please, God, don't make me go into this *house.*

3.

ALICE FROZE, AND FOR a moment she thought that the wind that wrapped itself around her entire body like a frigid apron had finally encased her in ice.

There was a man in the window, a handsome man, she guessed, supposing he was capable of ridding himself of the dark circles around his eyes and the frown that seemed etched on his narrow face. At first she thought that it might have been a mannequin, some sort of crude anti-theft device, but when the man wiped at his eyes with his sleeve, Alice realized that he was indeed real. Real, but strangely dressed in a mish-mash of multi-colored outerwear, topped off by what looked like a dark grey wool cap. Squinting her eyes in the twilight, she noticed that the interior of the house was nearly completely dark, and with this came the stark realization that the man must be without power—which would explain his ridiculous outfit.

What's he still doing here?

Her eyes darted to the two cars in the driveway, and the answer to her question became glaringly obvious: there was no way that these cars would be able to get out of the driveway, let alone navigate the snow-filled road that she had just painstakingly trudged through—no way.

Why doesn't he just walk somewhere? One of the neighbors must have a generator.

Alice's ears perked as she tried to pick up the sound of an engine whirring.

Nothing—just the wind.

Although she had spent most of her time just concentrating on her footing as she followed the faded blood trail from the smashed car, she couldn't remember seeing a single neighbor—not a house, not a barn, not even snowmobile tracks.

She shivered hard, and this time her body kept trembling after the initial sensation passed, thrumming like a plucked violin string.

I have to get inside.

She had lost feeling in her nose and ears some time ago.

Even if they don't have heat, I need to get out of the wind.

Having made up her mind, she turned, imagining the invisible layer of ice that encased her body cracking and then shattering to the snowy ground. It took some effort, but Alice managed to take the first of many large, deliberate steps toward the forlorn man in the window.

*   *   *

Even in the dusk that had begun to settle, the form was clearly distinguishable from the white snow.

Cody froze.

What the fuck?

He blinked again, but the figure did not disappear—did not pixelate and become part of the snow like a wintery mirage. No, there most definitely was a woman walking in the same direction that the injured man had traveled not long ago. In fact, she seemed to be following *exactly* in his footsteps, if for nothing else but to make her passage through the thick snow easier.

"What the fuck?" he sobbed. "Leave us alone."

This was what he had been fearing.

He did not *come*, as the wind had begged. And now, *it* had come to them.

"No," he moaned. His eyes darted to his sleeping family, all lying on the couch.

I'm sorry, he thought, tears streaming down his face. *I'm supposed to protect you, and I can't. I... I just can't.*

Then, inexplicably, the woman turned to face him and their eyes met.

It took Cody several more moments to acknowledge that the woman with the frozen black hair was actually coming his way—she was coming for *him.*

Something inside Cody snapped.

She is coming here. She is coming here to get us—to steal our things. What things? Our heat. Our food. She is coming, just like the voice said. She is coming. Come. Come. Come. Cooooooome.

Cody sprinted toward the door, accidently nudging Henrietta slept as he passed, and the infant awoke with a start. She immediately broke into a wail, but Cody paid her no heed. The sound just seemed to meld with the now ubiquitous wind, becoming one long, semi-coherent cacophony.

Coooooooooooooome

Cooooooooooooooooooooooooooooooome

She may be coming, he thought, an odd grin forming on his thin white lips. *She may be coming, but she's not getting in—she will not get us.*

Cody's thickly gloved hand latched the deadbolt moments before the woman's frigid face filled the door.

His thoughts returned to his family asleep on the couch, oblivious.

Maybe I can't protect you, but I'm sure as hell going to try.

4.

IT WAS JARED WHO acted first, despite his churning guts. He wasn't as squeamish as he used to be—case in point him stepping up and dealing with Corina's broken leg—but *this* was too much. Making sure not to look down at the skin puddled at his feet like a discarded pair of track pants, he hissed at his brother.

Oxford didn't move. Instead, he remained rooted, unable to draw his gaze away from what had once been Mrs. Wharfburn. Jared resisted the urge to follow his brother's stare.

He hissed again.

"Oxford! We need to get the hell out of here."

Nothing.

"Oxford!" Jared whispered again, louder this time.

When Oxford still didn't move, didn't even blink, Jared set to motion, intending on stepping over Mrs. Wharfburn's skin— his stomach did another barrel roll at the thought—and grabbing his brother and darting for the door. But before he could take a single step, what little twilight entering the house through the open door suddenly dimmed, and Jared's plans immediately changed. While he did follow through with the first part—hopping over Mrs. Wharfburn and grabbing his brother's arm—instead of making a beeline for the door, he pulled Oxford backward, deeper into the home.

The simple tug on his brother's biceps was enough to snap the man from his stupor, and his wide, dark eyes raised to meet Jared's.

"Skin," he mumbled, spit dripping from his lower lip.

Jared ignored the comment.

Let's go! he mouthed, trying to load the unspoken words with all of the desperation that he felt.

Mrs. Wharfburn's foyer darkened another few degrees as something or someone stumbled through the open doorway. Jared caught enough of a glimpse of the shape to confirm that it was indeed a man before he trained his eyes on Oxford and yanked his arm with such force that his brother nearly toppled onto Mrs. Wharfburn's boneless legs. Three pairs of pants and two coats were not conducive to agile movements, and that was before considering the bag and gas can still clutched in Oxford's hands. Still, despite all of these impediments, they somehow managed to make it to the staircase without falling.

Gripping his brother's biceps, Jared took the stairs two at a time, trying and failing to tread softly, quietly, *discreetly* in his heavy boots. When they reached the top of the twisting stairway, Oxford pulled back on his arm, indicating that he needed to stop. The man's face was white and he was breathing heavily through his nose, the air coming in thick, mucousy bursts, and against his better judgment, Jared obliged. While Oxford bent over at the waist trying to catch his breath, Jared quickly glanced down at the man in the foyer. He took a deep breath of his own, and immediately recognized his mistake.

The smell was so putrid that his eyes started to water, and the horrific stench, the sudden exertion, and the ungodly sight of the two eye holes in Mrs. Wharfburn's beef jerky face suddenly coalesced into one oddly tangible sensation, and he leaned over and vomited. Jared closed his eyes against the pressure, feeling the hot, mostly liquid puke fill his mouth before splashing noisily to the ground. Somewhere far away, he recognized the taste of one of the last things he had eaten — tuna sandwiches that Mama had prepared — and this made him vomit again.

When the sensation finally not so much passed as abated, he dared to open his eyes, terrified that the man standing in the foyer, the one responsible for skinning Mrs. Wharfburn, would be staring up at him and Oxford with a lecherous grin plastered on his face. And this face would be one of the last things that they would see. But after blinking away the tears in his eyes, he realized that this was not the case.

"Let go," he heard someone whisper.

The man downstairs was still in the center of the room as Jared had predicted, but he wasn't staring up at them.

"Jared, let go."

Instead, the man seemed to be staring at, well, at nothing. It was clear from the way the man was standing that he was injured: his left leg was bent slightly behind his right, with only his toes touching the ground. The man's eyes, which Jared could see even in the poor light that spilled through the doorway, were vacant, the pupils large and unfocussed. There was a welt that spread from the inner corner of his left eyebrow and extended all the way to his closely cropped hairline, and there was a steady trickle of blood spilling from a gash in the middle of his forehead.

Something suddenly struck the side of Jared's face, dislodging the last remnants of vomit from his bottom lip. Startled more than hurt, he turned to his brother, who was looking at him with a pained expression.

Oxford had slapped him.

He had placed the gas can on the ground, reared back, and *actually* slapped him.

"Let go of my fucking arm," he hissed, and Jared immediately obliged.

He hadn't realized that he was still grasping Oxford's right biceps, which seemed near impossible with his brother buckling over to catch his breath and his own furious bout of vomiting. But the stiffness in his fingers implied that he had been gripping him hard, and by the look on Oxford's face, his brother had felt the squeeze even through his many layers of clothing.

Jared turned his gaze back to the foyer, not because he was interested in the limping man—who did not seem to pose a threat as he had initially thought—but to figure out the fastest way to get to the front door and leave this horrible place. But with the man just standing there and what was left of Mrs. Wharfburn and the wolf skin just begging to trip them up, he didn't see how that would be possible.

"Who—who—*what* could have done this?" Oxford asked suddenly, and Jared looked at him.

Tears were running down his brother's cheeks and he was trembling. The terror on his face was so palpable that Jared cringed. To make things worse, his right hand clutched at his chest as if he were having a heart attack.

Jared gulped hard and collected himself.

"Calm down and be quiet."

Simple instructions... and impossible to implement.

Calm down? Really? After what we just saw?

Jared glanced nervously back at the man in the foyer, but ever since he had limped his way into the center of the room, he seemed to have stopped moving.

Maybe it was the visible head injury, or maybe it was his unfocussed eyes, but for some reason, Jared wasn't so much afraid of this man, but of—*Come*—someone or something else. He was terrified of whatever had skinned Mrs. Wharfburn, which he was beginning to strongly suspect was most definitely not this man standing in the foyer.

Jared looked around. He and Oxford were squatting just a

few feet beyond the top stair of what appeared to be a landing that connected two stairways, one on either side of the foyer. The sun had sunken so low now that most of the light inside the powerless home had egressed to a dim grey, making it hard for him to make out any specific features down the length of the hallway behind them. Directly off to one side was a plain white door to what must have been a small room or closet, as it was inset and disconnected from the main hallway.

We will go there, Jared decided, not knowing or caring what was in there, only somehow knowing that *in there* would be better than *out here,* squatting, exposed.

This wounded man was only the appetizer. Something else was coming, something far worse—he could feel it in his bones.

And the last thing he wanted to do was be exposed when it arrived.

Jared reached out to grab Oxford's arm, but his brother realized his intentions and quickly pulled away before he was gripped again.

Jared's brow furrowed. Sore arm or not, they needed to get the hell out of the hallway.

Let's go, he mouthed.

Without taking his eyes off the man in the foyer, Jared eased himself and his brother backwards, doing his best to stay hunched and crouched. Reaching behind him, Jared grasped the doorknob, feeling relief wash over him as it turned easily in his hand. Then, keeping his eyes fixated on the man, he opened the door and gently pushed Oxford back into what he was now fairly confident was just a broom closet. Jared followed, driving Oxford deeper into the closest as he backed up. It was damp and stuffy in there, but Jared started to close the door nonetheless, stopping an inch before it was completely shut, affording him a splinter of the foyer below. It was then, just a

split second after he and Oxford backed into the closet, that the
man with the injured leg started to slowly and methodically
remove all of his clothing.

Jared grit his teeth and brought a hand to his head.

*Oh fuck, oh fuck, what is he doing? What in God's name is he
doing?!?*

Less than a minute later, the man was back to standing as he
had been before, only now he was completely naked. Even
through the sliver of light that entered the closet between the
door and the frame, Jared could see that the man's left knee was
horribly mutilated, the kneecap swollen to the size of a
grapefruit and jutting out from the side of his leg. He had other
bruises, too, including a particularly gruesome purple line that
ran from above his left shoulder and traveled across his body
before disappearing behind his right hip.

What the fuck is he doing? Why the fuck is he naked?

For a few moments, nothing happened; the man just stood
there, unmoving, fixated on a point somewhere in the depths
of the house that neither Jared nor Oxford could see.

But then they heard it.

Mixed with the sound of their own heavy breathing, they
heard the voice.

Come

The word was clearer than ever before, despite the fact that
there was no wind in the strange, warm house.

Jared felt his eye twitch, and was overcome with a sudden
urge to throw the door wide, to succumb to whatever evil was
summoning them.

Yes... yes, I will come. I will —

An image of Corina lying on the couch, her leg, ragged and
bloody, flashed in his mind, snapping whatever trance gripped
him.

No.

He bit the inside of his lip hard enough to draw blood.

No.

A heavy plodding like heavy footsteps came next, and he felt Oxford lean heavily against his back, trying to catch a glimpse of whatever was causing the uncomfortable pressure inside both of their heads. The extra weight pushed Jared forward into the door, and it swung open several more inches. For the briefest moment, the heavy, rhythmic steps coming from somewhere to their left—from the other staircase—paused.

Jared inhaled sharply and quickly pulled the door closed, shoving his body backward into his brother to make room for the both of them in the tiny closet.

He held his breath, hoping that whatever the thing was hadn't heard them.

The temperature rose in the confined space, and the pungent smell of rot intensified as the heavy steps slowly descended the stairs.

Neither of the Lawrence brothers wanted to see what monstrosity was heading down to greet the naked, wounded man.

Seeing is believing, as they say, and nothing that had happened today was by any stretch believable. None of it was *real*—it just couldn't be.

Jaaaarrrrreeeeeeed.

Jared's heart fluttered in his chest and he squeezed his eyes tight.

5.

"OPEN THE DOOR," ALICE demanded calmly.

The pale, handsome face staring back at her did not change—didn't even acknowledge her. She could see that not only had the man locked the door, but he had his hand on the knob keeping it from turning as well, just in case she had a key.

Why the fuck would I have a key?

"Open the door," she repeated in the same monotone voice.

When the man still refused to move, she threw her head back in frustration, her frozen hair poking into the back of her neck.

My hair is frozen. And my nose... my ears... my fucking toes.

Alice took a deep breath and then slowly lowered her gaze, staring intently into the man's dark pupils.

"Open. The. Fucking. Door."

Every word deliberate—a hard stop between each syllable.

To her utter dismay, the man still did not budge, didn't even flutter an eyelash.

Alice took another deep breath.

"Listen," she spat from between pursed blue lips. "I'm from the sheriff's department."

Alice wasn't sure why she had said that, but when something flickered in the man's eyes, she was encouraged to continue.

"The sheriff—Sheriff Dana Drew—sent me."

Alice was hesitant, watching to see if the man would react again. And then he did. His hand slowly fell from the doorknob to his side, and Alice could have sworn that she saw his pupils constrict, even though the interior of the house had remained consistently dim. To further corroborate her story, she reached up, unzipped her jacket partway, and pointed a frigid finger at the ACPD symbol over the breast pocket of her shirt.

"He—he sent me to check up on residents up here."

Were they really *up* here? Were they north of town? Alice couldn't think straight; the cold seemed to have penetrated her brain as well as her bones.

"He sent me here to make sure everyone is all right, seeing as you have been without power for—" She glanced at the darkening sky and then at the dark lightbulb above the door. "—for a few days now."

Something in the man's face broke and his expression changed from pure apathy to despair almost instantly. His hand went back to the door, but this time, instead of holding the lock firmly, he turned the deadbolt.

Seizing the opportunity, wanting to make sure that this strange man didn't suddenly change his mind, Alice grabbed the knob and pushed the door. The speed of her movements startled him, and truth be told, it had startled her as well, and he stepped back awkwardly to avoid being struck by the opening door. Immediately after she entered, the man sprung forward, reached behind her, and closed the door quickly, trying to keep the cold—or something else—out.

To Alice's disappointment, the interior of the house was only a couple of degrees warmer than outside; but this she probably should have guessed, given that the man was wearing what looked like two jackets, a pair of gloves, and a winter hat.

The man before her was tall, over six feet, with a narrow face, large blue eyes, and a straight, almost Parisian nose. But while Alice wouldn't hesitate to call him handsome, it was hard to pin down exactly how old he was, as the desperation that clung to his features dug heavy grooves around his nose and mouth could have been permanent or simply a reflection of his situation.

As Alice watched, the man opened his mouth to say something, but then quickly closed it again. His face, which had been stark white, suddenly reddened, and Alice became acutely aware that he was ashamed and embarrassed of how he had acted.

Well, no time for grudges.

"I'm Alice," she said abruptly, holding out a frigid hand.

The man looked down at her outstretched fingers as if she were offering him a rotting fish. Eventually, after another few awkward seconds, he grasped her hand and shook it—one appropriately frozen, abbreviated pump.

"Cody," he said, still trying his best not to meet her eyes.

There was no time for further formalities.

"I—" She hesitated. "I, uh, I was in an accident."

Alice brought a hand to her side to indicate the area, even though there was no chance she was going to lift her jacket to show him and expose her flesh to the cold. She performed the charade anyway, her mind still trying to work its way through the meandering maze that was the last two days.

You fucking cunt, come back with my H!

The man looked confused, and she was grateful that she had washed the blood from the cut above her eye off with some snow before approaching the man's house—*that* would have been a difficult sell.

"I thought you said—"

"I was in an accident," Alice interrupted, "and I need your help."

Silence.

Alice grimaced a little more obviously, partly from the pain and partly as an act to try to get this man—this *Cody*—moving.

"Wait—are you from the sheriff's office or not?"

As he spoke, Cody slowly shifted to directly in front of her, blocking her path. Alice didn't interpret this as a particularly aggressive maneuver—nothing at all like the man with the beard walking and stalking and stroking his way toward her. This was more defensive.

He is protecting something.

Now it was Alice's turn to pause.

"Yes, I am from the sheriff's office. But I need your help. Someone else was in—"

Cody's brow furrowed and he cut her off.

"Do you have a car? Some way to plow these roads so that we can get out?"

The pitch of his voice increased with every word.

"An ambulance? Is an ambulance on its way?"

He was almost screeching now.

Ambulance? Why does he need an ambulance?

The man suddenly reached out and grabbed her shoulders with both hands and leaned in close, his eyes finally meeting hers.

"You said you were from the sheriff's office, that Sheriff Drew sent you."

Alice raised an eyebrow, her numb forehead crinkling uncomfortably. As she watched, anger started to usurp some of the desperation on Cody's face, and Alice gently pushed his hands away before the situation escalated.

"Well, I am," Alice said, pretending to brush some snow from her pants. "Kind of."

"Kind of? What do you mean kind of? I let you in here!" Cody threw up his hands. "I let you in here when God only knows what's coming!"

The word *coming* sounded odd to her, with undue emphasis on the first syllable.

"Do you know what I've seen?"

As before, hysteria began to creep into his voice.

"First, I see wolves and bears running across my lawn—together, for Christ's sake! Then a fucking zombie—some guy with a limp wearing no goddamn gloves or hat—then I fucking see you!"

Alice tried to interrupt, but the man's roller-coaster of emotions frightened her and she hesitated. Cody suddenly reached out and grabbed her arm again and pulled her toward him—*You fucking cunt, come back with my H!*—while at the same time backpedaling. At first she resisted, confused, scared, but when it became clear that he was meaning to show her something, Alice allowed herself to be led. Together they passed through a small kitchen and into another room, a large, open space with couches and a TV mounted on the wall. Alice's gaze lingered on the pile of gifts by the corner of the room—some half opened, others still wrapped—before she saw the girl, and her breath, a frigid puff of air, caught in her throat.

Lying on one of the couches was a girl who looked like she was just entering her teenage years. Her legs were propped up on the lap of an older woman with long, dark hair who appeared to be sleeping soundly. But as odd as this scene was, it was the young girl's face that had caused Alice to stop short. Her face was so pale that it bordered on translucent, and her eyes were sunken and partly closed. With every breath, the girl's cheek twitched in what was obvious pain.

"My daughter has a broken leg," Cody whispered from between clenched teeth.

Then he gestured at the sleeping woman who was holding the younger girl's legs, and Alice noticed that her eyes were closed as well.

"My wife just sleeps, and—and—and my other daughter—"

When the man's voice hitched, Alice drew her eyes away from the stagnant scene on the couch and looked at Cody. He was crying now.

Another daughter?

"And my other daughter—"

He couldn't finish.

Alice followed Cody's outstretched finger and saw a toddler with a small upturned nose and bright blue eyes sitting on the floor and staring up at her. The girl was bundled in so many layers, including a purple and white snowsuit that looked two sizes too big, that under other circumstances Alice might have laughed. The toddler was trying to flip a puzzle piece over, with her tongue poking just slightly out of the corner of her mouth, but the task was impossible with her thick mittens.

Jesus Christ, they are going to freeze to death.

"And my mother—goddamn it—where the fuck are you, Mom?"

Cody turned away from Alice and looked upstairs to the loft.

"Mom? Mom! Where the fuck are you?"

6.

NOTHING HAPPENED FOR A long time. So long, in fact, that if it weren't for the bitter cold nipping at all his tips—fingers, nose, ears, and even penis—Deputy Coggins might have thought he had fallen asleep. And what happened next did nothing to confirm or deny this feeling.

What. The. Fuck.

Like in a demented dream, the man, the crooked man with the limp, the one whose back he had been staring at for the past hour, suddenly began to disrobe. Undress. *Get naked.*

It was such an absurd act that Deputy Coggins could only crouch behind Sheriff Drew's open cruiser door and watch, mesmerized. In a matter of moments, all of the man's clothing unceremoniously fell to the floor, and now he stood there, just five feet inside the open doorway, still as a mannequin.

As if that weren't enough, there was something else strange about the scene, and it took Coggins a few minutes to realize exactly what was making him uncomfortable: it was the wind. The ubiquitous wind that had been hissing and blowing for what seemed like three straight days now had suddenly died down, and instead of wrapping the house in a blanket of whirling snow, Mrs. Wharfburn's Estate was suffocating in a mysterious calm. Something strange—no, strange was too benign a word for it—something *abnormal* was happening here, something that transcended the naked man.

As Coggins watched, the sun slowly started to dip, and the man's naked back, which he believed at this point he would probably be able to identify out of a lineup of about fifty, became increasingly shrouded in darkness. The maze of tree branches, sticking directly into the lawn like the bars of some tribal cage, weren't helping, either.

Squinting against the fading light, Coggins realized that eventually he could no longer make out the man's back. It would have been easy—logical, even—for him to assume that the shadow that had slowly been filling the doorway had finally swallowed the entire entrance, but that just didn't seem *right*. There was an opaqueness to the shadow that convinced Coggins otherwise.

It wasn't a shadow. It was something else. Something hulking. Something dark. Something *wrong*.

7.

JARED DIDN'T DARE OPEN the door until the heavy plodding, the deep, low-frequency depressions, reached the bottom of the stairs. Although the closet was pitch black and deathly quiet—even his and Oxford's heavy breathing seemed inaudible—he turned to his brother and brought an index finger to his lips. It was unlikely that his brother saw this gesture, but he hoped that somehow his sudden shift in position conveyed the messaged. Only then did Jared dare ease the door open just a sliver and peer down into the foyer with one wide eye.

The first thing he noticed after opening the door wasn't visual; the first thing he noticed was the stench. Even though he had become accustomed to the general funk of Mrs. Wharfburn's house, the sour, caustic smell of battery acid mixed with rotting meat, this new smell had an almost thick quality to it—so much so, in fact, that it seemed to coat his nose and throat, triggering the umami taste buds on the back of his tongue. A hard swallow, and he fought the urge to vomit—again.

Goddamn it.

Jared forced himself to breathe through his mouth, and when the water finally cleared from his eyes, he turned his attention back to the foyer.

At first he could only see the naked man with the twisted knee, standing naked, dumbstruck, oblivious, as he had been ever since inexplicably removing all of his clothing. Blood still trickled from the wound above his eye, but the stream was slower now, lazy and uninspired. Jared sensed that there was something behind the man, something just out of view, but he didn't dare open the door wider to get a better look. As it was, he had to open the door more than he felt comfortable doing just to see the naked man, who was turned so that Jared and Oxford were stuck staring at his side and part of his back.

And stared they did.

For several moments, nothing happened, and when Jared felt the pressure of his brother leaning against him ease, he debated closing the door again.

Maybe I imagined it, he thought, but a cursory rub of his tongue on the roof of his mouth reaffirmed the horrible, thick taste. *That,* at least, was not imagined.

Movement suddenly caught his eye, and evidently Oxford's as well, as he felt his brother lean against him again, trying to get a better look. There was a blur, and Jared made out the silhouette of something big—not enormous, but thick, like a muscular man covered in a layer of fat—hovering over the naked man's back.

What is that? Another man?

Jared supposed that someone else *could* have slipped in behind this man when he had closed the closet door. And indeed, the shape did appear to have a human-like form, but... but it wasn't *right*. For one, the thing had a *heaviness* that was difficult to describe, a denseness that seemed to draw Jared and Oxford toward it—*Cooooooome*—a *tugging* that took considerable effort to resist.

There was another sudden blur of movement, a flash of color—dark green, maybe, or a deep blue—and Jared, mesmerized by the scene, saw what could only be described as two claws reach up and come to rest on each of the naked man's shoulders.

How can something that large—that dense—move so quickly?

But before he could contemplate this fully, the claw on the naked man's left shoulder curled into a fist, and Jared heard what sounded like the twisting of a dry leather belt. A thin green finger brandishing an inch-long silver nail slowly ratcheted out from the fist, accompanied by that same brittle sound. The nail first went to the top of the man's head, pausing above the matted grey hair for a moment before inexplicably, almost gingerly, tracing a line behind his ear, following the contour of his jaw. Jared thought he saw the man shudder, an almost imperceptible tremor, but it was difficult to tell if this was real or imagined. Oxford's breathing, previously inaudible, had grown tight and shallow, his heart pumping so hard that it gently rocked both their bodies.

Then, without warning, without even a hint of what was to come, there was another spark of movement and the claw traced a line down the man's back with startling, almost impossible speed. In fact, if it weren't for the dark red line that followed the nail and ran from the base of the man's skull to just above his bare buttocks, Jared might have thought he imagined that as well.

Someone or something grunted, and then Jared saw the claws, two of them this time, reach up and delicately probe the red line. As he watched, the hands suddenly turned and the fingers spread, the silver nail at the end of each finding its own spot along the streak of blood. That was when Jared noticed the flayed pale streaks on the thing's wrists, as if the green claws had burst from soft pink flesh.

A gasp escaped his lips and he quickly brought a hand to his mouth, trying to force the sound back in. Oxford tensed against him, and they both waited without breathing for several moments. Only after the hands resumed their cryptic movements did the Lawrence brothers allow themselves another breath of the foul air.

Please, God, Jared nearly whimpered, catching the words in his throat at the last possible second. He could barely comprehend the scene that unfolded before him.

It was the nails; they had worked their way to roughly half their length into the line of blood. Without warning, the trance, or hold, or whatever it was that had kept the naked man so silent all this time, suddenly broke and a shrill scream filled the foyer. The sound was so loud and unexpected that Jared could not help but bring his hands to cover his ears. At the same time, he felt Oxford's weight on his back ease as his brother shuffled into the dark recesses of the closet.

Jared, on the other hand, found himself unable to look away.

8.

A SCREAM FILLED THE cold, dark winter air. The high-pitched sound immediately vanquished all of his tenuous apprehension, and Deputy Coggins stood, his frozen nubs all but forgotten. As the sound droned on, he realized that it wasn't *just* a scream; there was another sound intermingled with the cry, a deep, bass-like rumble that he could not quite place.

Deputy Coggins immediately sprang to action, ignoring his knees, which protested audibly from being locked in the same position for so long. Moving swiftly now that he had rid himself of the snowshoes, he quickly made his way to the back of the car.

A moment later, he was in the trunk pulling out Sheriff Drew's shotgun. In one fluid movement, he loaded two shells into the chamber, shoved several more into his coat pocket, and closed the trunk.

The scream, which had been going on for so long now that it was almost an afterthought, slowly transitioned into a horrible moan. The rumbling, however, remained.

Dana, get down, Deputy Coggins thought strangely. And then he started to run—waddle, really—through the thick snow toward the open door of Mrs. Wharfburn's Estate.

I'm fucking coming, whatever you are.

9.

THE HOUSE WAS SO dark now that from his vantage point, Jared could only make out the man's back and the side of his face. And those hands—he could still see those green claws meticulously bobbing up and down, working their way deeper into the man's back, dissecting his flesh with a practiced touch.

Jared couldn't tear his eyes away. It was like the car wreck to end all car wrecks: no matter how much he wanted to just keep on driving, to resist the temptation to slow, he... just... couldn't... look... away.

When the fingers had worked their way just beyond the second of what might have been a half dozen knuckles, the digits tensed. A split-second later, just before the claws pulled, a ribbon of pink flesh the size of a shoelace tore and fell from the beast's wrist, revealing a green that was softer, milkier, than the other exposed areas.

When the claws yanked, the sound that reached Jared was like nothing he had ever heard. It was a grunt of sorts, he supposed, but it was so low and guttural that it reverberated in his eardrums, and it took all of whatever willpower he had left to resist rubbing his ears until they bled. As he watched, the claws pulled backward, lifting the man's skin at the red seam like a sheet from a tightly made bed. Then those dark green fingers pushed and the man's screaming suddenly stopped.

In an instant, the man's naked flesh flipped forward, and like a corn kernel suddenly unfurling and popping, his sinewy under layer was exposed, red and wet. And raw—*my God*—the maze of striated muscle looked so *raw* without the skin covering it. Blood not so much poured as it seemed to bead and sweat from the entire surface of the man's body all at once. The droplets, small at first, soon merged with their neighbors until the man's body birthed a new skin: a glistening red blanket of blood.

Even though the man had stopped screaming now, his mouth, previously spread wide, now formed a lowercase 'o', and a quiet yet perceptible undulating moan originating somewhere from below his diaphragm escaped him. His skin hung in front of him like the last vestiges of cellophane clinging to deli meat, with only his face still attached. Thankfully, for this man and for Jared's constitution, the horrific display only lasted another moment. One final grunt and the man's face was completely unstuck, his skin shed and tossed aside like a wasted rag.

Chapter Seven
The Day After Christmas

1.

ALICE DIDN'T KNOW WHAT to say, but she knew what she wanted to do: she wanted to get the *fuck* out of there—and she wanted to do it as soon as possible. The toddler was veritably *bawling* now, and although Alice didn't have a maternal bone in her body, her heart cried out for the little one.

Go to her. Go to her, for fuck's sake.

But the man, this *Cody*, instead insisted on trying to elicit a response from his wife, who was nearly as catatonic as his eldest daughter. And judging by the way the girl's eyes darted back and forth beneath partially closed lids, his teenage daughter was under the influence of some sort of opioid.

In the end, it was the two girls, the oblivious baby and the injured, drugged girl, that kept Alice from turning around and just bolting—consider it *human* instincts, as opposed to maternal ones.

She needed a drink. Or something stronger—it was all too much.

"I don't know what to do," Cody admitted, fighting back sobs. "I am helpless, just sitting here waiting for someone to come rescue us."

The man finally stood and made his way to Alice, scooping up the toddler as he passed. It was clear by the way he ignored the wails so close to his ear that this was not a new occurrence— that he was used to the sound. She, on the other hand, was not.

Alice looked at him, unsure of how to respond. Clearly, the

man wanted reassurance or support or *something,* but comforting was also a gift she lacked.

"What kind of father—what kind of *man*—does that; just sits around and waits? I'm supposed to *protect* them."

Alice was standing in the family room staring out into the cold darkness, watching what was left of the failing light reflect off the blowing snow. It had been a while since they had seen the last animal—an elk, Alice thought—traveling east on the snow-covered road.

Where the fuck are they all going?

Alice caught Cody's reflection in the glass just in time to see his face contort with the onset of another sobbing bout. He reached for her then, switching the young girl to his other arm, but Alice instinctively pulled away. Cody's pale face quickly transitioned to a deep crimson, and the urge to cry seemed to pass.

"Sorry," he grumbled, turning his attention back to the window.

"You should leave," Alice said suddenly, and then immediately bit her lip.

Why did I say that?

She turned to him nervously to see how her remark would be taken. To her surprise, although Cody continued to stare out the window, she thought she detected a nod—a subtle yet perceptible nod.

Am I right? Should they leave?

Maybe it had been her own feelings projecting, her own strong desire to leave this place manifested in her words. She considered the mess that the roads had been and thought that maybe leaving *was* the right plan. It would be days, if not a full week, before the streets were clear enough for the plows to get out to Cedar Lane. The power might come back on sooner, but then again, maybe it wouldn't. Sheriff Drew would probably prioritize restoring power to those within the city first, if nothing else but to ensure that the plow companies could run around the clock to get out to this house and the other rural areas.

But Sheriff Drew isn't at the station, is he? And neither is Coggins.

Which left only Deputy White.

But it didn't matter who was holding fort at the station; the men, so very different in many respects, would nevertheless all prioritize the town over the outskirts.

Well then, what am I doing here?

Alice looked away from the window and turned her attention to Cody's wife and injured daughter lying together on the couch.

Could they leave, even if they wanted to?

"I should leave," the man whispered suddenly.

Alice turned to him again, confused by his choice of words. Surely, when he had said *I* he had meant *we.*

When he spoke again, his voice was hushed and his teeth clenched.

"I'm just—I'm just scared of what's out there."

Alice stared at the man, but Cody just continued to look out the window, eyes wide.

"There is something out there—something begging for us to come. Something *wrong.*"

Alice blinked hard and rubbed at her temples.

He couldn't be hearing that too, could he?

She was too tired to deal with this right now—not after what she had been through.

Fuck it. This man can do what he wants, she thought callously, *but I will be leaving pronto.*

In the back of her mind, Alice knew that she would likely be in a similar situation—trapped by the snow, cold and tired—once she met up with the sheriff and his deputy, but there was something to be said about being in the company of one's family, being with the people she loved.

"Listen," she whispered at long last, again feeling sorry for Cody. "I'm just going to use the bathroom, then I'm gonna go."

Alice tried to read the man's face as she spoke, but it had become a mask—an expressionless void reminiscent of when he had initially locked her out.

"And when I find Sheriff Drew, I'll tell him about you—he *will* come."

The man shuddered, and Alice immediately regretted her choice of words.

Come.

She heard it too, no matter how hard she tried to ignore it—she had been hearing it ever since the car accident. There was something out there, just like Cody said, a deep, harrowing voice on the wind.

Come.

"In the loft," Cody finally said, and Alice nodded.

She backed away from the man and his child slowly, thinking that sudden movements might break the thin veneer of calm that shrouded this place.

As she made her way up the stairs, she noticed photographs on the wall and found it impossible not to look at them. It felt intrusive, this gateway into Cody's life, but she was held captive to her curiosity.

The first picture was clearly a much younger version of Cody, his hair a little thicker, his face slightly more full. He had a coy smile on his lips, the kind that you made just when trying hard *not* to smile. The next photo was of a much skinnier version of someone who looked like Cody, with gaunt facial features, dark eyes, and, unlike Cody, a broad, beaming smile showing a row of perfectly white teeth—the man's younger brother, no doubt.

The next photograph was of a couple in their late sixties, maybe even early seventies: a woman, her white hair meticulously tied up into a tight bun, dressed in a slightly outdated yet somehow appropriate blue dress with small pink flowers. Beside her was a man wearing a beige newsboy hat and a matching sport coat with a light blue shirt and red tie; he looked like an old Republican congressman. His expression was stern, unforgiving.

Mama, Alice thought, her attention focused on the smartly dressed woman.

Despite the fact that she had met Cody less than an hour ago, this stairway—this passageway—through his life somehow moved her, and was a tangible reminder of how much she needed her own family.

I have to get to Sheriff Drew.

Two steps from the loft landing, with three empty spaces separating it from the photograph of Cody's parents, was another picture. And it was this photograph among all the others that made Alice's world spin.

"No," she moaned.

2.

WHEN DEPUTY COGGINS HURLED himself through Mrs. Wharfburn's open front doorway, shotgun in hand, all of his training went out the window. He was just an Askergan County deputy, not a member of the Los Angeles SWAT team, and no matter how ingrained his small-town police skills were, he was not equipped to deal with what he saw. In fact, before killing the poor dog, he had only fired his pistol once, and that time—when Mark Corning was drunk and refused to stop waving his loaded crossbow at him and Deputy White—it had only been meant as a warning shot.

The house was warm, dark, and goddamn him if it wasn't the rankest place he had ever been. Hot and sweet, like Korean barbecue, with deep, brooding undertones of rot and decay. It was so horrible that all of his bluster and bravado, like the screaming from inside the house, evaporated into a thin mist.

Only after he blinked the tears from his eyes did his vision slowly start to adjust to the darkness. And even then, standing four feet inside the doorway, it was not clear what he was looking at. There was a form before him, a large, bulky figure that appeared mostly white, but with either dark green or black vertical stripes marking the length of its body. These parts glistened even in the darkness and appeared hard, like glass or rock, but this wasn't what was so upsetting to Coggins. No, that honor was bestowed on something else. Although Coggins was confident that he was staring at a beast's back, he saw a silhouette of a man's legs out in front of the hunched form, the heels of which just barely grazed the floor. It was like Penrose stairs—an impossible illusion. And if that wasn't enough, there was something else, something that magnified the horror: he heard a strange sucking sound over the blood rushing through his ears.

What in God's name—?

But this was not God's work—not now, not ever.

Another wave of the horrible smell, which Coggins now realized was clearly emanating from this *thing*, struck him in the face like a splash of outhouse water, and it was all he could do to stop himself from vomiting. The shotgun immediately fell to his side as he protectively buried his nose and mouth into the crook of his left elbow.

Slowly, trying not to make any noise, he took two steps to his left. Somewhere in the back of his mind, Coggins knew that he was required to announce his presence—*Askergan County PD!*—but there was no fucking way he was going to bring attention to himself in *this* place.

He took another step.

Then two more shuffling steps.

From this new angle, the hanging legs and feet appeared red and glistening.

What the fuck?

Deputy Coggins took four more crow hops to his left and then vomited. It wasn't a full projectile puke, as he managed to squeeze his lips tightly to prevent the partially digested food from exiting his mouth, but there was enough volume that his cheeks puffed. Desperate not to draw attention to himself, he held the puke in his mouth, tasting the remnants of his paltry last meal: a muffin and a coffee. Staring at the massive form before him, he shuddered, and an odd thought passed through his mind.

No fucking way is my last meal going to be a muffin and a coffee.

It wasn't one form that he was seeing, but two: the hulking, striped beast was crouched over—*oh my dear fucking Christ, no*—another body that it appeared to be eating, consuming, *devouring*. Coggins took one more step and witnessed the impossible.

From the side, he could see that the naked man's head—and it most definitely was a man, judging by his wet and red exposed penis—was already inside the beast's mouth, as was one of his shoulders. It didn't make sense that all of *this* would fit inside the thing's mouth, but as Coggins watched, the thing's jaw stretched further—new green splits splaying laterally on the creature's pink jowls and neck—and the other shoulder was somehow folded and maneuvered inside the horrible orifice. Coggins shuddered, but finally managed to tear his eyes away from the horrific sight—*goddamn it, that suckling sound*—and allowed his gaze to travel down the man's legs. It was only then, seeing the maze of sinew and blood, that Coggins realized that the limbs were so wet and raw because they were no longer covered in skin.

Deputy Coggins gagged, and the puke he was desperately trying to hold in his mouth sprayed from between his pursed lips like a hot geyser. The liquid, which had the consistency of runny oatmeal, covered a surprising distance. To Coggins' dismay, one of the few large chunks bounced off the hardwood floor and struck the horrible, pink-and-green-striped *thing*.

The suckling sound stopped.

Coggins, with the crook of his elbow lowered to just below his chin and dripping with vomit, suddenly snapped to. As the beast slowly started to turn its head, the half-devoured corpse swiveling awkwardly in its mouth like the movement of an unruly appendage, Coggins raised his shotgun.

Come   Come   Come

The deputy heard this one word repeat over and over in his

mind, but he had no idea if these were new words—new *spoken* words—or if he was just remembering them from an earlier time.

Part of the abomination's cheek and nose finally came into view, and to Coggins' surprise they were both startlingly pink. He could also clearly make out what looked like ears, so fat and full that they were completely plugged, which explained why the thing hadn't turned when he had barged through the doorway. There were giant tears at the corners of the thing's mouth where it had stretched to impossible limits, and there were a plethora of small green splits like spider veins around the thing's hairline and temples. But the cheeks and nose and eyes were surprisingly pink and *flesh-like*—undeniably, inexplicably *human.*

> *Come*

"Come?" he shouted hysterically. "*Come*?! I'm here, you motherfu—"

All of his preparation, even his timely, quirky comment, were for not as once again Deputy Bradley Coggins froze and he felt his arms and legs go numb. When the thing's head finally squared up and Coggins stared into its eyes, recognition swept over the deputy. Even crouched on its knees, bizarrely prayer-like, even with a man's head and shoulders buried in his fucking mouth, even with wet, red, sinewy legs hanging from its face, and even with hard green carapace showing through splits and tears of pink flesh, Coggins recognized those pale blue eyes: he was staring into Sheriff Dana Drew's demented face.

3.

IT CAN'T BE. I made this up—like one of those times when I think about something imaginary for so long that I trick myself into believing it's real.

The desire to use at that moment was so strong that it was almost palpable. The memory of the man stroking his penis, running, shouting for his H, came flooding back, but this time instead of forcing the image away, Alice let it flow right through her. Not because it made her feel any better—indeed, it had been a horrific sight—but because she wanted heroin so badly at that moment that just the thought of it, of someone other than herself yelling about it made her fingertips tingle and her heart race.

What the fuck is going on?

Alice Dehaust was trembling on the final stair leading up to the loft, staring into the face of the man she had spent last night with—or the night before, or the night before that; the days had so melded together in this strange, circular week that she did not know. She had no doubt that *this* was the man—the same man that she had spent the night with, but who'd been gone before she had awoken.

Alice had almost completely forgotten about the man, and with it had gone her guilt of being unfaithful to Deputy Coggins and about relapsing despite her surrogate father giving her chance after chance.

How is it possible? she wondered, staring into the photograph.

But somewhere deep inside, she knew how; it was possible because of the voice on the wind... it was possible because the deer, bears, wolves, and dogs had come—and gone—this way. It was possible because of *Come*—it was possible because of that fucking voice that they all heard, but were terrified to acknowledge. The storm had done something to Askergan... changed it somehow. She had no idea how, or why, but she was certain that the county that she had lived in for the past decade, the county that her step-father presided over, was different now. There was something inherently wrong going on in Askergan County, something undeniably evil.

A deep, racking shudder ran through her with such intensity that it broke the spell. She stumbled up the final step, suddenly needing the railing for balance, and hurried toward the partly opened door nearest the landing.

She was dreading the smell—if it smelled anything like the other bathroom, she would surely vomit—but when Alice opened the door to the room and then quickly made her way to the en suite bathroom, she was struck with a surprisingly floral odor. Despite the still pressing urge to pee, she went straight for the medicine cabinet, surprised to find it half open. She tore voraciously through the contents, mumbling various curses with every non-opioid bottle or container she found. There was toothpaste, a bottle of mouthwash, some Band-Aids, a half empty bottle of erythromycin, and about eight or ten individual packages of dental floss.

"Who needs so much damn dental floss?" she shouted angrily before sweeping her hand over the top shelf, not caring when a nail file and set of nail clippers clattered loudly into the porcelain sink.

Nothing—not even some Tylenol with codeine.

An image of the young girl on the couch came to mind, her eyes half open and fluttering, moaning in pain.

There has to be something stronger in here.

Alice checked the lower shelves of the cabinet.

"Fuck!"

She slammed her fists on the countertop.

"Where are you?"

And then she saw it: an orange medicine bottle at the back of the sink beside the glass that held two toothbrushes—one green, one blue. Her rapid breathing returned as she reached out tentatively, like someone stranded in the desert seeing a pond and not knowing if it was a mirage. She was grinning.

I'm sick, she thought, but it was quickly followed by, *But that's why I need the pills.*

The lid was not on the container, and when she didn't hear the familiar *cha cha cha* when she grabbed it, her smile faded.

Inside was one lonely white tab.

She shook the container again, trying to force that pill to multiply, to divide, to proliferate. When that didn't work, she turned her attention to the label: Clonazepam, 3 mg. Without hesitating, she put the container to her bottom lip and tilted it back, allowing the white pill to flop onto her tongue. Despite its chalky nature, it went down easily.

Alice was about to toss the container into the sink when she saw another pill, identical to the one she had just swallowed, on the edge of the sink beside the glass of toothbrushes. Her smile returned, and she swallowed that one too. It tasted a bit like minty toothpaste, but that was no matter; actually, it helped it go down more smoothly. When she saw another pill on the top of the toilet, she swept it up and put it into the container.

What the hell?

There was another pill on the closed toilet seat. She picked it up and then dropped to her knees to see if she could find the cap to the container. Almost immediately, her grin became a full-fledged smile and her eyes began to glow. There were at least a half dozen pills—probably more—scattered around the base of the toilet and the edge of the sink. Alice snatched them up hungrily, putting them into the container one by one. Whether it was the pills taking effect—she hadn't eaten in many hours—or just the soothing and familiar *cha cha cha* they made when they joined their friends, Alice didn't know, but either way, the anxiety that had gripped her when she'd recognized the face of the man in the last photograph—*what was his name? Something stupid, like Bull or Chino*—started to subside. Even the chill that wrapped her bones seemed to warm.

The final pill was stuck to a thick yellow-brown goo right at the base of the toilet. Cautiously, she used her nails to grab it, careful not to touch the offending substance in the process. It was yellow, and there was a curly black hair stuck to the underside, the sight of which her stomach curdle. Blowing on the pill just caused the short and curly to flap, almost as if it were waving at her mockingly: "*Oh, hi there, Alice, I'm here to stay.*"

She threw it into the container with the others, shaking the contents so that this one quickly buried itself out of sight.

"Where's the lid?"

Then she saw it lying—thankfully—top-side down on the bathmat. After shuffling her body to the left, still on all fours, she reached for it and was about to stand when she saw one more pill—a single, solitary beacon—on the edge of the tub.

What the hell happened here? Did someone play 'Toss the Little Downers Around the Bathroom'?

On a whim, she grabbed the frosted blue shower curtain with her free hand and flung it open.

Alice's eyes went wide, then she screamed.

4.

DEPUTY PAUL WHITE YAWNED and closed his eyes for a moment. Sometime later, he opened them again when the phone next to his ear rang loudly.

Was I asleep?

It was possible—hell, it was more than possible, it was likely. It even seemed a bit darker in the office, but this was probably just a figment of his imagination; after all—he checked his watch quickly—it was only six thirty.

Going on fifty hours straight—Dana is paying me overtime for this, I don't care what he says.

He had slept in the office—over Christmas, no less—for the past two nights, trying to keep abreast of all these calls. Trying to keep things in order until Alice or Coggins or the sheriff came back.

The phone rang again. Deputy White picked it up and cleared his throat.

"Askergan County sheriff's office," he said, not liking the way his voice cracked with the word 'office'. If he hadn't been asleep before, he should probably invest in some soon.

"Paul? Why are you picking up the phones?"

The deputy's mind snapped into focus and he tilted forward, allowing the chair to straighten from its incline.

"I, ugh, I—I—"

"Paul," the woman's voice on the other end repeated, slowly and evenly, "don't lie to me, Paul."

There was a pause, as if the woman were giving him a chance to weigh his options.

"Why are you picking up the phones at the office? Where are

Alice and Dana?"

Paul was too tired to come up with an intricate set of excuses or lies.

"They're not here, Mrs. Drew," he replied robotically.

There was another pause as Mrs. Drew waited for him to elaborate. Although he was not in the frame of mind to lie, he didn't feel up to regurgitating everything he knew, either; he didn't want to worry her.

And worry was definitely warranted in this case. After all, it had been nearly three full days since he had seen or heard from the sheriff, and about half that long since Coggins had left.

"Paul?"

Even though the voice on the other end was as direct as it had been before, Deputy White detected concern in it, buried just below the surface. Not answering would be as bad as telling the truth, it seemed.

"Paul? What's going on over there?"

Deputy White settled for the middle ground.

"Power and phones are out everywhere east and north of the city center," he offered. "Sheriff Drew went out just shortly before the real storm hit."

"When did the power go out?"

Paul pushed a thick thumb and forefinger into his closed eyes.

"Couple of days ago—depends on where."

There was a long pause.

"What's he been doing out there for a couple of days, Paul?"

Deputy White sighed.

"Helping Mrs. Wharfburn and the other residents, I imagine. Listen, Mrs. Drew, I've called all of the volunteers that could get out of their driveways. Most of them are either snowed in, or they are out on Main Street, trying to help the firefighters deal with an eight-car pileup."

There was a pause that went on for so long that Paul thought maybe Mrs. Drew's phone line had also cut out.

"Mrs. Drew? You still—"

"And Alice? Where's Alice? Both of them missed Christmas dinner. Now I know that she was going to spend the holidays with her father, but they usually stop by, if nothing else but to—"

"She's not feeling well," White lied. "She called in sick on Christmas Eve, then got snowed in."

Paul quickly transitioned to talking about the current state of the roads, trying to circumvent questions about the lie before they were even asked.

Mrs. Drew was having none of it.

"When's the last time you heard from her?"

"Christmas Eve," Paul repeated, then he added, "I contacted both Darborough and Pekinish Counties to get some help out here, but of course they just replied by asking *us* for help. It's going to be a few more days before things settle back to normal."

He cleared his throat.

"Well, maybe normal is a little optimistic. A few days at least until the roads are cleared and we can figure out the full extent of the damage."

Mrs. Drew replied as if she hadn't heard a word Deputy White had said.

"The staff over at the Quaint Quarry called: Elmira Coggins said that Bradley didn't get out to her place for Christmas dinner. First time in nearly a decade."

Of course *this* Christmas of all Christmases was the one Coggins' demented mother would remember.

Fuck. Why would they call the sheriff's wife... or is it ex-wife?

Paul could never navigate his boss' complex family relationships.

"Like I said, Mrs. Drew, phones are out everywhere east of city hall; north is a disaster. Cell phones and radios are out, too."

White looked skyward, knowing that his weak attempt to avoid her questions was an utter failure.

"How is your power situation? Some people out in your neck of the woods are without power as well, and you never know—"

"I'm coming down there," Mrs. Drew said, catching Deputy White by surprise.

"Pardo? Mrs. Drew? I—I don't think that—"

But this time when she didn't respond, the line was definitely dead.

She was on her way, Deputy Paul White knew, and he had no idea what he was going to say to her once she arrived.

Where the fuck are you Dana? I need you… I can't do this by myself.

5.

OXFORD COULDN'T BREATHE. IT was as if someone or something was sitting on his chest, flattening his lungs so that the two sides kissed and could no longer inflate.

Even though he had turned away long before Jared, a glimpse, a mere shimmer of light illuminating what that *thing* was doing to the naked man with the twisted knee, was enough to nearly break him.

Oxford crawled into the farthest recesses of the broom closet and buried his head between his knees, his palms pressed so tightly against his ears that his wrists and temples hurt. Then, inexplicably, only moments after the man started moaning, he found himself moaning along with him, a dull, monotonous sound that he was only subconsciously aware was coming from him. Tears streamed down his cheeks.

Please go away. Make it stop — go away.

There's something evil in Askergan, something I can hear — something inside.

When the man's groans eventually stopped, Oxford somehow mustered the courage to peel his hands away from his ears. Then he reached for his chest, fearing that he was suffocating, all the while his own moaning continuing on and on.

What the fuck is that thing?

Come

It wanted us to come here — to unburden us of our goddamn skin and devour us whole.

Oxford grabbed clumsily at the zipper of his second coat, and eventually, when the pins and needles left his fingers, he managed to pull it down a quarter of the way. As he did, something fell out and landed on his knees with a soft plop. Oxford opened his eyes and stared at the object, his breathing all of a sudden coming more easily now, the pain in his chest not quite gone, but definitely subsiding.

Yes, he thought, his mind racing, trying to grasp at wisps of reality that seemed to be floating by in the noxious smell that filled the closet.

Yes, yes — this isn't real. I can make it go away. I can make this all disappear.

A shout from Jared, so loud and so clear, and yet seemingly so far away like words spoken underwater, snapped him back to his jumbled reality.

"Run!"

A single word, so benign on its own, but in this context it held so much weight, so much *power* — and it was all wrong.

Who should run? Oxford thought absently. *Surely not the naked man who was being —*

He banished the idea from his head.

No, Oxford, that's impossible.

But then he heard the word again.

"Run!"

Flashes of pink and green strips filled his mind.

No — no, no. Don't run, don't come here, don't let it know where we are. Don't give us away. Don't give us away!

"No, not up here," Oxford heard someone say, but he wasn't sure if it had been him or his brother who had uttered those words.

"Not up here. Outside, go outside!"

Who the — ?

Someone suddenly grabbed his open jacket and Oxford, who was still moaning, screamed.

"Let's go," a voice he barely recognized whispered gruffly, and then he felt the hand on his coat start to pull.

It was Jared. It *had* to be Jared.

Go where?

But instead of arguing—he was too weak, too confused to argue—Oxford allowed himself to be dragged to his feet, and a second later he was on the move. He felt something bang off his knee with the first stride, but the sensation barely registered with him.

The closet had been hot and stifling, but now that they were in the hallway, the heat was nearly unbearable.

They ran, and Oxford realized that they were now three: Jared, himself, and someone or something else. They hurried away from the winding dual staircases, driving deeper into the recesses of Mrs. Wharfburn's Estate. It was all he could do to resist the urge to look down into the foyer, to once again experience the horror that just simply could not be true—could not be real. Just seeing it once more, just viewing the absolute absurdity, the impossibility, would ease his mind—would reaffirm that this was all just a dream. Or a trip. A nasty, nasty trip.

Trip... my drugs.

The thought rang through his head like a flashlight piercing a moonless night.

My drugs!

Oxford dug his heels in and was nearly pulled onto his face by his brother who still gripped his coat. He caught himself, rooted his feet again, and brought the blade of his hand down across the front of his jacket, slicing Jared's hand away.

"What the fuck are you doing?" Jared shouted.

Then something hit Oxford in the back and he flew forward, narrowly missing his brother as he careened onto the hardwood. The image of the green-and-pink-striped beast flashed in his mind, and he opened his mouth wide in a silent scream.

"Fuck!"

Someone swore—someone who wasn't his brother.

Sweat beaded on Oxford's forehead, and he felt his diaphragm relax, his lungs finally filling with air—whoever it was, it *wasn't* the abomination in the foyer.

"Oxford! What the fuck? Get up!"

The man, who Oxford now saw was tall and lean, grunted as he pulled himself to his feet.

"I need to go back," Oxford huffed, rolling onto his stomach and then pressing himself to his feet.

He didn't wait for a response, but instead turned and took two large bounds back the way they had come, back to the closet where he had felt the leather case fall and hit his knee.

Fingertips brushed the lining of his coat, but Oxford took another step and they fell away without finding purchase.

Come

He needed his drugs; he needed his *H*.

Cooooooooooome.

6.

No One Came Running as Alice thought they might have. In fact, after her scream died, the bathroom, and indeed the entire *morgue* of a house, went back to being eerily quiet. Her eyes, blurring in and out of focus, remained trained on the woman who lay in the bathtub. She was at least seventy years old, probably older, dressed in a neat blue dress. Her silver hair was still mostly tucked into a tight bun with only a small patch hanging out where her head rested against the faucet. Even if her lips hadn't been blue and her face completely flaccid, Alice would have known she was dead based on the awkward way one wrist and an ankle hung out the edge of the tub.

It was Mama.

Alice felt like crying, which was odd given the fact she had never met the woman. It was all just so *sad*; the baby in the many layers, the young girl hopped up on—she glanced at the bottle in her hand—clonazepam, the almost catatonic wife, and the poor, handsome man, this Cody, wondering where his mother had gone.

Well, here she is.

Alice glanced at the woman's cold, dead eyes again, and this time she *did* cry; not a wail, but a few silent tears that streaked down her frozen cheeks.

Fuck.

She breathed deeply and wiped her eyes with her sleeve, then she closed the shower curtain, but not before grabbing the last pill from the edge of the tub. She took another deep breath, then put the pill on her tongue and swallowed.

Trying not to look in the direction of the dead woman, Alice quickly peed and then, with the drugs taking hold, she made her way back downstairs. Her progress was slow, deliberate.

Despite her scream, the scene downstairs remained unchanged, except that the young girl still clutched in Cody's arms had finally stopped crying. Only when Alice was within a few feet of Cody did he turn from the window.

"What happened?" he asked, his tone so flat that she wondered if he would have reacted even if she told him the truth.

"Nothing," she whispered.

Alice followed his gaze and stared out the window, her mind going blank. When she made up her mind to leave, it took considerable effort to peel her eyes away from the moonlight that reflected off the snow.

"I have to go," she said softly.

When he didn't answer, she thought maybe he hadn't heard.

"I have to—"

He turned to her then, his eyes wild.

"Come."

Alice took a step back, wishing she had stopped at two pills.

"What?"

"Come back. Don't leave us here."

Cody's eyes had returned to normal: pale blue—sad.

Alice took another step away, confused, and stared at him for a moment.

"I will send the sheriff," she said at last.

Her gaze fell on the girl on the couch, and she reached into her pocket and pulled out the container of pills. Following a split second of indignation, she opened it and pulled out two tabs and handed them to Cody. It was the least she could do.

"Only a half," she instructed, purposefully not indicating for whom the dose was intended.

Then Alice walked briskly toward the entrance, put her outerwear back on, and left Mama Lawrence's house without another word.

7.

IT ONLY DAWNED ON Deputy Coggins that he had dropped his shotgun after one of the men, the skinny one that looked as if he hadn't slept in a month, had unbelievably run back toward the thing—*Sheriff Drew*—with the greasy green flesh.

"In here," the other man hissed, and Coggins followed him into a room roughly halfway down the long hallway.

His mind was numb. It didn't make sense that he had run into the house instead of back out into the cold—*Come*—but he had. It didn't make sense that there was a hulking figure in the foyer of Mrs. Wharfburn's house devouring—*Jesus fucking Christ, swallowing*—the man with the limp and the bloody forehead. Least of all, it didn't make sense that the thing was—had been—Sheriff Drew. Sure, its face was stretched and torn at the corners of its mouth like a Muppet, and the pink skin was mostly ragged around the jaw and neck as if the thing had just ripped someone's—*Sheriff Drew's*—face off and wore it as its own, but it had been the sheriff; of that, even under these extreme circumstances, he was strangely certain. Bile rose in Coggins' throat and he swallowed repeatedly, trying to reject his body's attempts to empty itself again—he was already hollow.

"In here," the man whispered again, and suddenly they were inside a large, well-lit bathroom. Too well lit, in fact, and Coggins' eyes took a few seconds to adjust to the bright interior. It dawned on him that the house didn't have power, and it took him a moment to realize that the moon was shining directly into the bathroom window like a giant celestial flashlight.

Deputy Coggins caught his reflection in the mirror and the

sight startled him. He was pale and wet, the melted ice and snow having since mixed with beads of sweat that had formed inside the hot, dank interior of Mrs. Wharfburn's Estate. There was a spray of dried blood from the dog that ran from his left temple to the outer corner of his lips, and he looked as if he had seen a ghost—and maybe, just maybe, he had.

Coggins had come all this way—driving in the ridiculous storm, wading through waist-high snow in snowshoes—to find Sheriff Drew, and now that he had found him, he wished to Christ that he hadn't.

"What the fuck was that?" the man across from him suddenly shouted shrilly.

Coggins debated telling the man to be quiet, to not say a word, but then he remembered how the sheriff—*the thing*—hadn't noticed him enter the room until his vomit had splashed its leg. He also recalled the fat ears, so swollen and green that there was not a pinprick or even a hope of an ear hole.

The fucking thing can't hear.

The man who stood before him didn't look too much unlike his own reflection: pale and scared. Even his chin and jacket, like Coggins', were covered in drying vomit.

"What the fuck was that?" the man repeated. His eyes were wild and he was borderline hysterical. "Was it—was it—was it eating—?"

Coggins raised a hand, cursing himself again for having dropped the shotgun.

"Calm down," he whispered.

"It was! It was eating the man, wasn't it? Fucking eatin—"

The deputy took a step forward and repeated himself, louder this time, but the man ignored him.

"What the fuck is going on? How could it be—?" the man's eyes bulged. "How could it be eating the man alive?"

Tears were streaming down his cheeks and his face was turning a deep purple.

"Calm the fuck down," Coggins said forcefully, taking another large step forward.

Jared swallowed hard, but this time he took heed. As Coggins watched, the man began breathing in through his nose and out through his mouth—the classic move to avoid hyperventilating. When he spoke again, his voice was still shrill, but he had managed to regain enough control to temper the volume.

"What is that thing?"

Coggins' hand instinctively dropped to his hip and grasped the butt of his pistol. But any comfort that the weight offered vanished when he thought of the green stripes peeking through the pink flesh, so hard and shiny, like a husk, and he was left wondering if his bullets would actually penetrate the beast. Then he saw Sheriff Drew's demented face and wondered if he could actually do it; if he could actually shoot his boss—his friend—despite the abomination he had become. Sheriff Drew's eyes, despite being larger than normal, the irises thickened and elongated at the tops and bottoms, were *his* eyes. And despite the fact that his mouth—Jesus, his mouth was the worst part, so impossibly wide—was split at the corners almost to his ears, they were *his* nose and *his* mouth.

"I don't know," Coggins lied. "I don't know what it is. But it doesn't matter—"

"We need to get my brother and then get the fuck out of here."

The man's eyes were wild again, whites showing on either sides of his pupils.

Deputy Coggins slowly shook his head, his wits returning. With the hand not holding his gun, he unzipped his jacket.

"No way," he said. "We continue down the hall and see if we can get out the back way."

The man's face twisted; clearly, no matter how frightened or disturbed he was by what he had seen, it was not enough for him to abandon his kin.

"Listen," the deputy continued, "we can come back for your brother. But there is no way that we are going *back* toward—"

—*Sheriff Dana Drew.*

"—that *thing*."

Now it was the other man's turn to shake his head.

"We have to get my brother first."

Coggins swore under his breath. He had to give the man credit; even with him holding his pistol—drawn from its holster now—this man was defiant. He paused for a moment and listened. The house was eerily quiet, and he could thankfully no longer make out the disgusting slurping, suckling sound.

"What's your name?" he asked, changing tactics.

The man's eyebrows scrunched.

"Jared," he said in a small voice.

"Good. My name is Deputy Bradley Coggins."

Something changed in the man's face then, as if his resolve or reluctance, or maybe both, finally left him. Maybe it had been Deputy Coggins' authoritative approach, him saying the word 'deputy', or maybe it was something else; it was is if this Jared had been in control for some time, not out of desire but out of necessity, and now that Coggins was here it was a weight off his shoulders. A big weight. A fucking meteor-sized weight.

"We should go deeper into the house, see if we can find another way out. Then we can think about getting your brother."

Coggins saw an image of the man with the busted knee

hurling himself through the snow with no concern for the cold or his own wellbeing, and he wondered if Jared's brother hadn't fallen under the same spell.

As if on cue, he heard the voice in his head again, the airy, wind-like whisper that sounded mysteriously like *"Come"*.

"Yeah, yeah," he muttered, "I'm fucking here. I *came.*"

Remembering that Jared was still standing in front of him, he looked up in time to catch the last trace of a furrowed brow and sidelong glance.

"What about that?" the man asked, indicating the gun that Coggins now held in his left hand.

Coggins looked down at the piece, and despite the comforting weight, it looked pitifully small. The thing's green—skin? Scales? Armor?—patches had been so hard and shiny that they had seemed iridescent. Again he wondered if this nine millimeter would even make a dent; Coggins didn't know, so he said as much.

"That… that *thing* looked pretty hard. Now the shotgun…" Coggins let the words and thought trail off. Problem was, he didn't have the shotgun, because he had *dropped* the shotgun.

"I won't leave him," Jared said suddenly,

Deputy Coggins stared at the man's sunken eyes. When Jared didn't waver, he relented and nodded. Relinquished control or not, this man would not budge on this.

We'll get your brother, he thought, *if that thing doesn't get him first.*

He swallowed hard.

Or us.

8.

IT'S THE DAY AFTER Christmas.

The thought flew through Oxford's head like a clumsy, low-flying seagull.

It's the day after Christmas, and I have yet to unwrap all of my presents.

But the only gift that mattered was right in front of him, lying on the floor just inside the closet, lonely and ashamed. Like a starving man lunging for the last morsel of bread, Oxford leapt at the case and picked it up, caressing it once before tucking it safely back into the front of his coat. Despite the heat, he zipped his inner jacket all the way up to his neck, leaving only the outer layer unbuttoned.

No way I'm going to drop you again.

Oxford exited the closet and made his way into the hallway.

Two steps; he only managed two steps in the direction his brother and the other man had fled before he heard it: a deep, bass-like rumble coming from just below where he stood. Oxford slowly turned on his heels, and now that he had his drugs again, his mind was free to remember.

Please, no, was all he could think as his gaze unwittingly lowered.

The green and pink beast was still downstairs in the foyer, but this time it looked more green than pink. The naked man was almost completely gone now; all that remained were his shins and the bottoms of two dirty feet protruding from the thing's mouth, somehow stacked on top of one another. The thing moved its head slightly, tilting it forward and then snapping it back a quarter of an inch, and to Oxford's horror the feet hanging out from the gaping hole receded a few inches. It was at that moment that he realized that the thing was staring at him; those large, bloated eyes were *trained* on him. Yet despite their bulge, they seemed almost human.

Oxford, unable to look away, stared into those dark eyes.

"Why?"

He shuddered. The eyes were green, warped, and swollen, but oddly *familiar*.

"Why, Oxford?"

They were his mother's eyes.

"Why did you let me down again, Oxford? I did everything for you. I helped you—gave you a place to stay when you had nothing. Dressed your infections when you used dirty needles. Cleaned up after you when you soiled yourself. And this is how you repay me? Why, Oxford? *Why?*"

Despite the sweat dripping down his forehead, he froze. He even stopped breathing, and had it been possible for him to force his heart to stop beating, he would have done it.

"Oxforrrrd. Oxxxxfoooooooorrrrrrrd."

"Mom?" he whispered. "I'm sorry, mom. I'm so sorry."

As he watched, the thing hitched again, but this time the man did not move further into the beast's mouth; instead, Oxford saw movement in the thing's horribly distended and now almost completely green belly. The impression of a hand, like an overripe fetus pressing from inside its mother's womb, became visible. Then, as that depression faded, another hand appeared. A face came into view next, just the outline of a round head at first, then a nose pressed out from beneath the thick green scales. The head rotated and Oxford made out deep indentations where its eyes were. A mouth. He saw a mouth spread wide in a gigantic 'o' shape, and Oxford pissed himself.

The rumbling returned, and it took Oxford another minute

of paralysis before he finally figured out what the sound was: the thing was laughing.

The fucking thing was laughing *at him.*

> *Come*

The word echoed in his head, loud and clear.

There's something evil buried in Askergan.

Something broke inside Oxford.

Mama! Mama, I'm so sorry.

Oxford somehow managed to peel his eyes from the abomination and ran, hot urine tracing lines down the inside of both his legs.

Chapter Eight

H

1.

AFTER THE STRANGE WOMAN with the black hair left—and admittedly even when she had still been there—Cody's mind was a soupy, muddled mess. Everything was just so confusing, and the cold and dark only added to his numbness. Had his brothers been here? He supposed they had been, they *had* to have been; it was Christmas, after all, and they had all decided to head north to find a quiet place to mourn the passing of their father. They *had* been here, but where had they gone?

How long has it been since I've had something to drink?

His thoughts jumped around erratically, unable to focus on any one idea. At times, it felt as if there was someone else in his head, guiding him, telling him what to think.

Twenty-four hours? Seventy-two hours?

It was impossible to know—time, like the air and snow, had frozen.

Cody vaguely remembered his brothers saying that they would return, but when? He blinked three times, hard, and when his vision cleared, he realized that he must have been staring out the window for the better part of an hour. His legs hurt, his arms tingled, but it was all he could do to stay in that spot; something was calling—*pulling*—him away from this place, and he knew deep down that listening to that call would only end in tragedy—in something even worse than his current situation.

Come

The voice had gotten progressively louder over the past few hours, and Cody found it increasingly difficult to resist — his resolve was wavering.

Why shouldn't I go? Why shouldn't I leave this place?

And he knew that he *should* leave, just take Henrietta and go. Get help, send someone for Corina and Marley. Fuck, it had been four days — *three days? Five?* — surely some of the roads had to be clear by now.

Cody shook his head back and forth, trying to clear the frost from his grey matter. It wasn't leaving he was afraid of, it was where he thought he would go that was most terrifying.

A noise suddenly snapped him back into reality, and he turned to Corina, who lay on the couch, her legs propped on Marley's lap. She was staring at him, her eyes strangely vivid. It took him a moment to realize that it had been at least two full days since he had last seen her this way.

Maybe her leg wasn't as bad as they had initially thought.

His eyes darted down her body. One glance at the now greenish-brown bandage on her shin suggested the opposite.

"Daddy?" she said, her voice soft but clear.

Cody looked at her, tears welling in his eyes.

"Yes, sweetie?"

"I need to go, Daddy."

His brow furrowed.

Go? Go where?

As if she had heard his thoughts, she continued.

"I need to go to *him*, Daddy."

Cody stopped breathing.

Him?

A slow nod from his daughter, as if she was affirming this fact to herself.

"I need to go to *him*. He wants me—" Her breath caught in her throat. "He wants me to *come.*"

Cody started to tremble. The word *come* had been uttered uncannily like the voice he had first thought had been carried on the wind, but was now convinced had been in his head the whole time. As he watched, unable to move, unable to *breathe,* his eldest daughter's eyes rolled back in her head.

Cody gasped.

"Who?" he whispered, tears flowing down his cheeks. "Who wants you to come?"

No answer.

"Corina," he begged, taking an aggressive step toward her, "who wants you to come?"

When she still didn't answer, he took another step and crouched down, lining his face up with hers. Then, suddenly and without warning, her lids flickered and her brilliant green eyes stared directly into his.

"*Oot'-keban*, Daddy." She paused. "*Oot'-keban.*"

2.

THERE WAS NO TIME to think, and even if there had been time, thinking—real, cognizant reflection—would have likely been impossible; the *thing's* rumbling laughter, like a persistent, monotone thunder, scrambled Oxford's thoughts.

Mom; it has Mom's eyes.

But even in the absence of that horrific noise, the suffocating darkness and equally suffocating need for his heroin was all-encompassing, and Oxford couldn't remember which way his brother and the other man had gone. He ran right by the first and second doors, barely noticing them based on the fact that they were firmly closed, and then barged through the third, cringing when it banged loudly against the wall behind.

Squinting hard, Oxford looked around, trying to figure out what kind of room he was in. In the corner, he made out a leather lounge chair and a bookshelf on the wall to his right. There was also a large wad of something, like a huge stack of towels or blankets, piled up against the back wall, but it was too dark to make out what exactly they were from just inside the doorway. Oxford turned his attention back to the chair.

This will more than do, he thought, recalling all of the horrible places—alleyways, underpasses, and even once inside a dumpster—that he had shot up in his life.

Heart pounding in his chest, he unzipped his jacket no more than two inches and reached inside and slowly pulled out the black leather case. He couldn't remember how much heroin had been in there—a gram? Maybe two?—after he had shot up at Mama's house, but it didn't matter.

I'm sorry, Mama.

What mattered was getting the stuff into him. What mattered was to *forget*.

And, for a brief moment, he did forget. He forgot about the power going out, Corina breaking her leg, him nearly overdosing and shitting himself, his fight with Cody, and last but good fucking Lord not least, he forgot about the huge mound of glistening green flesh consuming a man whole. As was his habit, his mind slowly began to adopt one singular focus: *heroin*.

In the next instant, Oxford was sitting on the chair, both his inner and outer jackets removed, one arm hanging out of his green turtleneck. There was a lot in the case, much more than he remembered, which was good. Another few seconds, and the heroin was boiled and loaded into the syringe.

His belt was almost completely out of his pant loops when he heard it. The laughing was there, had always been there, but now it was getting louder and was accompanied by something else: heavy *depressions*, waxing and waning, alternating like footsteps. It was like nothing he had heard, or, perhaps more appropriately, nothing he had *felt* before—except for once. And that had been roughly ten minutes ago while he had been stuffed in the closet with his brother. Watching. Waiting.

It's coming.

The laughter intensified—slow and rumbling and, despite the lack of intonation, somehow mocking.

It's coming for me. The thing with Mom's eyes is coming for me.

Oxford wanted to inject the heroin, *needed* to inject it, but the laughter—real or imagined—grated him. It made him grind his teeth, it made him stomach churn, and it made his heart flutter.

Go away, he willed, his hand holding one end of the belt frozen in midair. *Go away.*

But the footsteps didn't listen; instead, their cadence

increased. It sounded like the thing had reached the top of the landing now, and Oxford's inner monologue shifted from "*Go away*" to "*Don't come here*".

Beggars can't be choosers, Mama used to say.

And this time, as if the thing had heard Oxford's unspoken plea, its footsteps paused momentarily. Slowly, like a vascular surgeon threading a final suture, Oxford teased the belt completely out of his pant loops.

I can shoot—

But then the footsteps returned—not slow and sauntering and deliberate as they had been before, but with renewed vigor—desperation, even. Three more steps and they doubled their pace again. Oxford's entire body went cold despite the stifling interior of Mrs. Wharfburn's Estate. It knew he was in here and it was coming for him, of that he had no doubt.

He dropped the belt, tossed the spoon and lighter back into the leather case, and, still tightly clutching the filled syringe in his other hand, bolted from the chair. When the heavy compressions—now frantic, excited, *aroused*—reached the door, Oxford had no choice but to dive headlong into the pile of towels or blankets at the back of the room, hoping— *praying*—that there wasn't a desk or chair hidden beneath them.

How does something that big, that heavy, move so fast?

His lunge landed him smack in the middle, and thankfully the blankets cushioned his awkward fall. Shifting his arms back and forth, Oxford swam his way into what he hoped was the center. The towels were horribly wet and sticky, making his progress difficult, and he found himself wriggling his hips just moments before the air in the room got incredibly hot. By chance, one of his eyes was left uncovered, and with it he spied the beast as it entered the room.

The failing light made it difficult to make out any distinct features, but the form was dark and heavy, that much he could tell—that much he already *knew*—and it smelled god-awful. Truth be told, though, he couldn't be sure if the smell was emanating from *it* or from the towels, which were themselves damp, sticky, and positively *fetid*. The heavy shape remained motionless in the doorway, and after a few seconds Oxford became aware of another sound: it was sniffing the room.

Oxford squinted hard with his one eye, trying to make out the thing's face. He could see a shadow of a nose, a wide nose—wide but undeniably human—and two dark hollows where the thing's eyes were buried deep in its head.

Please don't have Mama's eyes. I imagined that—please, please.

But the heavy shadows on its face thankfully prevented Oxford from making out its eyes.

The skin on its forehead was a lighter green than the rest, stretched tightly over its skull and the top of its head. Oxford saw the remnants of a pink scalp, complete with several tufts of short grey hair, but these seemed tenuous, swaying with every sniff as if they were ready to fall out in clumps.

It was from the nose down that things got sloppy: the skin around the lower jaw seemed extremely loose like the jowls of a morbidly obese man, an odd contrast to the thinly stretched green skin on the top of its head. Lower still, the sagging jowls eventually disappeared into shadows that somewhere became a massive torso. This, Oxford garnered, was a blessing: if he saw the imprint of the face inside the thing's stomach again, it would be the end of him.

The sound came again—rapid, shallow sniffs—and Oxford's cold body suddenly got hit with an adrenaline dump that sent his heart racing and made his face break out with sweat. He became acutely aware of the uncomfortable dampness around his crotch, and wondered if the thing could smell his piss. When the perspiration spread to his arms and then his hands, he adjusted his grip on the leather bag and syringe ever so subtly to make sure that he wouldn't drop them into the pile of towels.

Oh my God.

His eyes widened and he almost gasped out loud.

Oh my God, oh my God, oh my God.

The three words repeated in his head like a mantra, albeit with an urgency unsuitable for any form of meditation.

Oxford had somehow dropped the syringe when he had bolted from the chair. It took all of his waning willpower not to rocket to his feet, throw the towels off his body, and look for it. Biting the inside of his cheek so hard that he tasted blood, his eyes frantically scanned the room, rapidly oscillating back and forth.

Then he saw it: in the middle of the room, lying on the floor, the metal needle reflecting a sliver of moonlight.

How did I—?

But Oxford was not the only one who had seen the syringe. With two awkward, lurching movements, the shadow propelled its girth forward. The weight—the *heaviness*—of those steps made the fillings in Oxford's teeth vibrate.

Don't touch it! Leave it the fuck alone! Leave it alone, you fucking bastard! Don't touch my fucking heroin!

The beast hesitated, and this wasn't the first time that Oxford got the impression that it had somehow heard him. In the end, whether it heard him or not was irrelevant as it continued to move forward, one step closer to the syringe and one step closer to Oxford. With this latest movement, Oxford felt his vision blur from the strange increase in pressure. When the beast stopped advancing, his sight cleared just in time to see the thing bend over, or *fold* over, as it were, the body that it had consumed in the foyer somehow already mostly digested.

No, his mind whined, trying and failing to calculate how much dope he had left in the black satchel. Then it dawned on him that it wouldn't matter how much he had left; there, lying inches from those horrific silver claws, was his only syringe. If the beast took that, it wouldn't matter if he had a kilo or a milligram of heroin, he would not be getting high this day.

Just when Oxford neared his breaking point, something odd happened. First, the rumbling laughter ceased and Oxford felt some of the pressure that had been building in his head and ears over the past few minutes start to alleviate. But this relief was short-lived as the sound was almost immediately replaced by a guttural roar, a sound so deep and resonant that it vibrated Oxford's eardrums almost to the point of bursting. Still growling, the thing spun more quickly than Oxford would have thought possible given its size, and it bolted from the room, squeezing its dark green frame through the doorway. The sound and sudden movement did something to Oxford's mind, and he witnessed a blur of colors. The colors transitioned to monochrome, and his vision narrowed to a thin tunnel. He had felt this sensation before, and knew that it would be only moments before he passed out. But as the footsteps receded further and further from the room, and then down the stairs, the feeling began to pass, and his vision and mind slowly returned.

What the fuck just happened?

Oxford had all but conceded that he was going to be devoured by the thing with Mama's eyes, headfirst like the skinless man, and his only regret was that he hadn't shot up first. But then the beast had reached over and inspected the syringe, and—

Oxford's eyes finally focused on the needle lying in the center of the room. If he hadn't seen it with his own eyes, he would have thought that the beast hadn't even noticed it, let alone picked it up and—he squinted harder—depressed the plunger.

Something wet and sticky slapped against his cheek, and now, alone in the room, he shifted his stiff shoulders, debating whether or not he should wait a little longer before getting out from under the towels. When he moved again, the wet blanket on his face slipped over the eye he had been using to peer out into the room.

Sick.

He tried to shake his head to move it from his face, but for a towel, even a wet one, it had an unusual weight to it, and it stuck to him as if it were covered in drying glue. Cautiously, ready to freeze immediately should the hulking green form return, he fumbled with the leather case in his left hand, trying to work his fingers inside without disturbing his cover. His searching fingers eventually found the lighter and he pulled it out, moving it up near his face.

After slowly and deliberately raising the towel with one hand, he flicked the lighter once, twice, and on the third try it ignited, the spark so bright at first that it was temporarily blinding. The flame licked at the edges of one of the towels, causing a puff and a crackle. Oxford instantly let his thumb fall from the gas, once again ready to retract his arm and freeze should he hear something—*anything*.

Nothing.

There was *something*, though; not a sound, but a smell; something new, something different from the musty funk of the towels and the rot inside the house that he had become accustomed to. To Oxford, it didn't smell like a burning towel, it smelled like...

Burning hair?

He flicked the wheel again, but it had become slick and his thumb kept slipping; it took six tries to light. Moving the flame closer to his face, he inspected the towel that he had been holding up with the back of his other hand. It was only then that he noticed his entire hand and arm were completely red.

What the fuck?

Trying to keep the lighter lit, he rubbed his fingers together and was sickened by the way they stuck to each other.

Oxford allowed his gaze to move from his red hand to the towel and his mouth fell open.

No.

A sound — a noise somewhere between a scream and a moan — burst from his open mouth.

3.

IT WAS DARK, AND without the moonlight reflecting off the snow, Alice wouldn't have been able to see anything. As it was, when she first stumbled up to the squad car, she thought it was Coggins'. It wasn't until she got closer that she was able to make out three letters peeking from beneath a layer of snow on the driver's side door: *–iff*.

It was Sheriff Drew's car.

Which was fine, expected even, but as she surveyed the area further, worry began to sink in.

Where's Bradley's cruiser?

When she saw nothing but clean white snow along the road for the meagre few hundred meters that she could make out, she started to panic.

Tell me he didn't fucking leave!

The last thing she wanted to do was see the sheriff right now, especially without Brad as a buffer.

Alice took a step toward the squad car, comforted by the *cha cha cha* of the pills buried in her coat pocket.

I'll have one more, she thought, *to take the edge off.*

An image of the smiling face on the wall of Cody's house — the man she had been with what seemed a fortnight ago — flashed in her mind. Then she saw the old woman in the tub, with the one thicket of grey hair covering the side of her face. To Alice, the most disturbing part of that scene hadn't been the woman's eyes or face or even her blue lips; it had been her dress, so neat and proper, and her hair, meticulous, nearly perfect, save the part that spilled from her bun. It just didn't seem right.

Or maybe I'll have two pills.

The door to the squad car was unlocked, but she didn't find the keys inside. Not under the visor, where she knew the sheriff liked to keep them, and they hadn't fallen beneath the seat, either. But it was no matter; all she needed was somewhere to shield herself from the wind and a place to rest her legs while she had another clonny.

Even before she brought the small, inconspicuous pill to her lips, exhaustion hit her and she felt her eyelids droop. It had been an extremely long three days, starting with the horrible encounter with the filthy man with the scraggly beard — *where's my H* — and ending here, after running away from Cody and his dead mother.

Alice wondered how the poor man would react when he discovered the woman, and she hoped for both his sake and the sake of the kids that she was found *after* the power was restored, *after* some semblance of normalcy returned. Her mind turned to the little girl with the upturned nose, and how she had been crying incessantly nearly the while time Alice was there; even she knew that something was horribly wrong here in Askergan County.

The wind blew strongly against the open door, and Alice groggily tucked her legs in and then reached over and pulled it closed.

Come

"Shut up," she grumbled, bringing the pill to her lips. She swallowed and fell asleep before her head struck the headrest.

4.

JARED WAS PARTWAY OUT of the bathroom when he first heard the rumbling groan. Instinctively, his hands went to his ears, but while this muted the sound, it did nothing to block out the vibrations. For nearly thirty seconds, the sound rolled on before finally subsiding. The horrible sound was chased by rapid depressions that sounded like they were receding back down the stairs. After a few moments, Jared pulled his hands away from the sides of his head and ground his teeth in an attempt to equalize the pressure.

Then he heard the scream.

Jared immediately reached for the deputy's arm and squeezed it tightly. Even after the scream stopped, they stood with their backs pressed flat against the wall, frozen in fear. Jared's breaths came in short, terse bursts as his mind raced. Though the scream had an awful moaning quality to it, it most certainly *could* have been Oxford. And as far as they knew, he was the only other one here.

An image of the green beast with the pink, fleshy stripes flashed in his mind.

Correction, he thought. *The only other* human *here.*

They listened in silence as the footsteps made their way to the bottom of the stairs. Only then, after at least a full minute of not hearing any sound at all, did they dare move. When the deputy finally turned to face him, his narrow face was pinched and his eyebrows pushed down over the dark pits that housed his eyes.

He was tired too, Jared realized. Not as tired as he, surely, but tired just as well. There was sweat on his brow, and Jared noticed that he had once again drawn his gun. The small pistol looked tiny in his pale hand.

I'm going back, Jared thought, or maybe he said it out loud, because Coggins nodded.

"Get behind me," the deputy whispered, despite the fact that they had established that the thing had poor hearing, if it could hear at all.

Even after leaving the bathroom, neither the deputy nor Jared heard or felt any further movement from below. For a fleeting moment, Jared let himself believe that the thing had left, fled out the front door, never to be seen again—like the Sasquatch or Loch Ness. But he knew better; the temperature was the hint. The thing's bastardized metabolism—*digestion*; it was digesting the poor man—was generating the disgusting smell and horrible heat.

The first room off the hallway they entered was nearly empty, save a half-knitted scarf hanging from an old, wooden chair in the center. The second room was much the same, with the moonlight casting long shadows throughout.

It was in the third room that they eventually found Oxford.

This room was darker than the others, and it was dank as well, the warm air holding a strange meaty smell tinged with coppery undertones. Jared forced himself to breathe through his mouth as his eyes scanned the room.

Just inside the door, on their left, was a worn leather chair, and at the back of the room there was a large pile of what looked like towels or laundry, but before Jared could take a closer look at the odd shapes, movement from a rounded figure beneath the window drew his attention. At first he thought that this too was just a pile of clothing, but when he squinted hard, he wasn't so sure.

The deputy turned to leave, to check the next room, but

Jared blocked his path.

"Wait," he said.

He pushed by the deputy and took two steps into the room, trying his best to make out the figure in the dim moonlight. He paused, indicating with a raised hand for the deputy behind him to stop. Then he saw it: the slow rise and fall of what he now knew was his brother's back.

"Oxford!" he whispered loudly as he ran to his younger brother.

It was Oxford—it *had* to be Oxford—but as he approached, he realized that there was something different about his brother. Hunched over with his head between his knees and his back to Jared, his shirt and jeans looked wet.

What the hell?

Jared cautiously crouched behind his brother, tentatively laying a hand on his back, trying to lean around him to see his face. Immediately, Jared retracted his hand.

His brother's back was sticky.

"Oxford," he whispered, wiping his hand on his pants.

Oxford screamed.

Startled, Jared fell on his ass and then quickly scrambled to a prone position. He glanced quickly at Deputy Coggins, who had since crept into the room behind him. Together, they waited in silence, listening. Hoping. Praying.

Nothing—no other sound. Oxford's head had been so buried in his lap that the scream had been muffled.

They needed to get out of there—get out now.

Jared crab walked closer to his brother, again wiping his sticky hand on his thigh. This time, he didn't touch Oxford.

"Ox," he whispered. "Ox, it's me."

When that generated no response, he leaned in closer.

"It's your brother, Jared."

What the fuck happened to him? What did that thing *do to him?*

Oxford slowly turned his head and stared up at him. Again Jared was caught by surprise, and would have fallen backward had Deputy Coggins not come up behind him and gently pressed his shin against his spine.

Oxford's face was covered in blood.

"Jesus—"

"The faces," Oxford whispered.

Jared stared in horror. His brother's cheeks, nose, and even his lips were marred by streaks of the tacky dark brown substance.

The faces?

"Oxford, are you hurt?" he gasped, finally collecting himself.

"The faces," Oxford sobbed. "The faces are all staring at me!"

He reached for Jared with two bloody hands, but Jared stopped him by grabbing his wrists.

"Ox! Where is all this blood from? Are you hurt?"

Still holding the man's wrists, he did a cursory once over of his brother, but failed to identify the source of the blood. It dawned on him, however, that there was more than one thing that was wrong with this scene: Oxford was no longer wearing his jacket, and one of his arms had been pulled out of his turtleneck.

"Not hurt..." the youngest Lawrence brother murmured.

Shit.

"Oxford," he said, louder now, trying to get through to his brother, "did you shoot up?"

His hands still held in midair inches from Jared's face, Oxford answered.

"The faces..."

"Oxford!" Jared repeated, more forcefully this time. "Did you fucking shoot up?"

Oxford spat a spray of blood on the floor beside where Jared crouched.

It can't be his blood—there's way too much of it.

"The faces, Jared... the faces are all staring at me."

His words were slurred and his eyes seemed to bob in his head, unable to focus.

Jared ignored the nonsensical response and instead craned his neck to look at Oxford's back. The man's outer two pairs of pants had been pulled down a few inches, but this was not what bothered him. It was the base layer: Oxford's belt was no longer in the loops.

Jared quickly glanced around the room and eventually identified a belt lying beside Oxford's jacket by the leather recliner. And then he saw something else, too—a syringe lying abandoned in the center of the room.

Fuck. Fuck. Fuck!

Jared thrust Oxford's hands to his sides. Then it was his turn to reach out and grasp the man's blood-streaked face in his palms. His hands stuck uncomfortably to his tacky cheeks, but Jared, now convinced that none of this was Oxford's blood, tried his best to ignore the sensation—the disgusting feeling beneath his palms brought with it too many questions, ones that would eventually require answering. But there was one question that was more pressing, more *immediate.*

"Jesus," he heard the deputy whisper behind him, clearly noticing the blood for the first time.

Jared ignored him.

"Oxford, did you use?"

Memories of Oxford lying on the stairs of his mother's house came flooding back. If he was high, they were going to have to drag him out of the Estate.

Oxford tried to move his head, but Jared's grip held fast; the man resigned himself to looking at the floor.

Jared felt a gentle nudge on his back.

"We should get moving," Coggins said.

Jared ignored him.

"Look at me," he demanded, tightening his grip on Oxford's narrow, blood-covered cheeks. "Did you use?"

Oxford looked up, and Jared saw a deep sadness buried in his dark eyes.

"No," he finally whispered, "I wanted to, but..."

"But what, Ox?"

"...but *he* didn't like it."

Oxford's voice was so quiet now that Jared had to lean in close to hear. His brother's breath was stale and hot on his ear, but these smells were secondary to the nearly overwhelming coppery smell of blood. He felt his stomach flip.

"Who?" he asked, swallowing hard.

When Oxford looked away again, Jared squeezed his face even harder.

"Who didn't like it, Oxford? Who? Who the fuck didn't like it? The... the *thing*?"

Oxford pushed Jared's hands away and slowly nodded.

"*Oot'-keban*," Oxford whispered.

Jared made a face. He didn't recognize the word or words coming out of his brother's mouth.

"What? What the fuck are you saying, Oxford?"

His brother's entire body started trembling.

"*Oot'-keban* didn't like it," Oxford gasped, "and it doesn't *want us here.*"

5.

ALICE COULD FEEL THE beginnings of a migraine forming behind her eyes when she awoke.

Where am I? she wondered, staring out the windshield.

Then it came flooding back to her—the night out, the creep, the storm, and the dead woman in the bathtub.

What am I doing here?

But then she remembered that, too: she was here to meet up with Coggins and Sheriff Drew and get some help for the handsome man and his poor family—they were in a bad spot.

Alice adjusted her cap and sat up, her migraine inching closer to the back of her eyes with every movement. Slowly, trying to coax her headache into submission, she opened the cruiser door and tried to pull herself out of the vehicle.

A groan escaped her lips and she slumped back down into the seat. Falling asleep in the front seat of the cruiser had done nothing to help ease the soreness on her right side from the accident. Gritting her teeth, she braved the pain and this time managed to sit up and step out into the cold.

The wind had finally stopped blowing, leaving the air frigid but surprisingly tolerable. As Alice made her way through the snow, following in what must have been the sheriff's or Coggins' footprints, the oddness of the cruiser being left unlocked and the door to Mrs. Wharfburn's house thrown wide suddenly dawned on her. Now that the pills had mostly worn off, a new emotion—worry—started to build like the headache behind her eyes. Her pace quickened, and she found herself almost running to the door, stumbling, nearly impaling herself on the many large branches that dotted the lawn.

The blast of warm air that hit Alice when she was within a couple yards of the door almost went unnoticed—that came secondary to the smell.

Jesus.

Instinctively, she brought the arm of her ACPD jacket up to cover her nose. Then Alice turned her head sideways, took a massive gulp of cold air, and stepped inside.

It was dim in the foyer, and Alice struggled to make out anything specific. There were some piles of clothing scattered about the floor, and her first thought was that someone had robbed the place, which would explain the sheriff coming here, and maybe Coggins as well. In the center of the room, Alice noticed a reflective pool of something that could have been melted snow. She stared at the liquid for a moment and slowly began to convince herself that maybe it wasn't water after all.

It was too thick, too *coagulated.*

Against her better judgement, Alice took a quick breath in through her nostrils. She could smell blood underneath the foul scent.

Something had happened here.

Something bad.

Something *wrong.*

Alice pulled her gaze away from what she was now convinced was blood, and tried to look deeper into the house.

It was no use; the only thing she could make out in the darkness was two stairways that flanked the foyer receded upwards into darkness.

It was then, only after her olfactory senses had been desensitized by the inundating stench, that she noticed the odd warmth of the house.

Funny; I didn't hear the generator.

It dawned on her that the door had been open as well.

How the hell is a place as big as this holding heat with no power and the door wide open?

All of these questions made her feel tired again, and her headache crept a few millimeters closer to her retinas. She pulled off her gloves—technically Cody's gloves—and tossed them on the bench by the door. Then she undid her jacket down to her collarbone. With her now bare hands, she pulled out the little jar of pills and put three in her palm before resealing the container and putting it carefully back in her pocket.

Maybe they left the door open to air the place out? An animal crawled into the septic tank and a pipe burst, perhaps?

As she mulled this over, she heard the first of the scuttling noises coming from somewhere upstairs. Her hand made a fist and the three hard pills dug into her palm.

"Hello?" she shouted into the darkness.

Silence.

"Hello?" she repeated. "Anyone there?"

She heard more scurrying, followed by what sounded like an intense, whispered exchange.

"Hello? Sheriff?"

Her voice was more timid now, apprehensive.

What's going on?

"Dana? Brad?"

All of the shouting had matured Alice's headache, and it progressed to a solid throbbing in her temples and behind her eyes. She was about to put the three clonnys in her mouth when there was a sudden flurry of activity up above. A moment later, several figures appeared on the landing, and Alice squinted to make out their faces.

"Alice?"

A man's face came into focus at the same time he said her name, and relief washed over her.

"Brad!" she nearly shouted, but when his face contorted, her enthusiasm wavered.

"Alice, you need to run," Deputy Bradley Coggins whispered over the railing. "You need to get the fuck out of here and run. You need to run now!"

Alice's mouth fell open, and she would have thought it a cruel joke—it was not beyond Brad to joke even at a time like this—but it was his eyes, big, round, and black, that instantly clued her to the fact that he wasn't fucking around.

"What?" Her mouth hung open.

"Alice," he continued more desperately. "Go! Get the fuck out of here! Run!"

A shadow, one of the other figures, shuffled awkwardly toward the railing. After squinting for a moment, she realized that it wasn't just one person as she had first thought, but two; a slim man who looked oddly familiar holding the even thinner frame of another man. Judging by his posture—his head hung low, feet not firmly planted on the ground—this second man was either unconscious or very sick—and *wet*. For some reason, he also looked wet.

A reflection of moonlight flashed off something to the right of the two men, bringing her attention back to Deputy Coggins. His gun was drawn and he was holding it in front of him. In the five plus years that she had known him, he had only pulled his gun from his holster once. She knew, because she had helped him write the report.

"Alice," he pleaded, his eyes looking watery even in the dim light. "Just go. Please."

What the fuck?

Alice found herself tongue-tied.

The man to Coggins' left nodded vigorously.

"Go," the other man reiterated, his voice hoarse.

At the sound of the word *Go,* the sickly man lifted his head, and Alice saw his face for the first time.

No.

The single word flashed in her head like lightning. Then, like thunder chasing the boiling air, the migraine that had been slowly building exploded, sending her vision swirling and bringing with it a pain in her stomach like someone had driven a pickaxe between her lower ribs.

How could it be?

Although she couldn't remember his name, his face was unmistakable: it was the man in the photograph at Cody's house, the man from the night she had gone drinking after work, the man who had left before the bearded creep had appeared. His face was covered in deep crimson streaks, but it was the same man.

And now he is here. Here with Brad.

"Alice—"

At first Alice thought that the reason why she hadn't heard the rest of Deputy Coggins' sentence was because she had been deafened by the headache that pulsated in her ears. But when the deputy and the other man retreated from the bannister, and the third man's eyes rolled back and he fell limply to the floor with a muffled flop, she realized that she hadn't heard the end of Brad's sentence simply because he hadn't said anything else; he had stopped at "Alice".

But now the deputy spoke again, and Alice heard these three words loud and clear.

"Oh. My. God."

6.

CODY HAD BEEN STARING at the snowy lawn for a long, long time. The sun had set, the sky had darkened, and the full moon had appeared, illuminating the snow as if someone had laid millions of tiny white lights on the lawn prior to the storm. He had been crying off and on for the last few hours. It was a vicious cycle; he cried because of his inability to act, and when he cried he felt unable to do anything.

I have to leave. I have to leave this place. I have to leave now. I want to go. I have to go. I have to come.

He had been thinking this almost since they had arrived, and most definitely ever since the power went out. But what bothered him most, oddly, wasn't the fact that his brother had nearly overdosed and shit himself, nor that his eldest daughter had broken her leg, which had now turned an awful black and green and smelled of sulfur. It wasn't even that his wife was essentially comatose, or that his mother, God bless her, had been gone for so long that only the worst seemed realistic; no, none of that *pain* made him feel as sour as his desire to leave. Not to take his family and seek shelter — warmer, *better* shelter — but to leave on his own and to hurry east, like the man with the broken knee, the strange woman with the jet black hair, like the bears, the wolves, the deer, and the dogs. He was being *pulled* east. And this scared him — scared him more than anything.

I need to get out of here. I need to go west. South. I need to go south — anywhere but east.

He had selfishly forced his family to come to his mother's house, in what he now realized had been a desperate attempt to reconnect with his brothers following the death of his father. And to try and *rekindle* with Marley. But it had all been a mistake—a terrible, terrible mistake.

A gust of wind suddenly struck the house, flapping the cardboard window covering high above Cody's head.

Come

That was it. That was the last time he wanted to hear that word spoken, uttered, whispered, or thought.

"Please," he begged, "leave me alone."

If he heard it again, he feared that he might shut down, that he might further recede into the dark abyss that his mind had become.

Cody ground his teeth and was finally driven to action.

Corina was lying still on the couch, eyes fluttering, only now her lips were permanently downturned. Cody wiped the tears from his eyes and reached into his pocket, his sweaty fingers quickly finding the two pills that the strange woman had given him.

Half a pill, Alice had said, but she didn't know about this; she didn't know about *Oot'-keban.*

"Corina, sweetie, can you hear me?"

Cody crouched, bringing their faces level. He was nervous—nervous that she would awaken and look at him and speak *that* word. Tentatively, he reached out with the back of his hand and touched her pale forehead. It was cold.

"Corina," he whispered, and his eldest daughter's eyes fluttered and opened, only this time they lacked the lucidity of an hour ago.

He took the pills out of his pocket and stared at his open hand. The two chalky white discs almost blended into his palm. Then he picked the half-empty bottle of water off the table, reached over, and gently placed both pills in his eldest daughter's open mouth. He put the water bottle to her lower lip next and slowly lifted the bottom. Instinctively, Corina gulped and swallowed, her expression remaining tight, pained. Then her eyes closed again and Cody kissed her cold forehead and told her he loved her. He paused for a moment, deciding what to do next. Instead of standing, he turned to his wife.

"M—M—Marley," he stammered, trying hard to control his emotions. "Marley? Wake up, Marley."

He started to cry again, and his words became borderline incoherent.

"Marley, why the fuck won't you wake up? Why—?"

The wind gusted hard, and Cody turned his eyes to the cardboard-covered window.

"Fuck off!" he nearly screamed. "Fuck off and get out of my fucking head!"

As if in response to his cry, the wind gusted again, harder this time.

Cooooome

Cody bit his lip and drove his index fingers into his closed eyes so hard that he saw spots.

"Marley," he repeated, eyes still closed. "I can't stay here anymore, I can't handle the—" He caught himself before he said the word. "I can't handle the *wind.*"

To his surprise, when he opened his eyes again, his wife was staring back at him. Looking at those hazel eyes, which now seemed black, empty, he was reminded of the eyes of the deer he had seen blundering through the waist-high snow. She was gone, he knew—perhaps driven mad by the voice inside their heads telling them to *come,* and yet unwilling to leave her injured daughter. He knew then why Seth had just up and left—why he had opted to turn away from the injured man and head in the opposite direction. He knew because he felt it too;

he felt that if he stayed another five minutes in this place, he would succumb to the voice, to that ungodly grinding, foreboding, fucking *heavy* voice in his head telling him to '*Come*'. And Mama?

Mama, did the same thing happen to you?

Wiping the tears from his eyes, he stood.

"I'm going now," he repeated, unsure of whether or not Marley was *truly* there, if the fact that he was speaking even registered with her. "I'm taking Henrietta and going."

Marley made no move to rise or beg him to stay, and nothing in her face made him think that she wanted him to leave their youngest daughter, or to take her with them. He wanted that—needed it.

What's wrong with you, Marley? Can't you ask—beg—me to stay?

But she said and did nothing—she was gone.

Cody wiped more tears away with the back of his hand.

"I'll come back for you," he promised, trying to be strong, trying to sound genuine. The words, however, seemed hollow, and a vision of his two brothers, decked out in layer upon layer of clothing standing by the front entrance uttering those same words, flashed in his mind. Marley just stared.

"I love you," he whispered, but his wife's only response was to let her eyes close.

Still crying, he turned back to his youngest daughter, who was sleeping on the chair behind him. After quickly checking her body for exposed skin and not finding any, he picked her up and set about putting on his gloves and as much outerwear as he could find. Just as he was wrapping a brown and green wool scarf across his face, Henrietta grunted and woke.

"I want that, Daddy," she said in a sleepy voice. He couldn't remember the last time she had spoken—had actually stopped crying and said a word.

"What's that, sweetie?"

Cody's gaze followed her outstretched arm. The stuffed owl that Oxford had bought her with what must have been his last few dollars lay on the floor. For some reason, this made him cry even harder.

Eventually, the sobbing passed and he managed to pick up the stuffed animal and hand it to her.

Strong. I need to be strong.

A deep breath.

Cody offered a final glance at his wife and eldest daughter. They moved so little that he had to concentrate for a good minute to confirm that they weren't statues—that they were real. He felt angry at himself and at his father—*Fuck you, Gordon*—as without his death, they would have stayed home. They wouldn't have braved the storm and come to this place—to Askergan.

"Where we going, Daddy?" a sleepy Henrietta asked. "Mommy not coming?"

I love you, he thought, hoping that somehow, like the voice on the wind or in his head or wherever the fuck it was coming from, his own words would resonate with his wife and eldest daughter.

"No," he replied, turning from the family room and heading for the door. "No, Mommy not coming."

To his surprise, Henrietta didn't burst into tears and beg for her mommy as he half expected her to. On some level, Cody almost wished she had wailed—maybe this would have snapped Marley from her stupor. Instead, a look of understanding crossed Henrietta's round face, and the toddler simply nodded. At not quite three years old, she couldn't possibly understand, of course, but for some reason this acceptance by his youngest daughter gave him strength. The little girl almost seemed relieved; like Cody and the rest of them, maybe even more so, she knew something was wrong here. She wanted to get away from this place almost as much as Cody.

"Where we going?" she asked again.

"South, sweetie; we are going south."

7.

AT FIRST ALICE THOUGHT that Deputy Coggins had lost his mind and was shooting at *her*. From below, she saw three distinct muzzle flashes illuminate the darkness, but the loud reports and their echoes reverberated repeatedly off Mrs. Wharfburn's massive ceilings and walls, making it sound like a dozen or more bullets had been fired.

She did not turn, could not turn, but when the bullets missed her, she realized that Deputy Coggins was not aiming at her but was shooting at something *behind* her.

The first two reports were accompanied by the sound of breaking glass—clear misses. The third, however, hit something dense, making a heavy *thunk* sound that reminded Alice of the sound a large stone made when tossed into a lake. But to her surprise, no cry of pain or even an angry shout followed this *thunk*—she heard nothing, not even a grunt.

Then she remembered the animal tracks that she had seen in the snow on her journey from Cody's house to here.

Was it a wolf? Was Brad shooting at a wolf?

Alice was terrified, unable to turn and look, but somehow she doubted it; the expression on Deputy Coggins' face and the way he had said, *"Oh. My. God."* —just like that, three separate, complete sentences—suggested that it was something worse.

A bear?

Brad was yelling something at her, but her ears were ringing from the shots and all she heard was one muffled, unintelligible word that seemed to drag on and on. Her head pounded. Her side hurt. Her fingers were frozen. Her face was numb. Yet despite all of this, Alice somehow mustered the courage to turn.

It was the smell that hit her first. Even before she had fully turned, the horrible stench that filled Mrs. Wharfburn's Estate accosted her again, except now every putrid flavor of the smell that had made her gag upon entering the Estate intensified: rotting eggs and decaying meat, tinged with the spicy-sweet aroma of habanero peppers.

It was all too much for Alice and she vomited, the projectile kind, water and bile jettisoning from her open mouth and spraying at the base of a huge, dark silhouette that squatted mere feet from her. Her reaction was so sudden and vulgar and distinct that it reminded her of the time she had wolfed down six Quaaludes and had needed to sip ipecac in order to get them back up again. Hunched over, trying to regain control of her body, she felt a rumbling grow inside her head—or maybe outside of it, she didn't know for certain—a rumbling that rattled her molars, blurred her vision, and forced the pistol-induced tinnitus away like a pesky fly. Eyes watery, with more vomit rising in her throat, she forced herself to look up, trying to take in—to *understand*—what hell loomed before her.

Despite the fact that it was but a foot from her, the thing's face was shrouded in shadows. She saw what she thought was a mouth—a set of paper-thin lips extending in a slash almost all the way around the thing's head. Buried in the thing's mouth was a row of teeth, almost comically small in that horrendous gash.

It was a grin of nightmares.

Before her gaze drifted upward, the rumble coming from the thing's mouth increased and she felt something graze her hip. In the next instant, mired in horrible fascination, Alice felt herself being slowly pulled forward as if she were standing on a moving carpet at the airport.

Instinctively—and it was exactly that, instinct and nothing

more—her right hand, still knotted in a fist, shot out and smashed into the thing's lower lip.

Punching the beast was a preposterous act—pathetic, really—but several unexpected things happened next in rapid succession. First, she felt the odd sliminess of the pink skin, like raw chicken that had been left on the counter for too long, and then she felt the hardness beneath. Next, her hand rang from the force and the three clonnys that she was still clutching in her hand were crushed. The pain forced Alice's palm open, and the majority of the smashed pieces actually flew into the thing's cavernous mouth.

Alice retracted her hand immediately, her knuckles throbbing from the impact. The thing's lip quivered and the rumbling, which she now knew could only be one thing—*laughter*—increased in tempo. The piece of pink flesh that she had punched slowly fell away, revealing more of the same hard green shell beneath.

A hideous tongue, long and tacky, slid out of the thing's mouth and licked at where Alice had struck, and she caught sight of a dozen or so white clonazepam remnants clinging to it. The touch grazed her hip again, but this time the sensation did not linger as it had before.

The tongue suddenly recoiled, pulling back into its mouth with startling speed, and the thing quivered before twisting awkwardly to one side. The rumbling ceased, and Alice sighed as the pressure inside her head relented. The thing's neck, as thick and nearly unidentifiable as it was, seemed to bob; it was going to be sick. A horrible retching noise suddenly filled the air, and for the briefest moment the thing's head lowered and she caught a glimpse of its entire face, dead-on for the first time.

"Aliiiiice."

Despite the hard green skin and bulging eyes, the *thing* had an uncanny resemblance to someone she knew — someone she knew very well.

"Allliiiicccee."

Alice's bladder let go, but she barely noticed the warmth spreading down her legs.

"Allliiiiiccceee. How many chances did I give you, Alice? And now you go and *fuck* around on Bradley? After all *he's* done for you?"

She couldn't move, couldn't even *breath*.

"Allliiiiicce. I gave you a job, kept you out of jail. Gave you a life. Allliiiiiiiiiccccccce. Allllliiiiiiiiiiiiiiiiiiccccccccccce."

This last utterance of her name seemed to draw on into infinity.

"Dana?" she whispered.

Chapter Nine
Oot'-keban

1.

DEPUTY BRADLEY COGGINS WATCHED in horror as the thing—the dark green monstrosity—toyed with Alice, its elongated fingers brushing her waist almost erotically. But that wasn't the worst part; the worst part was the thing was laughing—laughing its horrible, deep, rumbling laugh.

He had fired at it—had hit the thing—but it had barely even noticed. If it weren't for his still ringing ears and the dot of blood marking the beast's shoulder, a splash of red on what little remained of Sheriff Drew's pink flesh, he might have convinced himself that he hadn't fired at all.

That act, firing his gun, had sapped all of the deputy's courage, and he felt his body go cold despite the incredible heat emanating from the monster below. He could not move; all he could do is watch. It was as if his mind could *think* about moving, could process the act, but somewhere just below his neck there was a conduction problem and the signal refused to continue to his limbs. He wanted to go there, he wanted to run downstairs and save his girlfriend, but he remained rooted, helpless.

The shadowy beast had a hand around Alice's waist now, the long, dark appendages completely encircling her body, and it was pulling her slowly toward its mouth, all the while still laughing. As Alice neared the horrible orifice, it slowly began to open as if being controlled by a massive hinge, and Coggins could see a row of tiny teeth—Dana's teeth—inside the hole. It was fucked up on so many levels, the least of which was the fact that Dana had rescued her from an abyss from which few return, but was now was sucking her into another dark, horrific pit.

Then Alice did something that shocked Coggins even after all he had seen: she hit the beast—she literally reared back and punched the thing—and it seemed to him that the laughing changed, becoming so low and guttural that his own teeth started to vibrate.

Images of the skinless man with the limp being devoured whole flashed in his mind. He couldn't—wouldn't—let that happen to Alice, or to anyone else for that matter.

But Coggins didn't have to do anything—something odd had already been set into motion. Instead of continuing to bring Alice closer to its open mouth, the fingers around her waist suddenly unfurled and the thing moved—shuffled? Slid?—a foot or so *away* from Alice. The thing's long tongue darted frantically about its mouth for a moment, and then its whole body, its entire thickness, started to contract, and Deputy Coggins realized that he was watching the thing gag.

This is your chance! his mind screamed. *Run Alice! Run!*

But Alice did nothing.

Why are you standing there? Run!

"No," Jared moaned from somewhere behind him.

And with that word, whatever spell Coggins had been under broke.

Deputy Coggins shook the paralysis from his body like a thin layer of dust and ran down the staircase so quickly that he nearly took a header when he tried to holster his gun at the same time. Stumbling, falling over the last few steps, he reached Alice in seconds. Trying his best to ignore the gagging, retreating beast and the foul stench emanating from it, he grabbed her around the waist with one arm, acutely aware of the eerie similarity between what he was doing and what the thing had done moments before. He tried to pull her back toward the staircase but she resisted, her legs remaining locked at the knees. Now that the laughing had stopped and the ringing in his ears and teeth was nearly gone, he realized that Alice was saying—whispering—something, a single word over and over again.

"Daddy... Daddy... Daddy..."

Coggins felt his heart wrench. Dana had been like a father to her, and if seeing him—*it*—like this was enough to make even the most stable of people go mad, he couldn't imagine what was going on in Alice's mind.

But there was no time for this now. He pulled again.

"Come on, Alice."

With his eyes still firmly fixated on the retching beast that receded further into the shadows with each gag, he tugged Alice again. This time she mobilized, or, in the very least, she became pliable enough to half stumble, half allow herself to be dragged to the bottom of the staircase. Keeping his eyes trained on the dark shadow into which the beast had retreated, he hoisted her up onto the first step with a grunt. Then the next, then the one after that. He had to stop to rest on the third step, breathing heavily.

"I'm sorry, Dana," Alice muttered, her eyes rolling back in her head. "I'm so Bradley. I'm so sorry."

"No!" Coggins shouted. "Stay with me Alice!"

He shook her and her eyes rolled forward again, seeming to focus.

"C'mon, Alice!"

To his surprise, she responded by stiffening a little, and when Deputy Coggins went to pull her to the next step, she seemed to facilitate the process.

"Keep it together, Alice," he repeated, and pulled her up another step. It was an impossible request, but, *fuck*, this entire day was impossible.

Once they reached the fifth or sixth step, Jared ran to them, tucking one of Alice's arms around the back of his neck as the deputy did the same on the other side. Silently, the three of them humped their way to the top of the stairs and then down the hallway. They entered the third doorway, the room in which they had first found Oxford, and dropped Alice's limp body onto the chair, where she collapsed in a heap. Oxford, Deputy Coggins noted, had been dumped unceremoniously in the center of the room where he lay face down, his back rising and falling rhythmically with each breath.

The deputy wiped the sweat from his brow with the back of his hand. His muscles were strained from the awkward movement of dragging Alice backwards up a flight of stairs, and he was so, so tired; he'd gone at least twenty-four hours now without food or sleep.

Sleep.

He wondered if he would ever be able to sleep again after what he had seen.

It was Jared who spoke first, his voice hoarse.

"We need to get out of here."

Thank you for that penetrating glimpse into the obvious.

Coggins stared at Jared; he looked as tired as Coggins felt. Then his eyes drifted to Alice slumped in the chair, eyes closed, and Oxford face down on the rug. They had tried their best to get the blood off the man, but without water it was a near impossible task; all they had managed to do was to streak his face, making it look like someone had rubbed earth-brown finger-paint on his cheeks. Then they had taken off his outer layers of clothing and tossed them in a sticky ball in the corner of the room.

They still didn't even know where the blood had come from—they only knew that it wasn't his.

Coggins shook his head.

Go? How can we go?

"It won't let us leave."

Jared raised an eyebrow, and Coggins shook his head again.

"It won't let us leave—at least, not out the front door."

Coggins didn't know if this was true, but if they managed to escape—break a window, say, and jump to the snowy ground below—where would they go? They would just freeze to death, and despite the thing below them, he wasn't sure that this was the best alternative.

Something washed over Jared's face, something that was difficult to describe—despair, maybe? Disappointment?—and it was clear that the man was thinking the same thing.

"What happened down there?" Jared asked after a long pause, his voice hoarse and dry.

Again Coggins shook his head, but this time he offered no reply. When it was clear that the man needed some answer—any answer—Coggins finally spoke.

"I don't know." He paused, trying to piece together in his mind what he had seen. "Alice hit him and it—it made him sick somehow."

Jared appeared to mull this over.

"That's it?"

"That's it." Coggins shrugged. "That's what I saw. I think it was gagging."

The two men stood a few feet apart in the stinking darkness without speaking for several minutes. When Coggins could take it no longer and finally opened his mouth to say something, a voice, one more delicate than either his or Jared's, interrupted him.

"I hit him with these," Alice said, holding an orange bottle in her outstretched hand.

2.

OXFORD WASN'T ASLEEP, BUT he wasn't fully awake, either. His limbs refused to respond and his mouth tasted like copper pennies. His head hurt. His back hurt. His *mind* hurt. He had seen things today that he would have previously thought impossible. The faces—he had seen the faces, the empty eye sockets of sheer hell staring at him—*into* him.

—she says she hears it inside—

The smell of burning hair, of his own piss. The wetness of tissue slapping his face. The *tackiness* of the blood.

But somehow, despite all of this insanity, his hearing was clear; clearer, in fact, than he could remember in a long time. It was as if the heavy footsteps had unblocked his ear canals. And what he heard, on this day of impossible things, oddly seemed to make sense.

"Think about it."

The deputy's voice.

"It makes sense. First, your brother tells us about how the thing touched the syringe full of heroin."

There was an awkward pause, as if the deputy anticipated an interjection. When none came, he continued.

"And then Alice hits it in the mouth with the pills."

Alice? Who's Alice?

Then he remembered the shape of a woman who had foolishly entered the house, and the thing had... it had... *embraced* her.

"So? What do you think? It reacted to the drugs?"

Jared now.

"Dunno. I guess. What other options do we have?"

"I checked the back balcony. Crazy Mrs. Wharfburn boarded it all up—windows, doors, everything. There's no way I can pry them off."

Boarded up? Why had she boarded up the house?

Mrs. Wharfburn... Mrs. Wharfburn, who had been devoured and whose discarded skin looked like unsalted beef jerky, had boarded up her own house.

There was another pause, which must have been preceded by an inaudible exchange of sorts, because the next sentence didn't seem to follow logically. Oxford tried to lift his head from the carpet, but his body still refused to respond.

"I'll do it."

Jared, forlorn.

Pause.

"Do what? What the fuck are you guys talking about?"

A woman's voice this time; Alice, presumably.

"We have one chance to get out of here," Coggins said. "You saw how that thing got when just a little clonazepam got in its mouth. How many pills do you have left?"

There was a rattling sound.

"Maybe eight more?"

"And I have this," Jared added.

"So, somehow, we are going to inject the thing, and—and—and what? Hope it ODs?"

Alice again.

"Brad, use your head. How will you ever get close enough to inject it? And what about the clonnys? Hand feed them? What the fuck, Brad! What if it doesn't die?"

"It can't hear well, we know that; it has some fucked-up cauliflower ears. And if I could just get my shotgun—"

"You would, what, shoot it? You tried that, remember? It didn't fucking work!"

"No, but I missed—"

"You didn't miss, I saw—"

"I missed the, ugh, the, the *fleshy* parts. I saw blood where I hit the pink part, Alice. We need to act fast before there is nothing left—"

"Nothing left of what? Of the fucking sheriff? Of your boss?"

The woman's voice suddenly escalated.

"Of Dana... of *dad*?"

This time when the deputy responded, his tone was softer.

"It's not Dana anymore, Alice. It may have been once, but not now. I—I just want to get out here."

Oxford's head was swimming. The sheriff was that *thing*? It didn't make sense... the thing with his mother's eyes—the thing that had whispered his name so hauntingly, that had spoken to *him* with his mother's voice—was this the sheriff?

There was another long pause, during which Oxford felt himself fading again.

"I'll do it. I'll go down there, strip like the man, and wait."

Jared again.

"If it doesn't work, you can probably run by and out the door, while it—while it—"

It was bullshit, of course. Oxford had seen how fast the thing moved, and there was no way they could outrun it. Even if they managed to slip by and get outside, running in waist-high snowdrifts was not an option he wanted to entertain. And even if they got away, the *call* might bring them back.

Oxford had had enough. Exacting all of his limited willpower, he managed to pull his head from the carpet. His eyes immediately fixated on the syringe clutched between his brother's thumb and finger.

"No," Oxford said, feigning confidence. "I'll go."

3.

Jared Was Adamant That he went and not Oxford. Coggins was out; he was the only one who could handle the shotgun. And Alice? Well, asking her to do anything to the thing that was once like a father to her was not even a consideration. Besides, she was in rough shape—worse than Coggins, Jared, and maybe even Oxford.

"I'll go," Jared pleaded, more so at Coggins than at Oxford. "It's better if *I* go."

Deputy Bradley Coggins' eyes darted back and forth from Jared to Oxford's blood-streaked face. It was obvious to him which of the two should act as bait, and it should have been evident to Jared as well.

Slowly but definitively, he shook his head.

"Oxford."

There was no glee or gloating on Oxford's face—just the opposite. The man swallowed hard.

"Him?" Jared said desperately. "He's a—he's a—"

Fuck up? Coggins thought, finishing the sentence in his mind.

"He'll go," Coggins interrupted, doing Jared a favor by stopping him before he said something that he might regret.

Like in the bathroom when Coggins had introduced himself—*My name is Deputy Bradley Coggins*—Jared let it go. The decision had been made, and he knew that Jared was secretly grateful that he wasn't the one who had to make it.

Coggins turned back to Oxford, whose breathing had suddenly gotten shallow. He remembered the naked man standing in the center of the foyer, his leg and knee twisted awkwardly, blood leaking from a cut on his forehead. He had never gotten a good look at the man's face, but when the man in this memory turned, he had Oxford's wide eyes, and the same deplorable, blood-streaked expression.

Come

Coggins shook his head.

This is fucking nuts.

"Will he have enough time before—?"

"I'll wear the faces," Oxford whispered, his voice dry, hoarse.

Jared turned to look at his brother, anger suddenly flashing across his features.

"What fucking faces, Oxford? What the fuck are you talking about?"

Coggins readied himself to step between them, but Oxford just lowered his head and pointed over his shoulder with one trembling finger.

"Those faces," he said, his voice cracking.

"The fucking towels?"

Jared took three steps toward the pile of laundry at the back of the room. His fourth step, however, was a little slower, tentative. At that distance, they didn't much look like towels; they were too heavy, too wet. Another step. And then another.

With Coggins watching, Jared raised his leg to take a final step, but instead of moving forward, he suddenly backpedaled so quickly that Coggins had to get behind him to prevent him from tumbling right out of the room.

"What?" Coggins asked, trying unsuccessfully to keep the fear from his voice. "What is it?"

Jared turned to him and swallowed hard.

"They aren't towels," he gasped, "they're *skins.*"

4.

ALICE BLINKED TWICE AND her eyes focused on Jared wrapping the man that she had awoken beside in a layer of skin—*human skin*—to protect him long enough so that he could inject a monster with a lethal cocktail of clonazepam and heroin. Oxford had stripped down to his boxers; then they had covered him in blood, first wiping their hands on some of the underside of the skins, then all over his body, even his face. They had even reapplied some on top of the layer of dried blood that marked his narrow face.

Although Deputy Coggins had initiated the search through the pile of thick, damp skins, he had only managed to flatten two of them before he was overwhelmed by revulsion and ran to the corner of the room to vomit.

It was Jared who had eventually found one that looked like it had belonged to someone about Oxford's height, and he had shaken it out like a damp sheet. The slit down the back was so precise that it was almost surgical, and Oxford easily stepped inside, pushing his fingers into *its* fingers like gloves that were just a bit too large. It was like walking into a hazmat suit, only this one lacked the convenience of a zipper. Instead, after they had lined up the eyeholes, they had resorted to pulling it hard from behind, squishing it against Oxford's nearly naked flesh, the blood they covered him with helping it stick. The only thing they didn't have to worry about were the feet; the skin ended around mid-shin, as if the beast had become anxious and had simply torn the feet out.

It was horrific; Oxford looked swollen to the nth degree, all puffy and distended. The top part of the skin, the part pressed against Oxford's forehead and scalp, was a matted mess of blond hair, thin and scraggly, clumps of it sticking to the face and scalp where they had accidentally smeared blood. Oxford's entire body, save his shins and feet, was covered in the pale membrane that clung tightly to him in some places—his hands, neck, and upper thighs—and hung awkwardly in others—his face, back, and the rumpled top of his head. Quite simply, it looked like he was wearing an ill-fitting human onesie.

Alice gagged; it was a repulsive sight.

"Give me the clonazepam," Coggins demanded, his hand outstretched.

Alice managed to draw her eyes away from the atrocity that Oxford had become, and stared up at the deputy with a strange, blank expression on her face. Slowly, almost robotically, she held out her hand, and Coggins snatched the container from it—*cha cha cha.*

He was about to turn, but instead he stopped and stared at the bottle for a second. Then he opened it and peered inside, his lips mumbling with mental math.

Without warning, he reached for Alice, drawing her in close with his wiry arms. The gesture surprised her, and at first she resisted, guilt of what had happened with Oxford coming at her in waves. But he pulled harder and she eventually relented, allowing herself to be sucked into his embrace. He smelled horrible, of course, they all did, but Alice didn't care; she hugged him back. She started to tremble, and they stayed in each other's arms for a good minute. Coggins was the one who eventually broke the embrace, kissing her gently on her sweaty forehead as they disengaged.

"Take one," he said loudly, allowing his hand to hover over hers for just a moment before turning to face Oxford and Jared.

Oxford had turned sideways, and was subtly shrugging his

shoulders, trying to realign his eyes with the eyeholes of the skin that he had stepped inside. Coggins didn't wait for a response, and instead found the man's swollen hand and dropped a pill into it. When Oxford failed to react, the deputy leaned in and said, "It's in your hand."

Oxford nodded, or at least Coggins thought he nodded, and then brought the swollen hand to his face. When the man began his uncoordinated attempts to try and push the pill through the torn mouth hole with puffy fingers, Coggins had to look away for fear of being sick again.

Alice, on the other hand, laughed—she couldn't help it.

To her, Oxford looked like a blind man trying to figure out where to put the round peg.

She laughed again, and this time Deputy Coggins turned and gave her a hard look. Even in the darkness, which she realized was actually becoming less suffocating as dawn approached, the fear in his eyes was obvious.

Coggins took a set of keys out of his pocket and used one to crush the remaining clonazepam inside the container.

"This is crazy. Fucking insane," Jared said suddenly, shaking his head.

Coggins paused.

"Of course it's crazy," he replied out of the corner of his mouth before going back to breaking up the pills.

"Maybe we should just go," Jared continued, his voice almost a whisper.

Coggins stopped what he was doing and turned to face Jared.

"Go where?"

Jared moved closer to his brother and tried to help him get the pill into his mouth.

"Go—as in leave this place."

"You don't think it knows we're up here? You don't think it's waiting for us?" Coggins voice was louder now.

"Maybe—I dunno. Maybe we can get by it."

There was a short pause.

"Maybe it won't get all of us."

Coggins ignored that last part; he wouldn't let *that* happen to anyone else

"So we get out; then what?"

No answer.

"If we leave here—if somehow we get past it—one of two things will happen: one, we freeze to death out in the cold. Or two, we walk around out there in the fucking blizzard and then wander our way back here."

Jared froze.

"Come back? What the hell are you talking about?"

"Don't tell me you haven't heard the voice."

Jared hesitated for a split second.

"Yeah," Coggins said, almost forlornly. "You hear it. I hear it."

He swept an arm across the room, hesitating only momentarily as his gesture passed Alice, who had a queer smirk on her face.

"Alice for sure hears it. Oxford, too. Think about it. Why are we all here? Alice? Me? You? The sheriff? Why did you come here? You could have gone anywhere—"

Jared turned away and went back to adjusting Oxford's skin.

"We came here to look for help. Because, because—"

"To this place? You came to *this* house for help? Why here of all places?

Coggins took two steps across the room and grasped Jared's shoulder. The man jumped, and when he turned to face the deputy again, Coggins could see that he had been crying. He loosened his grip and lowered his voice.

"Is this the closest place, Jared? Did you come this way because it is the closest place to look for help?"

"No—no I don't think so... but—"

"Why didn't you go the other way, Jared? Why didn't you split up? Why didn't you go towards town? Stop a car on the road, maybe?"

Jared took a page out of his younger brother's book and looked down.

"I—I—"

Coggins squeezed his shoulder again and the terrified man looked up at him.

"You came here because of *it*. Because it called to you... because—because—" He glanced around quickly before finishing in a harsh whisper, "—because of *Come*. For God's sake, man, I've had this fucking monosyllabic mantra repeating over and over in my head—*Come, Come, Come, Come*—for hours now, maybe even days, and you think after all of this it's just going to let us out of here?"

The deputy gritted his teeth.

"I can't get the fucking thing out of my head—I don't think I will ever be able to get that *feeling* out of my head, Jared. The only way to get rid of it is to kill the motherfucker."

And with that, Jared turned.

It was done. They would stick to the plan.

Deputy Coggins took a step backward and pulled the black case from his pocket and opened it. He crouched down on his haunches, spreading items out on the floor in front of him. When he flicked the lighter wheel, Alice made out what they were: a syringe filled with heroin, a spoon, and some alcohol swabs. Her eyes darted from the paraphernalia to Oxford in the skin suit and back again.

Of course!

She thought of the man with the beard yelling for his case, for his *H*, and things came into focus. Oxford had been with her that night and had left before she had awoken. But he mustn't have remembered, or, like her, he had blacked out, because there was no recognition on his face when he looked at her. This perhaps wasn't that surprising given that she had been half-naked, lying on her stomach, her back riddled with a rash when he'd left. But when Oxford had awoken, *he* was the *cunt* who had taken the bearded man's case of heroin. And now that heroin was here with her. Full circle—full fucking circle.

Come

The deputy tapped the crushed pills onto the spoon and proceeded to heat the bottom. With the flame from the lighter illuminating his face, he not only looked terrible, but he looked scared. His usual sarcastic wit, evident in his features—a wry smile, tight wrinkles by the corner of his eyes even when he wasn't laughing—was gone. His typically slicked black hair was knotted atop his head, and his eyes, usually his most striking feature—dark, but twinkling, especially when he was teasing Deputy White—were dull and sunken. The lighter flicked out, and she saw the silhouette of his hand shake and knew that the wheel had gotten too hot and he had burned himself. She had done the same thing numerous times back— *ha, back!*—when she was an addict.

The flame reignited, and Coggins was holding the syringe now, using one hand to pull the plunger back while his other hand held the spoon; no shakes, no quivers, no spills this time. Alice marveled at the ease with which the deputy filled the syringe with just one hand. She was impressed.

Maybe he was once an addict too.

Alice thought about that for a moment.

Everyone's an addict — everyone is addicted to something.

The lighter flicked off again and Jared turn to face his brother.

"Good luck, Oxford. I love you."

Jared leaned forward, intending to embrace his brother, to hold him close, but his arms fell short; even if he had the constitution to hug him, there wouldn't have been any physical contact — the extra layer of skin made that impossible. Jared backed away.

"Oxford?" he asked.

"Yeah?"

His voice was slow — tired.

"What did Mom say to you before we left?"

There was a long pause, and Coggins lost sight of Oxford's eyes; it wasn't clear if the man had closed them, or if the skin had slipped again.

"She said, 'Look after your brother, he needs you.'"

This floored Jared, and he took two quick steps backward. He opened his mouth to say something, but no words came out.

Coggins stepped forward to put an end to this awkward exchange; if the flaking, peeling pink flesh on the beast below them was any indication, which he thought it was, their window of opportunity — if there had ever been one — was closing.

"Take this," Coggins instructed, holding out the syringe.

It was enough drugs to kill an elephant, Alice saw, a murky brownish-yellow substance that filled the entire volume of the syringe. Enough to kill an elephant, but she had no idea if it would be enough to kill that *thing*. To kill the sheriff — to kill the closest thing she'd had to a *dad* in years. She started to cry.

There was another pause before Oxford's thick, trembling hand slowly extended and took the syringe. He manipulated the plunger awkwardly, like a baby trying to work chopsticks, but despite his fumbling, it appeared as if he would be able to inject it even with the extra skin covering his hands.

Alice looked down at her own hand through watery eyes and was surprised to see one lonely clonazepam sitting on her palm—the deputy must have put it there without her noticing.

"Are you ready?" Coggins asked.

There was a wet, muffled sound like someone speaking through a washcloth, but Alice understood the word anyway.

"No."

She put the pill into her mouth and swallowed.

Everyone is addicted to something.

5.

Jared Knew It Was time when he heard that singular word, the one that he had first heard more than three days ago, convinced then that it had been the wind.

Come

The affirmative glance and nod from Deputy Coggins wasn't necessary; reassuring, yes, but not required.

"Let's go, Oxford," he whispered.

Coooome

Cooooooooooome

Cooooooooooooooooooooooooooome

The voice was getting anxious, and they could literally feel its excitement manifested as an electric thrum in the air. Not only was this in itself unnerving, but it was a clear sign that whatever effects the clonazepam had had on the thing had evidently passed—it had recovered quickly. Jared pushed the negative thoughts away; there was no time to change their plan now. And besides, deep down he knew that Coggins was right—if they tried to run, they would eventually make their way back here.

Jared grabbed Oxford by the arm and, together with Coggins, guided the nearly blind man out of the room. They moved cautiously despite the lightening sky, their steps but awkward shuffles, tentative and scared.

"You are at the stairs now," Jared whispered.

A nod, a slip of the skin. Jared didn't bother adjusting it this time; the skin wasn't meant to confuse or disguise, but only to give Oxford more time to inject the thing while it removed it.

All the while keeping Oxford's own skin intact.

Jared bit his lip as penance. It should have been him wearing the skin; he should have been the bait. He was the one who had skipped his father's funeral; maybe if he had been there, they wouldn't have felt the need to get together over the holidays to mourn. Maybe the mourning, almost a year since their father had passed, would have already have been completed.

"You'll be okay," he said, more for his own comfort than Oxford's.

Mama told me to look after you, he had said.

But Mama had told Oxford the same thing.

Why had she done that? How could Oxford look after me?

Something clearly wasn't right with Mama. He longed for her then, knowing deep down that even if he made it out of this godforsaken place, he might never see her again.

"You'll be okay," he repeated, trying to focus.

Truth was, he doubted that any of them would be okay after this, let alone Oxford, who was fucked up to begin with. And the girl? This Alice, who somehow knew both Deputy Coggins and Oxford? He remembered her laughing at Oxford in his skin suit; well, she clearly wasn't all there anymore, either.

Whatever evil had descended on Askergan, it was messing with more than just their skin.

Coooooooooooooooooooooome

"Go," Jared said, fighting back tears.

Oxford took one quivering step forward, his foot searching for the top stair.

Jared turned and followed Coggins quickly across the landing to the other side. Alice bounded almost merrily in front of the deputy, his hand gently guiding her.

No, she's definitely not all there.

And then they had really come full circle, huddled in the broom closet, peering out into the foyer. But this time it wasn't him and Oxford looking down at a man with a twisted leg. It was Jared, Alice, and the deputy —*fuck, it sounds like the start of a bad joke*—looking down at Oxford.

Oxford in his meat suit.

Coooooooooooooooooooooooooooooooome

We're here, Jared thought, licking his lips with a tacky tongue. *Now it's your time to come.*

6.

SITTING? WHY THE FUCK are you sitting? Stand up, you fucking nitwit, stand up!

Jared couldn't believe it. His fucking brother couldn't even keep it together for five minutes. But now he wasn't just fucking up his own life, but they were all going to die.

I knew I should have gone! I fucking told Deputy Coggins I should be the one!

After making his way painfully slowly to the approximate center of the room, Oxford had stood there for a good minute or two as they had planned. But then there had been some shifting of the skin, which, granted, was not too surprising as it was likely as uncomfortable in its stench and the heat it retained as it was horrific to look at, but a moment later, his brother fell rather clumsily to his knees.

Get up, you selfish bastard! Get up!

It was so silent for the next minute that the only sound he heard was his own breathing and Deputy Coggins' equally shallow breaths. Jared leaned on the man's back, nearly driving him into the floor. Then he heard a deep rumble, followed by that uncomfortable pressure in his ears again; *it* was coming.

Jared's breath caught in his throat.

Get up! Get up, Oxford! Get up!

He felt like screaming, but plugged ears or not, Jared would not risk the thing hearing him—unlike his fucking delinquent brother, we would not put all of them in that spot.

Another depression, and then the unbelievable happened. Instead of rising back to his feet, Oxford collapsed onto his face, his arms not even reaching out in front to protect himself. There was a sick *thwack* like smacking a raw steak off a wooden cutting board as the skin struck the hardwood.

No!

There was another sound, too, one that seemed out of place in this world of deep, brooding noise—a tinkling, as if someone had dropped a handful of pennies.

No! I should have gone, I should have gone, I never should have—

Something grabbed his arm, and Jared felt his heart leap into his throat. Reluctantly, he pulled his eyes from his brother and looked down. Deputy Coggins had somehow managed to turn his body even with all of Jared's weight pushing down on him, his eyes so huge that it looked as if he had been born without lids.

"I'll go," Coggins whispered, spit flying from his lips.

Jared shook his head violently and Coggins let go of his arm.

"I'll go," he repeated. "You can't shoot."

Jared shook his head again; the deputy had clearly misunderstood.

"You—"

"No one goes," Jared nearly shouted. "We have one shot at this; we stay."

"But—"

"Why do you have a baseball?" Alice suddenly asked.

They both turned to her, matching looks of surprise on their faces; they had forgotten that she was even in the closet with them. The woman's slender hands, white with frostbite, were buried in the bag that Jared and Oxford had brought with them from Mama Lawrence's. As they watched, one of her hands pulled out of the open bag and held up a spherical object for them all to see. She had that same queer smile on her face.

What the fuck?

Jared was about to say something when he noticed the red

gas can tucked away in the back of the closet. Had Oxford brought it all the way up here? He couldn't remember, but thought they must have.

Can we use it? Burn the thing?

Jared shook his head. They had a plan, and it was going to work, despite Oxford. Maybe after—maybe after it was all said and done, they would use what was left of the gasoline to burn the *fuck* out of this horrible place.

Jared heard another few heavy steps and he pulled his gaze from the gas can and the strange girl who was still holding the baseball and looked back at his brother's fallen body. His eyes scanned the tiles around the fallen meat suit, and before long he identified what had sounded like change spilling. It was the syringe, and as he had suspected, it was empty. The selfish bastard had injected the entire volume into himself—he just wanted to get high. He had probably planned this all along, and it was the likely reason he had been so adamant about being the one to don the suit and head into the foyer.

Or maybe he wasn't selfish at all. Maybe he had sacrificed himself to save them.

Jared felt what little energy he had left flow from him.

Either way, it didn't matter now.

Tears welled in his eyes briefly before spilling over.

The thing will consume the heroin one way or another.

"We stay," he instructed Coggins, his voice wavering.

7.

JARED WATCHED THE BEAST peel off the outer skin—more amused than confused—and then the thing's long green finger extended toward the nape of Oxford's bare neck.

You fucking idiot! It wasn't supposed to be like this!

For a brief second, the thing in the foyer turned its head and looked up at him, their eyes meeting even in the dim light.

"Jarrrrrreeeed."

It was the same voice that had awoken him what seemed a fortnight ago.

"Jarrrrrrrreeed, you missed my funeral, Jared."

It was the voice of his father.

"Jarrrrrrreeeeeeeeeeeeeeeed."

Then the claws moved again and he heard a tearing sound, like thick curtains being cut with a dull knife.

Jared buried his face in his hands, opened his mouth wide, and screamed a soundless scream until bright white spots speckled his vision.

The rumbling started then, that dull, consistent rumbling that had become oh so familiar.

Laughing. The thing is laughing at us again.

8.

UNLIKE JARED, DEPUTY COGGINS couldn't help *but* watch, and it took all of his concentration to keep from leaping out of the closet and running downstairs, gun blazing.

We have one shot at this, Jared had said, and Coggins thought he knew what he meant.

They *had* to get the drugs into the beast somehow.

It was easier to see the thing now that the sun had begun to peek over the horizon, but Deputy Coggins wished that on this day it had taken its time. His heart sank. He could no longer make out any pink on its face or upper torso. Whatever transformation it was undergoing, it was clear that it was nearing an end.

Stupid, stupid, stupid fucking plan. Way to go, Columbo.

Without warning, the beast lifted its head to the sky and shook its neck violently, flaps of loose dark green flesh on its neck whipping back and forth like the jowls of a massive dog. When its head faced forward again, it looked to Coggins like its lower jaw had come unhinged, revealing a row of small white teeth amidst the black void of a mouth.

With its long, pointed fingers, the thing raised Oxford's limp, skinless body until its black lower lip rested on the poor man's glistening red forehead. With one undulating forward shift of its neck, Oxford's head disappeared into its mouth to the tops of his ears.

If he had had anything left in his stomach, Coggins had no doubt that it was at this point that he most definitely would have rid himself of it. But it had been so long since he had eaten anything that his stomach had lost its ability to regurgitate—

instead, it revolted by clenching into one solid knot. His abdomen contracted as well, and he almost resorted to the hide-the-face tactic that Jared had adopted ever since his brother had fallen to his knees. But his job wasn't done yet, and he forced himself to keep his eyes trained on the horrific scene unraveling in the foyer.

Slowly, the dark black lips inched their way over the back of Oxford's head like two thin, slow-moving caterpillars. The thing's large arms suddenly flipped Oxford over so that the man was now face up, lying with his neck and shoulders resting on the beast's massive chest and even bigger abdomen, his bare heels just barely in contact with the floor.

Cooooooome

Now Deputy Coggins did look away, and he found himself struggling to avoid receding into Jared's dark place.

It was Oxford's eyes that had done it, that had made the scene unbearable. Even though it was unlikely—impossible—that the man could be alive, let alone conscious, after injecting the caustic mix of clonazepam and heroin and being skinned, his lidless eyes were wide and they seemed to scream at Coggins.

Help me! Dear Jesus, help me! his eyes screamed. *I made a mistake! Please! Please, I don't deserve to be eaten alive! No one deserves to be eaten alive!*

It was true, of course; no one deserved Oxford's fate, especially not someone that was clearly well-meaning, despite his obvious flaws. It dawned on him that perhaps Oxford's decision to inject himself might not have been as selfish as he had first thought; maybe he done it to make sure that the drugs got into the beast, just as Jared had said. He didn't know the man well enough—didn't know him at all, really—but it was possible that the man's decision was more a result of martyrdom than selfishness.

Either way, it was Oxford or all of them — Jared's words — and the latter was clearly not an option. Besides, the man had been skinned, and while he was perhaps the furthest thing from a doctor, Coggins doubted anyone could survive that. There was nothing he could do but follow through with the plan.

The rumbling returned, but now it was more wet and muffled, the individual laughs acquiring a *thwub, thwub, thwub* quality with Oxford blocking its gaping orifice.

Coggins breathed deeply, trying to focus.

Come

He covered his ears, trying to block out the sound, but it was no use; it was inside his head.

Coooooooooooooooooome

It took less time than either Coggins or Jared could have hoped; it was no more than five minutes after the thing had flipped Oxford over that the deputy heard the first gag.

It was a subtle noise at first, and Coggins thought for a second that maybe it was just a normal sound of the thing's fucked-up anatomy, or a consequence of trying to devour a one-hundred-and-seventy-pound man whole. The second gag, however, was more pronounced, and Coggins forced himself to look again.

Oxford's entire head and most of his left shoulder were buried in the thing's mouth. He had been folded somehow, his shoulders crushed together so that they nearly met below his chin. But instead of trying to shove the other shoulder into its enormous, gaping jaws, it seemed to be trying to force Oxford *out*. Its gullet, so obviously engorged with Oxford's head, twitched and vibrated, an action that Coggins recognized even in this abomination: it was retching. There was a large undulation of the thing's gut, a massive wave that shuddered from the bottom of its stomach up to the spot where its neck should have been, followed by a horrible, wet sound that was muffled by the body that still filled its mouth. Even from deep within the closet, Coggins could see the thing's yellow eyes roll back and the scaly green nose, pointed nearly at the ceiling its mouth was spread so wide, tighten and scrunch. A whole gallon or more of a hot, putrid fluid bubbled out of its lips and soaked Oxford's dark red upper chest.

Another gag, another convulsion. The thing's eyes closed and Oxford's body seemed to slip out a couple of inches, with more of his upper arm becoming visible. It was like witnessing Oxford being birthed, inching his way out of the membranous lips a centimeter at a time. Another gag, then another. Coggins heard more fluid splash on the hardwood, but he couldn't see where it landed. The gags became so frequent that they seemed to meld together like a horrible bulimic cacophony, and before long, Coggins thought he could see Oxford's front deltoid and the base of his throat clear the thing's mouth.

It was now or never.

Okay, you motherfucker, I'm coming!

9.

THE THING DIDN'T NOTICE Coggins emerge from the closet, nor did it acknowledge him bounding down the stairs two at a time. When Coggins got to the bottom of the staircase, he was hit with an unbelievably hot wave of air that was so thick and foul that he nearly stopped short. Only adrenaline kept him moving forward, a hidden reserve he had no idea existed, and with his eyes watering, he made it within ten feet of the thing to his shotgun that lay abandoned on the hardwood.

In one fluid motion, he grabbed the gun, spun it, cocked it, and aimed it at the thing's head. At that very moment, what was left of Oxford's partially digested face spewed from its open mouth, accompanied by a deluge of more of that hot, stinking liquid. Coggins fought the urge to look at Oxford's horribly mangled face, and instead concentrated on searching for a patch of pink anywhere on the thing's head. It was a repulsive sight; the lips were like black elastic bands had been pulled too far and then let go, but refused to return to their original shape.

C'mon, c'mon...

The thing's green head, which Coggins now saw was indeed covered in thick scales, was all dark save for some blood at the corners of its mouth where its lips had split.

Then he saw its eyes; they were dark and distended, and if there had ever been any human in those eyes, any of Sheriff Drew, it had long since disappeared.

Still retching despite having unburdened itself of poor Oxford, the thing slowly turned toward Deputy Coggins and he started to panic. He whipped the gun back and forth, trying to focus on some—any—pink area on the hard green carapace. Unbelievably, the rumbling returned; despite its obvious sickness, the thing was laughing again, the individual rumbles intermittently interrupted by more spattering of the hot liquid. So much had spilled from the thing's mouth that Coggins had to make sure he didn't slip as he swung around the thing's body, looking for some flesh—*human flesh*—to shoot at.

You can't kill me.

The words were so clear, so *distinct*, that Coggins nearly dropped the shotgun again. Instead, he froze, his eyes remaining locked on the beast's lips that had remained motionless.

The words were in his head.

You can't kill me, Bradley.

Coggins swallowed hard, trying to will the voice away. It was foreign, yet at the same time familiar.

It was the same voice he had been hearing from the moment he left the station.

It was the voice on the wind.

I'm here... I'm here and so are my palil, *Bradley. I have returned—I have returned and this time I plan on staying.*

The beast continued to turn its head, trying to follow Coggins, but the motions were ratchet-like and it failed to keep up with the deputy's movements.

You cant kill—

Just when Coggins had given up hope, something flew into his peripheral vision and smacked against the side of the thing's head and the voice inside his own head suddenly stopped.

A baseball. A fucking baseball.

Coggins glanced up at the railing and saw Jared's grief-stricken face staring down at him. Alice stood beside him, and as he watched, she mouthed the words '*baseball*'. She was smiling.

A rumble drew his attention back to the beast. Although the baseball hadn't hurt the creature, it had turned to look up at Jared and Alice, and in doing so revealed a small patch of pink skin still tightly attached to its left temple, with only the bottom looking as if it had started to peel away.

Bingo.

"Dana," Coggins said, his voice hoarse and dry, "*don't* get down."

And then he squeezed the trigger.

A hot liquid splashed Deputy Coggins' face, chest, and arms, and he stumbled backward, once again dropping the shotgun. He clawed at the fluid, pulling it away from his nose and mouth in thick, goopy strings. Gasping for air, he finally managed to clear the sticky mess from his nose and took a deep breath. He couldn't see, couldn't hear; the shot had been so loud in the house that he was temporarily deafened.

Even though he couldn't hear, he *felt* a sighing sensation—a change in pressure like someone had slammed the front door. Instinctively, he took another two steps backward, still trying desperately to remove the sticky substance from his eyes. His mind was racing, wondering if he had killed the beast, or if it was coming for him now, intent on eating *him* next.

He finally cleared enough fluid from his left eye to force it open, and he realized that he was immersed in a thick fog, like humid, tropical air mingling with the smoke from the shotgun blast. As Coggins pulled more of the liquid from his face and ears, relief overcame him: the hot mist was coming from the spot where the beast's head had been. The thing's massive body stood in place for a moment, upright, but as he watched it slowly fell forward, its bulk spilling out at the sides as it collapsed onto what was left of Oxford. A dark green liquid slowly gurgled out of the thing's ragged neck, coating Oxford like hot oil, and Coggins gagged.

Then he heard another sound: a strange clacking noise, like someone rhythmically banging a hammer against the side of a piece of wood. Coggins took another few careful steps backward before turning to face the landing above. On the balcony, Deputy Coggins saw Jared crouched over Alice's seizing body, her heels slapping off the hardwood with every spasm. And then there was the laugh; somehow, Coggins still heard the thing's laughter echoing inside his skull.

It was a sound he would never forget.

Epilogue
Thaw

OXFORD WAS DEAD. MAMA was dead. Seth, Cody, and Henrietta were missing. Alice, the strange girl he had met at Mrs. Wharfburns, was in a coma. But as much as Jared had been through, as much as he had *seen*, there was no time for grief or self-pity. Not now—not while several of his family members were still missing.

"Marley," Jared said slowly, staring at the woman's blank face, "do you remember anything about where Cody said he was going?"

Marley turned toward him at the mention of her husband's name, but if Jared was expecting some sort of revelation, he was sadly mistaken; the woman simply shook her head. It was the same head shake she had given him when he had told her what had happened at the Wharfburn Estate—albeit a heavily edited and censored version. Even for him, having been there, having *lived* the horror, he wasn't sure what was real and what his mind had fabricated. In fact, if it weren't for Deputy Coggins, he probably would've believed none of it.

"He just said he was leaving," Marley replied matter-of-factly. "He said he couldn't stay any longer."

Her apathy pained him.

"Are you sure? He didn't say where? South? North?"

All of a sudden Marley's expression changed, as if his words had triggered something in her, and the Marley that Jared knew before this whole shitstorm happened—the tough yet compassionate, caring woman—returned. Only she was sad now—so sad.

"Did I do this, Jared?" she whispered.

Jared reached out and grabbed her hand.

"Of course not."

Despite his words, Marley nodded as if to affirm her own statement.

"I did this—I made him leave. I made you all leave."

Her voice cracked and she started to cry.

"Mar—"

"I was scared... I wanted you guys to go so badly—I—I—"

She sobbed, and Jared leaned in close, his own tears starting to flow.

"I—I just thought that if you guys left, *it* would leave me alone. That... that... it would be *gone.* Jared, am I a horrible person? I thought that if you guys left, *it* would be satisfied—that *it* would leave me and Corina alone."

Jared wanted to hold the woman, but he was racked with his own sobs—as cryptic as her words were, he thought he understood what she meant.

"After you guys left, I couldn't do anything. I was afraid that if I even so much as got off that couch that I would leave Corina and go to it. And—for fuck's sake—I don't even know what *it* is, Jared. But I was so, so scared."

Marley looked at Jared when she spoke, and a shadow passed over his face when she uttered the word *it.*

"But you—you know what it is, don't you?"

Her voice was barely a whisper, her eyes wet and wide.

"Was," Jared corrected her, "what it *was*."

Marley shook her head slowly.

"I don't ever want to know, okay? I don't want to know what you saw, what happened to Oxford. Not ever."

Jared nodded and first wiped her tears away, then his own. If it were possible for him to forget, to not know what *it* was, he would have made it so.

He wished to Christ it were possible for him to forget—to have never known.

Dad's eyes; it had Dad's eyes.

They sat in silence for a few minutes, both of them slowly recovering from the emotional outburst. Marley's face transitioned back to the mask she had been wearing for the past few days, and when Jared convinced himself that he wouldn't start crying again, he finally gathered enough courage to speak.

"Have you been out looking for Cody and Henrietta?" he asked softly.

He himself had been out all morning combing the area around the Lawrence house, trudging through miles of snow trying to locate his eldest brother and youngest niece.

"No," Marley said unapologetically. "There are hundreds of people out there looking, and I can barely walk."

As proof, she held up one sandaled foot: all but the big toe was covered in gauze—frostbite.

Jared nodded.

"Besides," she added, throwing a glance over her shoulder, "I need to stay with Corina."

Jared gently tapped her thigh and stood. He didn't blame her; the woman had lost more than the tips of her toes, and it made sense for her to latch on to the thing closest to her, the one thing she had left: Corina.

"I'm gonna go see her now, okay?"

Marley's expression was blank again, and he took this lack of objection as permission.

Corina had been lucky enough to get her own hospital room, thanks to Deputy Coggins—a significant gesture, considering that even with his influence he had only been able to get one single room, which he had given to her and not to Alice. There had been so many minor injuries—falls, dehydration, pneumonia, and of course frostbite—over the Christmas holiday that single rooms were at a premium. But after what they had seen at the Wharfburn Estate and what they had discovered when the power finally came back on at the Lawrence house, Coggins had given the room to Corina, and then he had formed a search party. Problem was, there were more than two dozen people missing, and although Jared knew where some of them were—what was left of them, at least— there were others out there, like Cody and Henrietta, that were lost in the snow. Seth was out there, too, although Jared was still trying to piece together exactly why he had left—and where he might have gone. Marley had told him that Seth had just up and left without so much as a goodbye, and as much as he was infuriated by the coward—leaving his family to freeze to death—he hoped that Seth had found somewhere warm to wait out the storm, somewhere out of the cold. And for all of his anger toward the man, he hoped beyond hope that he had left to *avoid* going east, instead of because of it. So when Jared was out searching for his family, he was also searching for Seth—all the while secretly hoping he never found him.

What happened to Mama was even more confusing and disorienting, and his mind had put up a wall to shield himself from the brunt of the devastation. After what he had seen—had facilitated—happen to Oxford, he was numb to death. Jared supposed that he should have seen it coming—her apathy, the way she was so disconnected from what was happening around them, the strange incident of her trying to get outside, to go find Gordon—but he really knew it was game over when Oxford had told him that Mama wanted him, his junkie of a younger brother, to take care of him. They were the exact same words she had uttered to Jared.

Ludicrous.

He knew then that she had lost it, that she had been driven mad from the situation—from the call. From *Oot'-keban.*

As before, as with the many times that all of these feelings bombarded him, Jared pushed them away. He knew that he would have to deal with them someday, but not now—and definitely not all at once.

"Later," he whispered.

He took a deep breath and stepped into Corina's hospital room.

The girl was sleeping, her face a mask of peace and comfort—medically induced, no doubt. Jared walked to the side of her bed and brushed a lock of blond hair from her face. Then he tucked her right arm that had fallen from beneath the white sheet back onto the bed, making sure that the heartrate monitor was still correctly positioned on her finger. She looked older somehow, as if she had gone from twelve to twenty-four overnight. It wasn't her features—those were still as smooth as a sheet of unbaked filo pastry—but it was something else, something he just couldn't place. Or maybe it was just him, his perspective on everything having changed. His own body was old and tired, like an eighty-year-old instead of someone in his late thirties, and his joints ached as if they had frozen during the storm and were still struggling to thaw. The idea of thawing reminded him of the way Oxford's partially digested head had looked, soft and mushy and—

Stop it! Not now!

Jared felt beads of sweat begin to form on his brow. He tried hard to force the horrible images away, but they lingered like a foul smell. His only hope was that his brother had been dead before he had been skinned. Clonazepam and heroin—enough to kill a horse. But enough to kill an addict?

Stop it!

Jared's eyes fell from Corina's face and continued down her body. His vision was starting to get watery.

You killed him. You could have —

Corina's right leg lay flat, but her left was hoisted by a strap wrapped just below her buttock and tethered to a mechanical hook that arced down from the ceiling.

— you could have saved him. All you had to do was tell Deputy Coggins to go down there.

Jared wiped at his brow and blinked hard.

You didn't even need to tell the deputy to go, you just had to let him.

Jared looked at the heavily wrapped stump halfway down Corina's thigh. It was so strange, having the leg end like that just before it reached the knee. Jared had to resist the urge to actually lean down and look under the hanging limb to make sure it wasn't folded beneath — an old stage trick.

"Why are you crying?"

The voice startled Jared, and he bolted upright and took a step backward. He had been so lost in his own head, so trapped in a horrible reverie, that he had forgotten he was not alone. Corina was staring at him, a curious expression on her face.

He breathed deep in an attempt to compose himself.

"It's just —"

— I killed your uncle, my brother. We could have come up with another plan, we could have all escaped alive.

Jared shook his head.

But we did have a plan, a good one — it's Oxford's fault for fucking it up. It's Oxford's fault...

" — it's just that I miss Oxford. And your dad; I miss Cody, too."

Jared didn't know if it was okay to mention her father given Corina's fragile state, but, shit, he was fragile, too.

Thankfully, the girl seemed unfazed.

"I miss Henri," she said, her eyes looking away for a brief moment before returning to his.

Jared wiped the tears from his face.

"Do you know where they might have gone?"

It was a stupid thing to ask, but Jared was worried that if he didn't say anything, the conversation would go to a place that neither of them wanted. In the end, it didn't matter—it went there anyway.

Something flashed across the young girl's eyes—something dark—and for a moment her soft, almost affected expression seemed to harden. In an instant, Jared knew exactly what thought had crept into Corina's head—because the same thing floated through his.

"No," he stated calmly, "they did not—"

Corina's eyes grew wide, and he knew then that just like her amputated leg, her wounded mind would never fully recover.

Come.

"*Oot'-keban*," she whispered.

Jared furrowed his brow and took an aggressive step toward her bed.

"No," he said forcefully.

Corina paid his advance no mind. Her gaze drifted upward until finally fixated on a point on the ceiling, or perhaps beyond.

"*Oot'-keban*," she whispered again, quieter this time.

"No," he almost shouted. "*Oot'-keban* is no more, Corina."

Jared paused, fighting the urge to recall the horrific green beast that had flooded Mrs. Wharfburn's front hallway with gallons of stinking fluid.

"It's gone."

She shook her head violently.

"It's never gone," she whispered. "You didn't get it all...I can still hear it."

"Corin—"

"You forgot about the animals—the animal skins, Jared. It's growing its *palil* and it's still coming."

Corina's eyes slowly rolled back in her head.

The animal skins?

The girl's eyes suddenly flipped forward and her gaze locked onto Jared.

"Four boys," she gasped, the words sounding like they pained her. "four boys will awaken *Oot'-keban's* children, its *palil*. And then no one will be safe. Not you, not me, not Askergan."

Corina's eyelids started to flutter and Jared started to cry.

He couldn't fight anymore.

"Who told you this, Corina? How do you know this?"

Corina opened her mouth wide and sucked in a massive amount of air, generating a strange groaning sound.

"Mrs. Wharfburn," she answered at last. "Mrs. Wharfburn told me."

An image of the elderly woman's flattened skin flooded Jared's mind, and he bolted upright, his face contorting into an expression of pure horror.

"Corina?" he managed to squeak.

The girl's eyes had closed, and she was lying peacefully again. But when Jared stared closely, he realized that her lips were moving. He was terrified of what she might be saying, but he couldn't help but lean in close. He had to put his ear nearly to her lips in order to make out the words.

"It's not dead," she whispered. "It's not dead... it's not dead... it's not dead..."

She repeated those three words over and over again until

Jared thought that he too—like his mother before him—would go mad. He bent over her and grasped her shoulders with the intention of shaking her out of her trance when her eyes suddenly flipped forward again.

Then Corina screamed.

*   *   *

"You all right, Coggins?"

There was a long pause, and Deputy Paul White checked twice to make sure that the green light on his walkie-talkie was still lit.

Finally, a static-filled voice on the other end answered.

"Yeah."

There was a shorter pause this time.

"Just tired. What's up?"

Deputy White hesitated before addressing the reason for his call.

"Well, I know you are off for a bit, but I know you were part of the search and I thought you should hear it from me first."

Another pause.

"They found the girl and her father."

Silence.

"Brad? You there?"

Paul turned to look for his new temporary partner—Deputy Andrew Williams, who was collecting some of the larger branches stuck in Mrs. Wharfburn's lawn.

"Hey!" he shouted. "Remember what I said! Stay away from the house!"

The man, deputized only two days ago, was inching his way closer to the charred open doorway, obviously trying to get a peek inside. The entire front porch was a blackened, burnt mess, and the foyer was much the same. He himself had only been inside once, and even then only briefly. It looked like the fire had started in the foyer, but there was also fire damage to one of the rooms upstairs. It was strange, the fire seeming to start in two places at the same time, and it just didn't jive with Coggins' story. If it hadn't been for the wind, the whole house would have gone up. Coggins clearly wasn't telling him the whole truth and nothing but—but that would come in time. If there was one thing he knew about Deputy Bradley Coggins, it was that the man had a penchant for telling tall tales—the truth would come out. White just wasn't sure he wanted to know.

"The yellow tape is there for a reason! Not safe!"

Deputy Williams grumbled something before making his way begrudgingly toward the center of the lawn.

The fire was probably a blessing, as whatever had happened in there—whatever had happened to Sheriff Drew—couldn't have been pretty. Mrs. Drew had come down to the station as she had promised, and the woman, stronger than he, Deputy Coggins, and the sheriff combined, had actually taken over Alice's duties—when she wasn't in the hospital spending time with the girl she practically called a daughter, that is. White was grateful. With the sheriff and Alice gone and Coggins on leave, it was good to have a face around that he recognized—even if he refused to share what little he knew of what had happened with the woman, despite her near constant requests.

The radio crackled.

"Bad news?"

It sounded more like a statement than a query. Paul took a deep breath.

"Yeah—good and bad."

Deputy White made his way toward a massive branch that was stuck in the ground like a spear, roughly ten feet from the front porch.

"They found them on the ice, nearly two miles from shore. They must have gotten lost—wandered onto the ice and lost their bearings. The man was without his jacket, lying face down on the ice—frozen. They found—" Paul's voice hitched.

Damn.

"They found the girl a hundred meters from him, buried beneath her dad's large coat. And—"

A long pause ensued as his emotions surged, and Paul distracted himself by moving the stick back and forth with his one free hand. Surprisingly, it seemed well rooted and barely budged even with a sharp tug from his meaty palm. He looked skyward, trying to force the tears away.

"And goddamn it, Brad, she was *alive.*"

"Shit."

Relief.

Paul nodded.

"Frostbitten, terrified, but *alive.*"

Another pause, one that was drawn out for so long that Paul was about to put the talkie back in its holster before Coggins spoke.

"Hey, White?"

"Yeah?"

"How did you know the answer to the Gretzky trivia?"

The question caught him off guard, and he took a moment to answer.

"Heard it on the radio a few days before you asked me."

There was a clicking noise.

"Fucking radio," Coggins said, and Paul couldn't help but crack a small smile. It was just like Coggins to come say something inappropriate at a time like this.

Deputy White pulled the stick a little harder this time, and it moved a quarter inch to the left. When he let go, it unexpectedly remained in that position instead of bouncing back.

"Get some rest," he said. "We need you back soon, Brad. This town needs us—needs the good ones."

His use of the sheriff's words surprised him, and he fought back tears once again. Sniffling, Paul put the radio back in his belt without waiting for a response.

The deputy turned back to the large branch sticking out of the earth. With two burly paws, he pulled it hard to one side, then, without letting it come to rest, he pushed it back the other way. He repeated this motion a second time. On the third such movement, he noticed something down by the base of the branch; the snow appeared to not only be displaced, but also— melting?

Paul pushed again, and this time he saw something else: a flash of color.

"Everything all right over there?" Deputy Williams hollered, but Paul, engrossed in what he had just seen, ignored him.

This time, he pushed with all of his strength and a small puff of colored air rose to meet him.

What the hell?

"Hey, Andrew," White shouted. "Come take a look at this!"

Deputy Paul White bent onto one knee and peered down the length of the branch into what was now a much wider hole.

Is that—pink? Why the hell is the bottom of the branch pink?

Deputy White's head snapped up. He thought he heard something, an airy voice carrying on the wind, something that sounded like—

"Hey, Andrew, you say something?"

—Come

The End

Author's Note

I hope you had as much fun reading SKIN as I had writing it. It was an absolute blast... of cold, winter air. See, this is what happens when you are forced to endure −40° winters in Montreal: you write books about skinning and devouring people.

In real life, I love the snow *and* the cold. But what I don't enjoy is six feet of damp snow in a twenty-four-hour period and weather so cold that it turns your nose hairs into deadly icicles. So I wrote SKIN to help me cope.

If you liked SKIN, you're gonna love CRACKERS. It's about basements... creepy, dark, musty basements.

I hate those too.

If you have a spare minute, please consider writing an honest review for SKIN.

As an Indie Author, I live and die by reviews.

So don't kill me.

Let me live.

I have many more stories to tell.

Thanks for your support and stay warm,

Patrick
June, 2016
MONTREAL

Acknowledgments

Special thanks to all of my early readers, in particular FTG and ALL, as veiled in your sarcastic commentary were nuggets of valuable information that undoubtedly made this a better book. Thanks to AAL, as every minute I spent on this book, you spent taking care of the rest of our lives.

Get Patrick Logan's Starter Library FREE

Sign up for my no-spam newsletter and get the short e-story SYSTEM UPDATE free, and be the first to know of new releases, sales and exclusive contests!
Just go to www.PTLBooks.com.

You can also keep up to date by 'liking' my Facebook page @authorpatricklogan

And don't forget to grab your copy of CRACKERS, Book 2 of the *Insatiable Series*.
Available now!

CPSIA information can be obtained
at www.ICGtesting.com
Printed in the USA
LVOW12s2235060916

503497LV00006B/250/P